DESTINATION CLIFFORD

By

DAN DRUEN

This book is a work of fiction. Places, events, and situations in this story are purely fictional. Any resemblance to actual persons, living or dead, is coincidental.

ISBN: 1-4140-6361-X (e-book)
ISBN: 1-4140-6360-1 (Paperback)

This book is printed on acid free paper.

1stBooks - rev. 02/14/04

Acknowledgments

This book is dedicated to my Great Grandfather, Valerius McGinnis, and all the men who served their States during the worst conflict our Nation has ever experienced. Those who survived went on to take their place in the reconstruction of a battered Union. Without their dedication and perseverance, the healing process wouldn't have been effective and could have lasted much longer.

These men, and those women they left behind to stoke the home fires, maintained that thread of devotion required to establish the nucleus for a new start. It wasn't an easy task, but with exceptional effort they replanted their roots and helped build our country into a United States that today stands proud.

* * * *

This tale would never have been completed without the help and devotion of my family and friends. Special thanks go to: My daughter, Ann who kept me straight on my computer, designed the cover, and was instrumental in making this manuscript printable; My late daughter-in-law, Gail Druen who was first to read my manuscript and make some sage comments; Joyce Maddox who took time from her busy schedule to provide some professional comments; Don Harten, an author in his own right, who insisted I publish this story; and all my friends who patiently read the manuscript and only made good comments.

Foreword

The mood in the room was solemn. Hardly a whisper rose from the lips of these few men clad in Grey. They were there to honor one of their own, even though age was now a factor, which curtailed their travel. The body of a comrade in arms lay serene in the adjacent parlor; one of the many who had lived on after the battles had ended. They had gone on to be productive people who helped reunite this torn country during those dark days of April 1865. These men had done their jobs. They had produced families who had carried on the honored traditions they had lived, and now died, by. The sands of time were slipping fast for them. But they were, and would remain, a proud breed that helped this nation survive one of its most painful periods. A catastrophe they hoped would never occur again.

My Great Grandfather was sixteen when he joined Lee's forces. He had followed in the footsteps of his father and older brothers, not due to any hate for the North, but because of his loyalty to his family and the upbringing of his surroundings. At eighteen the war was over and all he wanted to do was to return home to the girl he had left behind. He held no grudges nor did he feel despair over the fate of the South. He was ready to take up his life again, minus the two years of what he termed to be misery.

I was seven on this day of mourning, and as I looked at those few remaining men, I was sure they too had Great Grandsons who loved and honored them. I know I will never forget what this vibrant, gray bearded, gentle man had meant to me. He had been patient with my youth even though it must have tired him at times. We talked, or at least he talked to me about things I wish I could totally remember. However, some of his words to me during those last few years of his life did stick in my memory. He didn't often refer to those war days, but during one of several checker games (he let me win once in awhile), he made a statement I will never forget. His words were something like; 'If Lincoln hadn't been assassinated; the South wouldn't have known the grief it endured. Those were difficult times, and it's a wonder all these years have turned out as well as they did.'

This tale is about the plight of one young man. The honor and loyalty he exemplified represents the character of many of those who fought on both sides during our country's worst conflict.

Much has been written about both armies on what occurred during the fighting and after. This story is a small capsule of those harrowing days immediately before the surrender, the shock of peace at Appomattox Court House, and of the transition following. The only way home was to walk, and the many survivors did just that. It had to have been extremely difficult to know defeat and to realize life would go on, with or without you.

My Great Grandfather's first name was Valerius, and he did walk to his home in Clifford from Appomattox Court House, barefooted. Whether those last days of the conflict or the trek home were exactly as I have depicted, I will never really know. I do know he survived the war and he made the journey. I'm one of a long line of descendents to prove it. I am also very proud to have known this man and to remember his last years. I'm sure his genes had something to do with the fact that I answered my country's call three times when the chips were down. He, or I, wouldn't have had it any other way.

Chapter One

The Federal infantry came cascading down the hill from their temporary fortifications, which had been hastily constructed across a shallow valley separating our two positions. A raging bombardment had preceded their advancement toward our lines. The valley was mostly open fields with very little cover to protect them, however they were now well out of range of our muskets, and below the level we could depress our cannons. They were approaching a small snaking road, which dissected the land area directly below our earthworks. The road, nothing more than a thin brown line etched into the landscape, led to the Petersburg Turnpike some four miles to the Northeast. Once they crossed the road, they wouldn't have a very difficult time getting to our battlements.

A steady downpour wasn't helping our efforts. The mire and mud from over a week's worth of rain was making a difficult position even worse. It was bad enough fighting a determined enemy, much less battling impossible elements.

Our battery had been delivering deadly fire into their trench area to cover our infantry's advance. However, our boys had been unable to gain any advantage over the Federal unit, and now the tide was turning in favor of the Bluecoats. Our choices appeared to be either stand and fight from our present location, or withdraw to a less perilous position and save our guns.

Our battery consisted of two twelve-pound Napoleon cannons and one three-inch rifle. We were authorized fifty horses to transport these weapons, however, we only had thirty-seven at the time. So

1

movement of the guns was always a major problem with our diminished number of horses.

Our manpower was also less than authorizations called for. A light artillery battery, such as ours, was authorized approximately 123 men counting the officers and Non Commissioned Officers (NCO). We only had ninety-eight present for duty, which included two officers and two NCOs. We had been hard hit by casualties with little or no replacements since arriving in the Petersburg area.

I had joined this battery back in January; it was now the first part of April. Our total manning had never been at full strength, but we had managed to fulfill every task assigned with distinction. Captain Ball, our commander, was the key to our effectiveness. He stood five feet, eight inches and weighed 210 pounds. With his brown hair and bushy beard, he had the look of a two-legged bull; one you wouldn't want to be in front of when he got up a full head of steam. He motivated, planned, and executed every aspect of our mission. He was the key to any success and survival we had experienced.

Lieutenant Fitzpatrick, just the opposite in appearance, was his second in command. He was tall and slender with blond hair and he was devoted to the Captain. He was a nice enough person, but he didn't have near the experience or ability exhibited by Captain Ball. There had been a sergeant assigned as senior NCO, but he had been wounded in a small skirmish on our way to this position, and no replacement had been available. I was one of two corporals in the unit although neither of us had seniority over the other. There hadn't been any need for either of us to rise to a position of authority.

This unit had faced the enemy on several occasions, and had proven its merit with valor. However, events leading to this day didn't seem to be in our favor. We were a last minute insertion into this defensive area of Petersburg, which looked like a lost cause before it began. It was no secret the Confederacy was in danger of losing their bid to become an independent South. Morale was low. Not many of the units had enough food, ammunition, or equipment to continue the war. And, there was no apparent relief in sight. This wasn't one of our finest days.

There had been a slight lull in the action for several minutes. It seemed eerie. Suddenly Bill, our "Point" some few yards down from our location atop the ridge, yelled out, "The Federals will be across

2

the road in less than two minutes. If our infantry can't stop them, we're going to be in a bad way."

"Stay where you are until they start up the hill," shouted Lieutenant Fitzpatrick. "I will advise Captain Ball of your observations."

"Well, do it in a hurry Lieutenant cause them Bluecoats don't seem to mind the rain, the mud, or the bullets. They ain't slowing down for nothing or nobody." Bill's voice went into high pitch on his last few words.

To add to the desperation of our situation, the ammunition we had brought forward was running dangerously low, which was another major factor in our choices. It meant we would soon have to order our eight supply wagons, carrying our reserve ammunition and food rations, forward or fall back on their position. They were in a grove of trees about a mile and a half to our rear.

"Come with me Corporal McGrady," shouted Lieutenant Fitzpatrick, "I want to relay Bill's observations to Captain Ball and he might have some need for you after he gets the information."

I evacuated my location from behind a caisson and started to follow the Lieutenant as he moved toward the Captain's position. The Captain was farther back along the ridgeline near one of our Napoleons. As I neared the two officers, I could see the Lieutenant gesturing to the Captain, trying to explain Bill's words and concerns. I had stopped near the three-inch rifle to make sure it was ready to move out if, and when, the Captain gave the order. The decision to get off this hill immediately didn't seem too difficult to me. Captain Ball yelled over to me saying, "Corporal McGrady, tell Bill to pull back. Then you take ten more men, and cover our retreat. When the Federals start up the hill, return their fire to keep them from over running these ramparts, at least until we can move out. You can join us when we rendezvous with our supply wagons on the road towards Sutherland. The rest of you men, hitch the horses and let's get our guns out of here."

The words "out of here" had hardly left his lips when an artillery round from one of their batteries landed just over our heads. Captain Ball heard no more than the blast. A single piece of shrapnel hit him dead center in his chest. Fragments from the round also wounded two other men standing some twenty feet from the captain.

Lieutenant Fitzpatrick leaped to his side, but there was little assistance he could offer the dying man.

As more shells hit our position, screams went up from the wounded and dying. "Let's get out of here, let's get out of here." Their screams could be heard over the sound of the incoming shells. It seemed the majority of the men were cowering behind anything they felt would shield them from the barrage. Others were running around looking for direction. Since our commander had been killed, no one seemed to step up to command. Lieutenant Fitzpatrick was still holding the Captain's head and rocking back and forth.

Somebody shouted, "They've got us zeroed in, if we don't move quickly we'll all be killed."

Without hesitation, I shouted, "Men forget those Federals coming up the hill, get these caissons moving before we are overrun." Without letup, the shelling continued with more landing to our front, rather than our rear. A piece of shell fragment tore through the sleeve of my coat. At that point, I wasn't sure any of us were going to get off this hill alive, but I knew we had to try. There wasn't any way our musket fire was going to halt their attack, our own infantry was falling back as the barrage increased. Now the only thing to do was to get the horses hitched, and move our twelve-pound Napoleons and three-inch rifle to safe ground.

Bill was losing no time as he passed me on his way to his position on one of the Napoleons. He was short of stature and his chunky little legs were churning along for everything they were worth. His shock of black hair was blowing in the breeze as he yelled over to me, "Do you think we can get off of this ridge before they overrun us, Corporal?"

"You bet I do. Men, get those horses hitched, and get your backs into those wheels. We are never going to get away from these shells or mud unless we all pull together." The men jumped to the task.

Lieutenant Fitzpatrick seemed stunned; he stared at me without making any comment. He didn't agree or disagree with my order, so I didn't hesitate to insist we hurry.

The horses were very skittish, and it took every man to get them hitched to the caissons. "Robert, help Jim over there hitch that last team. I'll drive these two, or we'll be stuck here forever." I caught myself almost screaming over the noise of snorting horses, yelling men, and exploding shells. The rain and mud was even more of a problem than we had expected. Of course, the incoming fire didn't help things.

Men and horses were slipping and sliding in the dreaded mud. Unfortunately, the horses weren't any more immune to the incoming barrage than we were. Two animals were killed before they could even be hooked to their harness. Many of the men were using the animals as shields as they led them into their positions ahead of the caissons. If too many more were killed, we might have to pull these caissons off this hill by ourselves.

It took a monumental effort, but finally we were able to hitch the remaining animals and get the guns on the move. We were now receiving fire from three sides. Two men fell from the lead caisson, and one other slumped over on a trailing gun as all three weapons raced off the ridge.

The decision to abandon our position had been timely. Had we waited much longer, we would have been totally surrounded, and the only thing we could have looked forward to was capture or death. Thank goodness we didn't attempt the holding action voiced by Captain Ball, although at the time I'm sure he thought it was the proper course of action. It was after he got hit, and the barrage became so heavy that I thought it best to insist we use all the men to help with our exit. Otherwise, I don't believe we would have had a chance to get out of a very tight situation.

Lieutenant Fitzpatrick had finally come to his senses, and had started taking part in our departure. He was on the lead caisson as we started down the ridge. He was hanging on for dear life, while at the same time yelling at the top of his lungs. "Men, keep those animals moving. Do you hear me? Keep those animals moving." Most of us wondered why he didn't quiet down; we were doing our best getting out of this hellhole. It made you wonder just how much leadership ability some of our officers possessed.

The race off the ridge and down the hill towards our supply wagons was breathtaking. We had finally outdistanced the barrage. Now the shells were falling just to our rear. The caissons were sluing from side to side, almost tipping over as they careened down the steep slope. The men were hanging on for dear life. I thought more than once I would be pitched off before we reached a safe haven. We finally eased up in our haste once we got out of range of their artillery. But it was still tricky controlling the guns on this muddy and slippery road. We slowed even more as we approached the area of our wagons.

To our benefit, the Captain had planned ahead, and had outlined a departure route just in case we were unsuccessful with our attack. In fact, our part in the attack was only meant to be a holding action to allow the bulk of Gordon's brigade to proceed westerly out of the Petersburg area towards Amelia Court House. Supposedly, additional rations and supplies were reported to be waiting there.

If we had been successful in routing the Bluecoats, then General Gordon could have used the opportunity to force the Federals well south of the Southside Railroad. Unfortunately, that didn't occur. As it turned out, we became just a small part of General Pendleton's overall evacuation, which saved the majority of the mobile ordnance fighting in the Petersburg area.

Here I was, almost an eighteen-year-old Corporal by the name of Valerius McGrady, getting my first real chance to help decide our fate. It had been a tight spot, and I didn't panic.

I was big for my age, close to six feet tall and weighed 170 pounds. My sandy hair was longer than normal, but it blended in with my mustache and goatee. I also had a prominent nose; some called it a Roman nose. I called it a hooked one. However, it served its purpose, and I never had any trouble knowing when supper was ready.

Most people called me Vee, a few referred to me as Mac. I had only been with this battery for a few months. Shucks, I had only been in this war for barely over a year and a half. I had done well and had won promotion shortly after my first six months of duty. Both corporals in my first unit had been killed, and I was first in line to get the stripes. One's life span seemed to be measured in hours rather than years, as our status of forces grew more critical.

Sometimes it seemed like I had just left our small farm near Clifford, Virginia, other times it seemed like I had been fighting all my life. I had enjoyed those early years. Life on the farm hadn't been complicated. I had my chores, and we had enough to keep us alive and well. I had gotten my schooling, and had learned my numbers and letters well. Every Sunday the family would go over to Saint Marks Episcopal Church, which was just a bare mile away from our house. There we would see all our neighbors and have a joyous gathering. There was even a young girl I had gotten to know very well. She lived over near New Glasgow. Elizabeth and her family attended church almost every Sunday, and I always looked forward to being with her. On more than one occasion she stayed overnight at our house.

One day every month my daddy would take the entire family into Amherst Court House to shop for the few essentials we were unable to find in Clifford. Clifford itself was only a cross roads with one small store that served as post office, stage depot, and local gathering place. But it was home, and I longed to return there when this war ended.

My two favorite things in the world, besides Elizabeth and my family, were on that farm. Duke and Sam, the two best bird dogs in the entire county, maybe even in the state, were waiting for my return. Those dogs could point up birds better than anything I had ever seen before in my life. My daddy had given them to me for my eleventh birthday when they were just pups. I sure missed hunting with those dogs.

My daddy had enlisted first, right after the war started in South Carolina. He had been wounded twice during the first two years of the war, but was still on active duty someplace near here, to the best of my knowledge. Then my two older brothers, Ted, nineteen and Ben, sixteen, had enlisted a year after my daddy. That had left only me, a fourteen-year-old, to work the farm. When we learned of Ben's death, I knew I had to join, or I couldn't have lived with myself.

My daddy had told me when he was home on convalescent leave after his first wound that he was afraid this war was going to be a long one. He said for me not to be too anxious to enlist, and get myself killed. He said he knew I would be going in because there had never been a McGrady who had shirked his duty. He just wanted me to get some growth on me before I took on the toil and despair of fighting a war. Especially a war whose cause was obscure to some people in our part of the country.

The word was we were fighting the North because of the slaves. If that were true, it would appear there should be a better way to settle the differences. Then some said it had to do with the Rights of States. Maybe that was it, I really didn't know. I knew we didn't have any slaves, and not many of the small farmers around our part of

7

Virginia did. A lot of the war those first three years had been fought in Virginia, and it looked like there would be many more conflicts before it was over. We had been lucky that not too many battles had been in the vicinity of our farm. Many of the men from our area had taken up arms so, as a Virginian, it was my duty to fight for the South. I guess I also needed to defend what my daddy and brothers had set off to do before me. Luckily for me, due to the advice from my daddy, my mother, and sister, I was convinced to wait until I was sixteen. I'm not sure, but I felt my mother and sister had no desire to be left alone with the care of the farm.

Shortly after joining, I heard my oldest brother Ted had been badly wounded in the head and wasn't expected to live. I had hoped to join his unit, but when I learned of his wound I knew there wasn't any way we could serve together. Instead, I was initially attached to a light artillery unit, which was all but annihilated during the battle at New Market Heights. After that engagement I moved toward Richmond and was placed in a replacement pool. I had been there only a day when I was assigned to Ball's battery of Gordon's Brigade, which happened to have a vacancy for a corporal.

We immediately became aware of a disruption as we closed on our supply wagons. They had been under fire without us being cognizant of their peril. The ones carrying our small food reserve had been stampeded off by raiding Union cavalry along with several of the ammo wagons. Only two ammo wagons were still remaining and able to move. At that point I would have just as soon had the food supplies. We hadn't consumed a decent meal for over a day, not to mention there had also been very little feed or fodder for our stock.

We gathered in the two remaining wagons and started to move westerly on what looked to be a safe avenue of escape. The surface of the road was muddy and deeply rutted. It looked like it had been well traveled previously, but for now there was no other traffic to slow our progress.

There was a lot of grumbling as we moved out. "When are we going to get something to eat?" "If we don't eat soon, I'm taking off to forage for myself." "Let's leave this equipment here and save ourselves." It sounded like we were becoming more of a rabble rather than a military unit whose record had been so exemplified over the past few years. Despair was beginning to show in a once proud unit of the Confederate States of America. Men could go just so long without proper food and rest before desperation started to show. How much longer could we keep fighting and expect to win? At this rate, not too many more days in the minds of most.

I said, "I'm just as hungry as you, but if we don't get something for these animals, we are going to be pulling these caissons and wagons ourselves." The grumbling died down a little, but I agreed that food and staying alive were the major items on all of our minds.

We weren't exactly sure where this road terminated, but it really didn't matter as long as we had an uncluttered avenue for withdrawal. Federal cavalry wasn't pressing us at the moment, which was a plus. We had proceeded about a mile down the road when it appeared to turn in a more northwesterly direction, which was fine. Captain Ball's plan, which he had issued when we first went into position on the ridge, had been to proceed northwesterly in an effort to rejoin with General Gordon's main force. But for now, we were on our own without a lot of leadership. Plus, we were isolated without knowing how far we were from either friend or foe. It might be said we were somewhat disoriented.

It was April the third and getting late in the day. The rain had started to come down in buckets again, so conditions could only worsen. The horses were straining under their loads, so we put men by the wheels to keep the caissons and wagons from miring down. We knew we were south of the Appomattox River and the Southside Railroad. We knew we needed to move northwest towards Amelia Court House to join with other units of Gordon's brigade, but we weren't exactly sure of the best way to get there. Also, we were almost certain the enemy was to our south and maybe in other quadrants as well. We needed food for men and animals and we needed some rest.

Lieutenant Fitzpatrick finally emerged in what could be called a commander's position. He called the unit to a halt in order to take stock of our situation. At least he thought the rest would let us gain some strength to continue on later during the night.

He walked out in front of the men and raised his voice so all could hear, "We'll rest for a half hour, then move on towards the Southside Railroad. I feel it would be best if we find the Appomattox River, and follow its direction northwest, at least until we can junction with the railroad. There we should make contact with the major part

9

of our army." This unusual expression of leadership was at least a positive step in regaining some semblance of order to our unit.

There were murmurs from the gathering; most sounded as positive 'Yeas' with very few 'Groans.' Many were too weary to voice an opinion one way, or the other. It was going to be a difficult march regardless of the direction.

The Lieutenant looked around and said, "I need a volunteer to scout out our position."

Before anyone could react, I jumped forward and said, "I'm your man, Lieutenant. I will find out just how far we are away from the river and if there are any friendly troops in our area."

He said, "OK McGrady, select two men to accompany you. Depending on how long it takes to gather some needed information, we should be able to join up again a few miles up the road from this position. The rest of us will depart this location in another twenty-five minutes. I want us to be as close as possible to the Southside Railroad by morning."

I motioned for Privates David Hubert and John Peebles to join me. They were two strapping farm boys from Virginia who had served well for the short time I had observed them. They looked enough alike to be brothers, both with brown hair and eyes, although David was a couple of inches shorter than John. They appeared a bit reluctant as we moved out through a heavy stand of trees bordering the road.

I didn't remember until I got into the forest, but I was barefooted. I knew my shoes had disintegrated when we were getting that last wagon unstuck. There hadn't been much left of them when they disappeared in the mud, so I didn't try to retrieve the remnants. At first, I noticed some discomfort, but I had been shoeless before, so the bottoms of my feet were pretty tough. I could make it; I would have to because there sure weren't any available shoes around to replace them. In fact, probably thirty percent of our unit didn't have shoes or a warm coat to keep the rain off.

As soon as we were well out of sight of the road, both David and John stopped and turned to face me.

"Just what do we expect to accomplish by going off on this wild goose chase, Corporal?" David's words were almost a whisper.

"Yeah Mac, why did you select David and me to go wandering off to nowhere? We would have been happy just to wait back there with

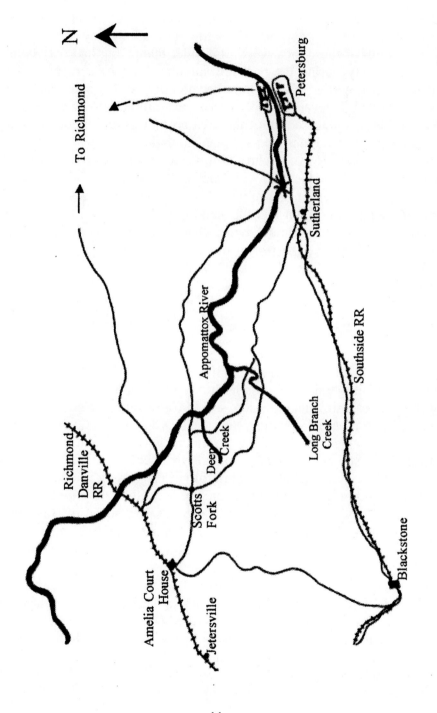

the others while someone else did the scouting." John sat down and leaned against a tree, appearing to settle in for a long stay.

Both of these men were a bit older than I, but had only come on active duty during the past few months. I wasn't sure why they hadn't joined earlier; maybe they had families and hadn't wanted to leave them. Whatever, it really wasn't my problem to worry about. My problem was to scout out the area around us and report back to the Lieutenant. And, that's what I planned to do.

"Listen you two, I chose you because I thought I could trust you if and when we meet up with trouble. Everyone else is either sick, wounded, or useless in my mind. I want to get out of this war alive, and I thought you might feel the same way. My theory is if we keep on the move we have a much better chance for survival. I didn't want to sit back there like the rest of our crew who, in my mind, are just stagnating and waiting for the Bluecoats to come grab them. Also, we just might find some food."

"OK, if that's the case, I'm with you Vee," said David.

John stood up and nodded his approval and said, "Lead the way, Corporal."

We had traveled about a half-mile through dense woods trying to make as little noise as possible. It had been slippery going with the wet undergrowth, making each step an adventure. We had barely entered into a partial clearing when we heard a commotion off to our right. I motioned for David and John to get down until we could determine just who or what was making the racket.

There was a small ridgeline off in the direction of the noise, which would provide us some cover. We crept forward until we came to its crest. Lying flat we peered over and saw a squad of Bluecoats attempting to bivouac for the night. They didn't seem to be attempting to keep their noise down, although we did see a Non Commissioned Officer motioning to some of the men making the most noise.

The Federals had put out several sentries and were starting to eat what rations they had. It was raining so hard; it didn't appear they could get any fires going. Regardless of whether their food was hot or cold, it was more than we had eaten in the last twenty-four hours. I had had some cornpone and beans about twelve hours before we moved into the positions above the small valley with the road dissecting it. But now, that seemed like weeks ago. I didn't know

12

when David and John had last eaten. It was all we could do to keep from rushing in and demanding food.

We could see a fair-sized river not too far from where they were camping. It had to be the Appomattox, so we had at least located its position. I made a small sketch showing its relation in conjunction with our group back on the road. Since I didn't have any paper and it was raining hard, I used the point of my bayonet to scratch an outline on the back of the leather part of my knapsack. I hoped the Lieutenant would appreciate my effort.

John whispered, "What do you think, Mac, should we try to take them, or just move on?"

I said, "I think there may be too many for the three of us. Best we move around them to the north to see what else we can find. We should be able to work our way around to the river without them knowing we were ever here."

So we waited there in the rain-soaked forest until nightfall set in. With the darkness helping to cover us, we started moving in what we hoped was a wide enough arc around the Federal encampment. Noise wasn't a problem since the dampness underfoot and the continuous falling rain muffled out any sound of our movement. We were able to skirt around to the northwest side of their position to the bank of the river without being detected.

The water had to be muddy from all the rain, but we were thirsty, and since we couldn't see the color, it at least tasted cool. We stayed put for several minutes, trying to look out across the river for any movement or lights on the far side. Only a sea of black greeted us, and the few sounds were those still coming from the Federal encampment we had just circumvented.

We started upstream hugging the bank of the river, trying to make as little noise as possible. We had moved approximately a half-mile when we were forced to rest for a moment to catch our breath. A bit refreshed, we continued, but going was still difficult due to the thick underbrush, which contained more briers than brush. More than once we were slapped in the face by unseen branches and twigs. The briers tore at our clothes, and before we could untangle ourselves we were almost shredded alive.

We hadn't looked like much before, but now we really looked ragtag in a variety of tattered pants, coats, hats, and a few shoes. Our appearance could be the reflection of our possible future, which seemed somewhat doubtful at this point. The Army of Virginia was becoming more threadbare as the days went by, in more ways than one.

At last I threw up my arm, we needed to get away from these briers. We had come to a stop in a small opening alongside the riverbank. I said, "I don't think we are going to find out anything in this darkness. We had best get back to our unit, and see if they have been able to forage any food. We certainly haven't found anything edible. Or, we could go back and see if we could stampede those Bluecoats out of their bivouac. Maybe we could find some food there. Any suggestions?"

David jumped right in with, "Let's go back and make those Bluecoats think an entire brigade is upon them. If we spread out and fire from three sides, we might be able to move them southeasterly towards the river."

John shook his head slowly and said, "I think all we would do is get ourselves kilt. They didn't look like they had much food when we saw them over an hour ago. Let's see if we can find Lieutenant Fitzpatrick and the other guys so we can keep trudging towards Amelia Court House. That's where some food is for sure."

"You might be right, John," I said, trying to sound like a seasoned NCO. "I don't think we would have much luck attacking those Bluebellys at night. We would only confuse things and probably not get any food for our efforts. Let's move out to the south and see if we can find that road again."

Regressing away from the river wasn't as difficult as moving along its banks. At least we were out of the briers, which gave us some comfort. Even the rain had eased up a bit. The trees had thinned out some, but there still wasn't much light coming through to see by. We took our time not wanting to fall into some unexpected hole and break a leg. That would have been the final blow after all we had been through on this day.

We had gone about a quarter of a mile when suddenly a rush of horses could be heard coming at a gallop. Also, scattered musket fire could be heard in the distance. We rushed forward and found the road only a few yards away. Just as we reached the ditch on the north side of the road, a squad of Federal cavalry came into view towing what looked like one of our ammo wagons.

The noise was almost ear shattering as the horses and wagons passed close abeam. I dropped to my knees and blasted a shot as the marauding horsemen came abreast our position. Two bluecoats slumped in their saddles, so I figured either David or John had been able to fire also. The others in the group didn't seem to notice that two of them had at least been wounded, for they continued on without slowing their pace. We stayed crouched in the ditch until we were sure they wouldn't turn around to find out who had been firing on their group.

As the clamor of hoof beats faded, everything went silent. We let it stay that way for a full three minutes before starting down the road in the direction we thought our unit should be. It took us ten minutes of brisk walking before we came upon a totally disorganized group of Rebels.

Men were scattered on both sides of the road. Only one Napoleon gun was upright and appeared serviceable. The other was on the ground with broken wheels. The three-incher was hub deep in mud. One of our remaining supply wagons was on its side in the ditch. Lieutenant Fitzpatrick wasn't in sight, and several of our comrades were lying dead in the road. We rounded up about twenty survivors and started piecing the particulars together.

"They came out of nowhere!" cried a wounded soldier.

"We hardly got off a shot. Most of us had fallen out on the side of the road again. We should have posted some sentries," a squatty wagoner mumbled, shaking his head in despair.

"Let's surrender and get this over with before they kill us all," a tall and slender cannoneer, with a bloody sleeve, shouted.

Compiling the fragments of information the best we could, it evolved that the Federal cavalry had completely surprised them. The Bluecoats had come through the trees while our boys were taking a much-needed rest. They had been worn-out by their continuing attempts to move the stuck equipment. The lack of enough horses to keep the caissons and wagons moving at a proper pace had been too much for them after their earlier efforts. Plus, the recent rest hadn't done much to help them regain their strength. When they had stopped for the second time, many of the men were too exhausted to even try and set up a perimeter of defense. Some wanted to spread out and forage for food rather than worrying about the guns or the wagons. Discipline had completely broken down.

15

At this point Lieutenant Fitzpatrick's senses left him. According to a wounded wagoner, he started to rant and rave, going back on his orders to allow a second rest. He started making threats in an attempt to get the men to move the wagons, but he had only been wasting his breath. Then, from out of nowhere, the Federal cavalry had hit them. There had been little resistance left in the group.

Lieutenant Fitzpatrick, along with two other of our boys, was found dead over in the trees bordering the north side of the road. I guess he had tried his best, but unfortunately he just didn't have the experience to lead a group of men, especially a group who were hungry, tired, and miserable. Now we were without any officers; both Captain Ball and the Lieutenant were gone.

Looking around, it suddenly hit me. I was the only NCO left alive. I was the ranking person. I was it. It was my duty to save what little there was left of this once fine artillery detachment. This unit and the men involved had served so well over the past years; had done so much when called upon in so many battles and skirmishes, never failing. Now it was down to twenty or so men with two guns and a supply wagon with only a portion of the ammunition normally available.

The war must surely be in its closing days. Would I be able to survive until the end? General Lee couldn't possibly hope to continue on and win. The Confederate States of America had attempted to win its difference with the Federals, but their abilities had been exhausted. There weren't any more resources available to wage such a conflict. There were no more allies to come to our aid. Our ports were blockaded, which shut down help from overseas. Further efforts to continue this conflict would appear to be futile. It would seem we were whipped. Just look at this once proud unit, only a few men remaining out of over a 120 on the original roster. No food, few shoes, no warm clothes to keep the rain off, a desperate group to say the least.

Not too many choices left at this juncture. We could sit down here on this lonely road and wait for the enemy to capture us. Or, we could all scatter and each try to find their way home. If given the opportunity, many of these boys might select one of these options. But, I wasn't going to give them the chance.

I didn't come into this army to sit down and wait for capture. My daddy has given his blood twice, and my older brother has a wounded head to show for his efforts. Too many Virginians have given their lives for the cause, including my brother Ben. I'm a Virginian and to the best of my knowledge, we aren't quitters. I know for sure the McGradys aren't, and I'm not ready to be the first one who does. Let me get this group together and move out of this place.

The three-inch rifle mired in mud could be retrieved, but the Napoleon with the broken wheels was beyond repair. It couldn't be moved. That left only one of the Napoleons still serviceable plus the three-inch rifle once we got it out of the muck. Also, there was only a partial supply of ammunition available for the guns even if we could get them to a point where they could be put into action.

"All right men, this is what we are going to do!" The words sounded hollow to me at first, but my voice got stronger as the men started to move in the right direction.

"Let's get that broken gun off the road and into the woods far enough so it can't be easily found. Get that three-incher out of the mud, we're going to need it before this thing comes to an end. Pull the dead into the woods; someone will have to bury them later. Get the wounded into the wagon and get the Napoleon ready to move. I mean for us to join General Gordon before noon tomorrow, and remember, if we can get to Amelia Court House, there is supposed to be rations waiting."

I'm not sure if there was a reversal effect from the Federal cavalry blasting down on them unexpectedly, or if my words of order joggled them into action, but it didn't take long before everyone had their back to the task. Maybe there was really a chance we could in fact join up with General Gordon.

The day was dawning with only a light mist. At least the rain had abated, but the muddy road still prevailed. It looked like the sun might even come out, something we hadn't seen for several days now. We fed the horses the last of their fodder; they would have to make it on that until we could find them more.

As I looked around at the remaining men in this group who had fought so hard to survive, I wondered where we would all end up. There weren't two individuals whose appearance looked like they were in the same army. Nobody had on a complete uniform. A few had coats, most had a hat that had seen better days, and there were many, like me, without shoes. We didn't even have a fire to warm our hands, and of course no food. Someone had the last of some coffee grounds he had found, although with cold water it didn't taste like anything you had ever had before. Food was still foremost in our minds, and we hoped to find some soon.

We moved out with only two guns and a wagon, which made our task easier than it had been previously. The mud wasn't any thinner, but we had less to push through it. We were a tattered crew but we intended to remain a part of what was left of Lee's army. The Richmond - Danville Railroad had to be some place up this road. We started forward to rendezvous with General Gordon and get some of those rations at Amelia Court House.

Thoughts of home flashed before my eyes. I could almost smell the bountiful meal table my mother used to set after we returned to the farm from Saint Marks on Sundays. Elizabeth and her family were often with us. It was comfortable for me being near her. The quiet conversations between our families passed the remaining hours of those peaceful occasions. War had been the last thing on our minds during those beautiful pre-cessation days.

Would I ever see those times again? Would Elizabeth be waiting for me when I returned? I certainly hoped so, for she was my chosen one.

There might be some hope of being alive when all of this fighting and bloodshed was over. The thought of getting back to Clifford will always be foremost in my mind; although many times during the previous months there were moments when an inch one way or the other could have been fatal. But, I've never dwelled on "what ifs." I've always tried to stay positive. I've grown to believe in predestination, contrary to my earlier Episcopalian upbringing. So what will be, will be. At this point, only the Lord could know.

The column was finally on the move and for the first time in days a bit of sunlight showered our path. "Let's keep our backs to those wheels, boys. We should be seeing that railhead before long. I can almost smell the grits."

Someone came back with, "Make sure there's some brown gravy on mine, Mac."

"If there isn't, you can have mine." I just hoped my voice sounded better than my spirits, for we were a long way from being out of the woods.

Chapter Two

The sunshine was brief, lasting less than forty-five minutes. But, even those few tiny rays had given us a shot of much needed adrenaline. Our step was a bit quicker, and it appeared we were moving with a purpose.

With the return of the overcast, the temperature dropped again, and I could feel the cold biting into my body. I pulled what was left of my coat collar up around me in an attempt to keep warm. My feet seemed a bit numb, but I was sure frostbite hadn't set in. I kept stamping them on the ground every now and then to make sure the blood circulation continued. If it got much colder, I would have to strip off some of the material from my coat and wrap them. As for now, I felt I could make it as is.

David Hubert was walking beside me and said, "Vee, do you really believe we can join up with the rest of the army today? We may be on our own if we don't find General Gordon. And, if we don't find him soon, I'm afraid the next time the Federals hit us, it will be all over."

"I'm positive we will make contact with General Gordon, so don't worry about that. However, if the Federals hit us before we join up with him, then we will have a problem." I continued with, "Let's not concern ourselves with what may happen, let's worry about keeping our small group moving toward the railhead."

David looked at me and shook his head as if in wonder, "OK Vee, you haven't led us wrong yet. The rest of the men are with you, and so am I." He moved off towards the Napoleon, which had just

21

mired down in a muddy spot. I watched him as he put his shoulder to the wheel and helped get it moving again. He was doing his share, which is all I could ask of any of us.

It seemed like the world had turned a total shade of gray. The sky was gray, the ground was gray, and even the trees were gray. It didn't make for an upbeat atmosphere at a time when we needed all the fortitude we could muster.

Despite the gloomy surroundings, we were moving along at a good pace. The road had drained well after the rain had stopped so the guns and wagon were, for the most part, rolling more easily than before. Even our underfed horses seemed to be straining less against their load as we progressed towards the railroad.

Conversation had increased and there was even some banter back and forth between the walkers and riders. Morale seemed to improve somewhat as we continued along without any Federals harassing our progress. At least it appeared higher than it had been last night. I believed the men had put the previous happenings of the attack by the Federal cavalry behind them. The few who survived that attack must have felt they were lucky to be alive. Now if we could just find some food we could really get back in stride.

It was approaching eleven o'clock in the morning and we were taking a five-minute rest before ascending what I hoped to be the last ridge before coming in sight of the railroad line. The two-man rear guard trailing us came into view and plopped down a few yards to our rear. Both William Sands and Trevor Crawford had been with the unit for more than a year and presented themselves as responsible men ready to do their duty when the time came. Bill Sands was from the Tidewater area of Virginia, while Trevor hailed from near Bedford. Both were tanned from being out in the sun and wind and they seemed to work well together.

I said to them, "Keep your eyes on that road behind us, I don't want a repeat of last night." They nodded in the affirmative, propping themselves against a tree trunk beside the road while maintaining their muskets at a ready position in case they were needed.

Our "Point" man was just a few yards from the ridgeline so I went forward to talk with him. His name was Ben Anderson. He was the serious, quiet type, never saying much unless spoken to. He made a perfect "Point" man for he liked to be on his own and ahead of the pack. Ben had been with the unit since February, and always projected a fairly positive attitude. I said, "Ben, let's ease on up to the ridgeline and take a look before we start out again."

He said, "Fine with me, Mac; I was planning on going up there anyway before we moved out. I didn't want to be surprised when I was so close to the crest of this ridge. I just hope it's the last one we have to climb over for a while."

The countryside was mostly wooded, with an open field every now and then. It seemed our route of travel since leaving Petersburg had taken us over one tree lined ridge after another. It was up one side and down the other, and of course the rutted road always snaked back and forth, both going up and coming down. It would have been nice if the road could have traveled along between the ridges for at least part of the journey. But alas, all the ridgelines run southwest to northeast in this part of Virginia, and we were traveling to the northwest.

As we reached the crest, my spirits soared. There, off to the east, lay the river winding its serpentine way through the countryside. I was pointing it out to Ben when he exclaimed, "Look, a bit to the left of the river, I can see the tracks. There are people there and it looks like there are Stars and Bars above the station." Sure enough, there was activity in the distance and it looked like we were finally going to join up with the main body of the Confederate force.

The rest of the men saw our excitement, and moved forward to get a look. It was all I could do to calm them down and keep them from racing towards the rail line.

I turned to John Peebles and said, "John, take one of the horses and see if those people down there are Confederates or Federals. If they are Bluecoats, escape in any direction you can and join us back here on the ridgeline. If we see you take off, we will dig in and prepare to defend. If it appears we would be wasting our time trying to defend, we will try to move out to the west. If you can move in that direction, we can link up later. I want to avoid a major encounter at all costs." I shook my head slowly and muttered, "Let's hope they are our boys."

John nodded and said, "Don't worry, Mac, I think they are our boys. I sure hope so anyway." With that, he dashed off in the direction of the railroad.

23

We watched him proceed towards the tracks, holding our breath for what seemed like long agonizing minutes, waiting to see what action he would take. They just had to be our boys. If not, Lee's entire army had ceased to exist. It had been reported earlier that units would be coming out of Richmond to help bolster our strength as we moved west in an effort to gain some superiority in the area. However, I wasn't sure if they would be this far south.

Leaving Richmond unguarded was more or less a last ditch move as far as I could tell. Hopefully the Federals were mostly to our south and if we could hold out and win a battle or two, then Richmond could be occupied again before the Federals got to it. We needed a victory of some magnitude if we expected to continue our offensive. Without some fresh troops it would be near to impossible for we were highly outnumbered at this point.

We watched as John continued his gallop towards the activity at the rail line. Suddenly he slowed when he was about halfway to the tracks. He seemed to inch forward at only a walk, finally stopping altogether. He remained in a fixed position for what seemed more than a minute. We could see him as he turned in his saddle and started waving for us to come on forward.

Thank the Lord; they were our boys.

As we approached the tracks I was surprised to see there was no more than a platoon of men. For sure, it wasn't the main body of Lee's army and it wasn't General Gordon's outfit. Well, at least they weren't Bluecoats and maybe they had some extra food.

I located the sergeant in charge lying under a tarpaulin he had stretched out over two limbs of a small tree. He didn't seem to be in any hurry to go one way or the other. My very first words to him were, "Do you have any extra rations? We haven't eaten in a day or two."

He said, "Neither have we except for the few fish we caught in the river yesterday, and they were small."

"Who are you waiting for? We are trying to join up with General Gordon and we thought he would be here at this rail line."

"He ain't here, this is the Southside Railroad. He must be up on the Richmond and Danville near Jetersville or Amelia. It's about twenty or so miles farther on. Supposed to be some rations up that way, or so I've been told. We got to blow up that road bridge over yonder before we can leave. Seems General Lee don't want any Yankees coming across the Appomattox at this point and slipping up behind him. We were supposed to wait for the last troops out of Petersburg before we blow it."

"Well, we didn't come that way, but I guess there could be some more of our boys expecting to cross the Appomattox this far up. We've been south and west of the river since we left Petersburg."

"As far as I'm concerned, you're the last ones I'm planning on waiting on. We been here too long now, and I'm expecting the Yankees to be a coming along any time now."

"Well, you got to do what you got to do," I said as matter of factly as I could.

The sergeant slowly got up and stretched, just like one would do when getting up from a deep sleep. He turned and yelled for one of his men to come over. He said, "Get the men together, it looks like it's time to blow that there bridge." As I departed, he was outlining something in the dirt. Maybe it was their escape plan, I didn't wait to see.

It was well past noon on the fourth of April as I walked back to where our guns and wagon were parked. The boys were resting in a small grove of trees, trying to expend as little energy as possible. The entire group jumped up as I approached. "Well men, this isn't General Gordon's headquarters. He is farther to the northwest on the Richmond and Danville Railroad, this is the Southside. These boys here have been left to blow the bridge over the Appomattox after the last of our troops make their getaway from Petersburg. And, we are the last according to their sergeant. Unfortunately they don't have any rations, and have been without for almost as long as we have. It's at least another twenty miles to Amelia Court House, which is a mile or two east of Jetersville. Amelia Court House is where the trains from Danville are supposed to have additional supplies for us. And, I'm hoping General Gordon will be in that vicinity also."

"Well, there isn't any use of us staying here," said John. "I say we light out for Amelia before the Federals catch us here."

"I couldn't agree more. There is some water over at that well. Get your canteens filled as quickly as possible, and we will be on our way. Depending on what's between here and Amelia, we should be there sometime before morning if we travel all night." I tried to sound as positive as I could.

We were just getting ready to pull out when the platoon sergeant came over to us. "Listen Corporal, after we blow this bridge, we plan to take off south and fend for ourselves. The Confederacy hasn't got a snowball's chance of surviving. Richmond has been abandoned, Grant has ten times the number of troops Lee can muster, and all we could do is get ourselves killed or captured. Why don't you guys come with us? We could be a fair sized fighting force, what with your guns and my men."

I looked at my small group who were staring at the Sergeant as he spoke. Before anyone could say anything, I said, "Sergeant, I didn't come this far to quit now, or move off on some wild exploit that may or may not be productive. I'm planning to join up with General Gordon and see what happens during the next few days." I turned to the men and said, "Does anybody here want to go with the Sergeant and his men? You are free to do as you please."

The air was heavy with suspense and it seemed like time stood still. There were a few sideway glances but not a hand raised. In a way, it surprised me as much as it pleased me.

The Sergeant continued talking, making sure he got in his entire pitch. "We plan to head down towards North Carolina. We feel we can get past the Federals to the south. They are busy moving west trying to cut Lee off before he can join with General Johnston. So, there should be some openings in their lines that will enable us to sneak through. We will either join up with General Johnston before he gets with Lee, or fade away into the surrounding countryside. Most of us are from the Carolinas anyway, so we might as well just head home."

I looked again at my troops to see if anyone came forward. "I guess you don't have any takers Sergeant. Most of us are from Virginia and figure we might as well keep fighting here until the end. Good luck. I hope you and your men make it all the way home."

It was getting harder and harder for me to even visualize home. At times, I could only remember a faint outline of the house and could almost see Duke and Sam running forward to greet me. But beyond that, everything was out of focus. Even the faces of my mother, sister, and Elizabeth had grown dim when I tried to concentrate on them.

Was this war worth it? I was beginning to think I had gotten myself into more than I could handle. Well, it was too late to quit now; I was going to see it through, come "Hell or High Water." I just hoped it wouldn't be any worse than "High Water;" I might be able to manage that.

The secondary road to the northwest was hardly more than a goat path. There had been some fallen trees that had to be moved before we even got started. Also, there were briers and tall weeds to each side of the path as we made our way towards Amelia Court House. The sergeant had said Amelia was no more than twenty miles away. He had said the road got somewhat better about two miles up the way. I hoped he was correct, for getting the two guns and our wagon through this first part had taken longer than I had expected.

We finally put what I hoped was the roughest part behind us and began moving forward on a stretch that could hardly be classified as a road. It did have deep parallel ruts that had been caused by some heavy traffic, but not recently.

We had gone at least a good five miles when we took our first break. Most of the men were beginning to show increasing signs of fatigue, falling to the ground immediately as soon as a halt was called. I couldn't blame them, they had been without rations for a long time now, and we really weren't sure if or when we would find food.

If nothing else, the horses could stand a break after coming across the toughest section of countryside we had faced to date. I wasn't sure how much longer they could pull their load without some feed.

I said, "Let's get the guns and wagon into these woods before we rest. That way we will be off the road in the event someone comes along unexpectedly. William and Trevor, you continue to watch out to our rear, I'll move forward to see if anything unusual is up ahead."

"Mac, let me go with you. It will be better to have two of us scouting ahead in case we find trouble," John Peebles said, as I started to move forward.

"Fine with me, John, if you don't feel that you need the rest." I was glad to have him; he would be my first choice to have around in case trouble raised its evil head.

27

We had gone a full mile and a half along the twisting road, which wound its way up a slight rise before crossing a wooded ridgeline. The road then dropped down to a ford, which crossed what was normally a small creek. It might have been Long Branch Creek, but I wasn't sure. It was running at near overflowing, due mainly to all the rain we had experienced in the past few days. The banks on both sides were heavily wooded in all directions.

It was going to be a lot more difficult to cross when we brought the guns and wagon forward. The water looked rather swift where the ford was located, but we would worry about that when the time came. For now we just wanted to see what, if anything, lay ahead of us.

We finally located a narrow spot up the creek where we could cross. Precariously negotiating some swift white water, we reached the other side of the creek, only slightly wet. Without drying out, we climbed up through the trees to an open area, which gave us a view of the surrounding countryside for at least two miles ahead. At first there didn't seem to be anything but more ridgelines and forest. We couldn't see the railroad or any signs of civilization. I was hoping to be able to see the church spire at Amelia Court House, but I guess we were still too far away. The only thing unusual was some black smoke rising up on the horizon and it had to be at least six or seven miles away.

John said, "Mac, it doesn't look like there is too much of a problem between us and Amelia. Best we get back and get the guns moving before darkness sets in on us. You want me to go back while you stay here and make sure the situation doesn't change?"

"Naw John, I think it best we both go back together. The boys are going to need all the help we can muster getting over that creek.........GET DOWN, JOHN." I almost pushed him into a tree as I grabbed him and pulled him to the ground.

"What the Sam Hill?" he whispered.

"Keep quiet, horses coming and I don't think they are ours," as I pointed up the road. We both moved farther back into the woods as the riders came closer.

"They are Federal cavalry for sure, Mac," said John, just as they were approaching the crest of the ridge.

"Right John, let's just lay low and see where they go. I think we can stay hidden in these trees. At least enough so they won't know we're here."

28

There were at least thirty mounted Federals on some mighty fine looking animals. It was a sure thing fodder hadn't been spared on those horses. They cantered by in a clamor and turned down towards the creek. Just short of entering the ford, they reined in on their officer's signal. Several riders went in each direction along the creek; it looked as if they were trying to decide the best way to cross over the swollen tributary.

"Take five and water your mounts," we heard the officer in charge say from a distance. It looked like they were going to rest for a while, and that placed them squarely between our men and us.

"John, it looks like they plan to stay put for a while. One of us best get back to our troops and let them know what's going on. You stay here, I will get the word back."

"No, Mac, let me go."

"No, I'll go. I just might have a plan to upset these Yankee's apple cart. I'll bring the rest forward as quickly as possible. We might be able to surprise them if they plan to bed down for the night. It is possible they are here to guard the ford."

"What is it you've got in mind, Mac?" John whispered as we moved out towards the creek.

"Let's work our way back across the creek first. Then you can take up a position where you can keep an eye on their movements. When I get the guns, I'll come forward and make contact with you. You can be looking for places to position the guns so they will have the best fields of fire. If it works out without too much difficulty, we can raise havoc with them. What do you think?"

"Sounds good to me," John said with enthusiasm. "Let's keep moving so we can hit them before dark. How long do you think it will take to get the guns back up here?"

"Not much over two hours if we are lucky," I replied, as we briskly moved back to the south side of the creek. The going wasn't too difficult for the trees and bushes weren't as thick as they were closer to the ford. We were forced to go farther up the creek to make sure we wouldn't be spotted, and were able to find some logs spanning across a narrow place. We didn't even get wet.

We circled around on the high ground until we got back to the roadway. John found a well-concealed position where he could observe the Federals.

"I'll be here when you return, Mac. Make it as fast as you can."

"Don't worry, I will. Being able to hit them while we still have good light will mean everything." I moved out to get our boys who had been left with the guns and wagon.

It didn't take long to get the group moving. I had given them a quick briefing on what was up ahead, and what I thought we could accomplish if we were able to surprise the Federals. The key was going to be getting in position without being detected. One thing to our advantage, if nothing had changed, was the Federals were on the north side of the creek. If they hadn't put sentries across, their reaction time could be a problem for them. It would take them a few minutes to get across to our side, and maybe by then it would be too late.

We eased up towards the ridge, which overlooked the creek. I halted the group some fifty yards before the ridgeline and went forward to find John. He saw me coming and met me halfway.

"They appear to be getting ready to spend the night. I think you are correct; they are here to guard the ford. Also, they haven't put any sentries over on this side, at least not yet anyway. Let's get the guns up here as quietly as possible. I've picked out two strong positions that will give us good fields of fire. We should be able to hit them at point blank range."

"That sounds good. I think the men are ready for a little action."

It took us only fifteen minutes to get the guns in position. There were four gunners handling each gun, and they went to their duties in precision manner just like they had done on many earlier occasions. We had very little ammunition left, so they knew they would have to make every round count. I placed three men with muskets on each flank just in case the Bluecoats tried to come in from either side. I sent John and David back across the creek by the way John and I had come previously. I wanted them on the north side in case we needed to move in on them in a hurry. If we were successful, we might be able to catch a few of their horses. Anything would be a plus.

That left only four men, counting myself, to provide protection for the guns in case the Federals charged our position. It wasn't much, but it was all we had.

It was coming on to dusk, however the light was still good but it wasn't going to stay that way long. If we expected to make an impact, we needed to do it now. I raised my arm and dropped it quickly, signaling both guns to fire.

The booming cannonade in this peaceful and quiet glade was close to deafening.

Our first volley was directly on target. We had caught them completely by surprise. Fire and smoke utterly covered the far side of the creek, and shouts could be heard coming from the chaos. Their officer was one of the first to fall, and that left the rest in utter confusion. Many were scrambling for their horses, which had bolted when the first shells hit their mark. A few got to their saddles, and went riding away at a fast gallop. They were last seen crossing the ridgeline on the far side. The few who were left afoot tried to form a skirmish line back in the woods. They were starting to fire in our direction when our second volley put them to rout.

I motioned for the men on the flanks to move forward as I did, all of us reaching the bank of the creek at the same time. There wasn't any musket fire coming from the far side, so we started across the creek unmolested. The swift water knocked one man off his feet, but luckily he was able to reach the bank safely without any help. The rest of us got pretty wet, but we made it without further incident.

We were amazed at the havoc our two volleys had caused. It was a gruesome scene with several mangled bodies in the area. We quickly gathered up three wounded Federals and moved them into the trees. They were hurt bad, but might be able to live if they got to some medical treatment soon.

I could see John and David coming down through the trees preceded by two Federals who were leading four horses. They had captured them as they were attempting to make their way through the wooded area north of the ford.

Upon reaching the area of the three wounded Federals, one of the prisoners went to his knees and started to babble. I couldn't tell whether he had gone into shock, or was begging for his life. I pulled him to his feet and said, "What's wrong with you man?"

"My name is Will Brown. I was captured last summer and spent six months in Charleston prison in South Carolina. You can't send me back. I was exchanged fair and square, and although I promised not to fight again, my commanding general ordered me on this patrol. I swear to you, I won't fight against you Johnnies, ever again. I will go crazy if I have to go back to that awful place. Men are dying from everything from malaria to scurvy. It was awful to be there. Please don't send me back."

"Don't worry, we don't plan to send you anywhere. We can hardly get to where we are headed with what we have, much less take prisoners along. Are there any more of you Yankees planning to come along this way?'

"No sir. We were sent down here to hold this ford, and capture any straggling Rebels we might come across. Supposed to stay here until day after tomorrow, then join up with General Grant's forces who will be marching into Richmond soon."

"Well, if General Lee has anything to say about it, none of you Yankees will be marching into Richmond. For sure, those three up there in the trees won't be going anywhere. You got any medical experience?"

"Only a little. Took care of some of the sick in prison. Don't know much about wounds."

"Well, you and your friend here," I pointed to the other prisoner who had been standing by watching the scene at hand, "better try. Those three up there need some attention. Maybe after we leave, some of your other friends might come back for you. Better hope so anyway."

"Mac, come on. This guy is trying to stall us, hoping another patrol will come back before we get on our way. Remember, a couple of these troops got away. Let these two care for their wounded, unless you want to shoot them." At the word shoot, Will dropped to his knees again. John just shrugged his shoulders and grinned.

We released the two prisoners to tend their wounded comrades with the assurance they wouldn't attempt to follow us. They said they wouldn't even remember what direction we were headed. They thanked us for not shooting them. Although why they thought we would shoot them was unknown to me. John's sense of humor must have really hit home. He was still grinning as we started to round up the rest of our unit.

To my knowledge, neither side had ever intentionally shot prisoners, and I hoped it stayed that way. Looking at these boys was almost like looking at yourself. Except for the uniforms, we were the same kind of people. We had worked the earth and tried to live a godly life. What had gone wrong to cause this catastrophe?

Now I understand why this war is so immoral. It is truly pitting brother against brother. However, 'Duty' is a strong divider between 'Right and Wrong'. And, I have pledged my 'Duty' to the South.

It was dark by the time we got everyone and the equipment on the north side of the creek. We hadn't lost a man and the best part was, we had found a few rations in the saddlebags left by the Federals. There were also some oats for the horses. Not an over abundance of either, but more than we had had in the last few days.

We had captured two prisoners and four horses to show for our efforts. Our guns and wagon had made it across the ford without too much difficulty. All in all, a successful engagement which did a lot for our morale.

However, we didn't feel we had much time to revel in our success. Most likely there would be more Federals coming our way if the survivors were able to make contact with their headquarters to let them know what happened. We had maybe an hour or two to keep moving towards Amelia Court House.

I put Ben Anderson back out in front to scout ahead as we started up the road. If we could put some miles between the ford and us before dawn, I felt we would stand a good chance of avoiding any other Federal troops. Hopefully, that cavalry unit wasn't part of a larger group.

It was near midnight when Ben came back and said, "Mac, the way is clear for at least two miles up ahead. This might be a good place to rest before we make our dash for Amelia. We should be able to get there by sometime early tomorrow, hopefully before noon."

"Sounds good to me," as I called for a halt. "OK men, let's take a little rest here for a while. You sentries, fan out to make sure we don't get surprised. We should move out of here just before daylight. Any questions?"

Someone piped up with, "Mac, do you think there will be any food in Amelia?"

"I sure hope so. I could stand a good meal, those few rations we found at the ford didn't do much for my stomach." I was sure everyone felt the same way I did. "Let's get some rest; hopefully tomorrow will be a good day for all of us."

A slow spring drizzle greeted us as dawn approached on the fifth of April. Ben and John Peebles had moved out ahead our main group. I elected to put two men on 'Point' this time, for I didn't want any surprises when we were getting this close to joining with General Gordon.

We had been on our own for too long, I was in over my head. We had been lucky back at the ford. I was sure we couldn't continue such luck if we ran into another Federal unit. I was afraid surprise would be on their side the next time.

Even though the drizzle didn't let up, the road condition didn't worsen. We were making good time considering the condition of the horses. We had cleared two more ridges and were resting by a small pond when Ben came rushing back.

"Mac, Mac," he was yelling as he came to a stop. "The railhead is just a mile or so ahead. John has made contact and it is General Gordon's unit. We've made it at last."

"Are there any rations? What is that smoke I see coming up over in the distance? Where are General Gordon's headquarters located?" I seemed to be all questions and Ben wasn't answering fast enough for me.

"I don't know, but you can find out for yourself. Why don't you go forward and see what's going on."

Ben always seemed to have a good suggestion when one was needed. I was on my way after I told David to continue bringing the guns and wagon forward. I told the men I would be back as soon as I could find out some answers, and I would bring rations with me. I got a big "Hurrah" and was on my way.

I was led to General Gordon's headquarters by a sergeant I had met back in Richmond just before I joined Captain Ball's artillery unit. General Gordon's headquarters was actually a few miles east of Amelia, but well in sight of the railhead.

34

I reported in with as much military presence as one could muster in a tattered uniform and shoeless. "Sir, Corporal McGrady reporting."

General Gordon was just as stately as I had expected. He stood tall and seemed every inch a leader and a warrior. It was evident he had earned respect as he had progressed up through the ranks to his present position of leadership. General Lee himself could only have topped my awe. I was more than impressed to be in his company.

He said, "Please let me have your report."

I explained in as much detail as possible what had occurred to Captain Ball's unit since the start of action outside of Petersburg. The general was very patient, letting me finish without interruption.

"You are to be commended, Sergeant McGrady." My eyes widened as he continued, "Yes, I said sergeant. You had been slated for the promotion after some of the action in Petersburg. Now it is even more appropriate since your outstanding feat of successfully bringing what was left of Captain Ball's unit to join us here at Amelia. We can use every able-bodied man and gun to continue our fight."

"Sir, we were told there would be rations and supplies here at Amelia Court House. My men haven't had a decent meal for days, I need to draw food for them and the horses."

"I'm afraid I have some bad news for you, McGrady. The trains didn't get through from Danville as promised. It will be a few more miles before we can expect to be supplied. Now, it looks like we can meet the supply trains in Farmville."

"That could be a few days from here, General. I hope we can make it." I couldn't explain the let down I felt in the pit of my stomach. Also, it was going to be extremely difficult to explain the situation to the men, but I would try.

"I know how disappointed you and your men must be, Sergeant, but we are all in the same boat. The promised supplies didn't make it this far up the line. General Lee has ordered wagons out to see what can be gathered from around the area, but I don't think we can hope for much from this already devastated land. Our best bet is for us to get to Farmville." The General didn't raise any false hopes; he told it like it was. "Your men and the two guns will be added to Major William Sandiege's artillery unit.

I want you to pick another man to assist you with a special project I have in mind. I need a good man for the job, and I think you

35

are the right person. You will be relieved from your present assignment, as will the man you pick to be with you.

First, see to your men, then report back to me for further orders. Your unit will be in good hands with Sandiege's outfit."

I said, "Yes sir! I will be back inside half an hour if that's all right?" He nodded that it was. I saluted as smartly as I could and took off to deliver the bad news.

No rations was a hard blow to take, but the men didn't grumble about it as much as I had expected. I think when we had seen equipment and ammunition being blown up on our way into Amelia Court House there had been some doubts raised in our minds about the overall condition of our army. Also, we didn't see any extra rail cars on the tracks, which would have been the transportation for additional rations. And, we hadn't seen any great quantities of food being consumed by any of the troops in the vicinity - another let down that had brought despair to many of those who heard the news before us.

Now Farmville was the new hope, which was another twenty-three miles farther down the road. How many would be around to get there?

I explained the new organization arrangement about Major Sandiege. I knew it was going to be difficult getting used to a new outfit, but I was sure the men could handle it, being the veterans they were. I said some quick farewells and gathered up John Peebles so we could report back to General Gordon. I didn't want to keep the General waiting.

John was all questions, "What does the General want with us? Why can't we stay with the boys? Are we in trouble, or do you think this might be a good deal?"

Of course I didn't have any answers for him, I just said, "John, you will know as much as I do when we both hear it from the General. I have no idea why he would want two people for something special. He asked me to pick a man I could trust, and I picked you. If you want out of it, tell me now so I can get someone else."

"No, I'm all for it. I just thought you might know something additional. Let's get on with it, I'm ready for anything."

"I believe it will get us out on our own for at least a short period of time, and I always feel I have a better chance at survival when I'm on my own. No telling what he will want us to do, but I think it will be something interesting."

As we approached the General's tent I was as excited as John to learn just what we were getting into. But regardless of what it was, I knew I could count on John.

Chapter Three

Heavy drops were pounding the side of the tent as John and I stood in the corner waiting as General Gordon finished addressing the men gathered before him. We had been told by the Adjutant to get in out of the downpour, which was passing through the area in the form of a full scale, bolt and lightning, thunderstorm. Many times in the past it had been difficult to tell nature's roaring, booming voice from that of our own guns or those of our enemy. This time there wasn't any doubt. The drops were so ponderous they almost penetrated the heavy canvas shelter.

The general rose from behind his desk and said to those before him, "Now, you all know what is expected of your units. I've been given the duty of keeping the Yankees from swallowing up the rear of General Lee's army as we move west towards Farmville. General Longstreet will be spearheading our armies, and will be coming from the direction of Jetersville and Rice. He is bypassing Burkeville, which has been overrun by the Federals. So, that rules out making use of the railroads which junction there.

Our best means across the Appomattox River will be at High Bridge. That will put us north of the river again and enable us to reach Farmville along the Southside RR. You know what an endeavor this will be, so use all your efforts to accomplish this task. Now, get out to your troops, we will be moving within the hour."

I wasn't sure John and I were meant to hear all of that, but the general didn't seem to mind as he waved his hand for us to come over to the desk. As we approached, he came around and unfolded a map,

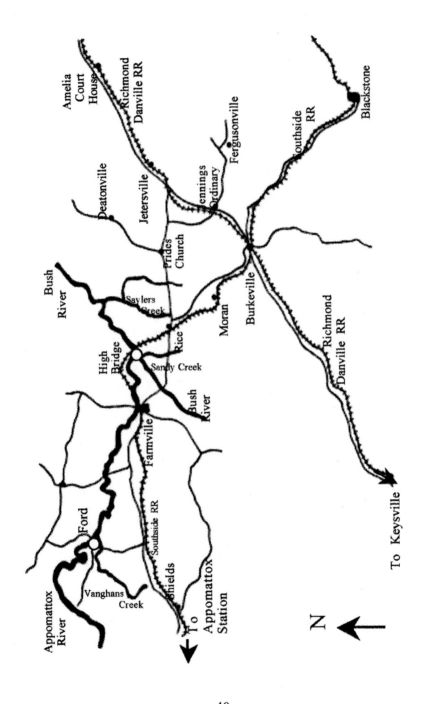

spreading it by putting a candleholder on one corner and his revolver on the other. We could see the meandering trail of what must be the Appomattox River curling its way through the center of the parchment. Closer inspection affirmed that it was indeed the Appomattox, showing its relation with our current area of operation.

The general pointed his finger at Burkeville and the junctions of the Richmond and Danville RR and the Southside RR. He said, "I've been informed that the Federals presently have control of this junction, but I'm not sure just how strong a force they are retaining there. What I want you two to find out is just how many Federals are there, how long they've been there, and if they appear to be moving out. If so, it could change General Lee's entire strategy. For the present, we plan to move our forces towards Farmville. There will be rations there for our starving army, of that I have been assured. However, if we could strike back down the Southside RR and recapture Burkeville, it could give Lee a better means of uniting forces with General Johnston. Also, the railway might then be opened again all the way to Danville." He paused seeming to wait for comments. With none forthcoming, he continued, "I believe two lone horsemen can get into the Burkeville area without being detected. If you can get into town, possibly at night, perhaps you can gather enough information to assess our chances there. It won't be easy, and if you get captured you may be regarded as spies." He looked me squarely in the eye; his gaze was penetrating. "What do you men think?"

John and I stared at the map for several minutes. Finally we turned to each other and gave knowing nods. John gestured for me to be the spokesman, so I said, "Well sir, we think the mission can be accomplished without too much difficulty. As for being captured, we'll just have to chance that possibility. It will take us a little while to get down to Burkeville and back to you, wherever it is you want us to meet you. Today is the fifth, it will take us at least until late tomorrow before we could get you any information."

John spoke up and said, "Sir, I have some relatives who live in the Burkeville area. They could possibly be of great help to Mac and me. At least, we may have a place to hole up if things get tight."

"Good, I knew I could count on you two. There are a couple of strong horses saddled just outside which should enable you to cut down on the time element. Report back to me before midnight tomorrow on the north side of High Bridge. That will be the sixth, or I should say the beginning of the seventh. Hopefully I will have gotten all our units over the river before then. Both the High Bridge and the Wagon Bridge below it are to be burned after we cross. Also, we can't be sure just how close the Federals may be pursuing us. You could have some difficulty."

"Do we have any leeway on that time limit, General? We could have a bit of a problem getting back across the Appomattox if those bridges are burned before we can get there," I said, somewhat warily. "We could be a bit later on the seventh, but we will do our best to be as close to midnight as possible."

"OK, McGrady, you and Peebles do the best you can. If you run into trouble, I'll understand the delay. But I'm hoping you can get back as quickly as possible. The information you gather could determine the fate of the Confederacy." The General paused, seeming to be thinking of some last words, then with a slight smile he said, "Oh yes, McGrady, take a look at some shoes my Adjutant has in his tent, they could make your feet more comfortable on the trip."

We saluted and went out into the rain, which had slacked off considerably from the downpour it had been. Now it was barely enough to wet your clothes. We inhaled the clean smelling air, fresh from nature's washing. It gave us a much-needed lift, as we were about to enter into an unknown adventure.

One pair of shoes fit. They felt good after two days of being without.

The horses were in good shape and it was nice to be mounted after the long trek from Petersburg. There were two pistols holstered on each side of the saddle horns and we had slung our muskets over our backs. We weren't going to be short on firepower. We didn't intend to take on a Yankee brigade by ourselves, but we did want to be prepared for a small squad if we ran into one.

It was going to be a good ten-mile journey to get to the Burkeville area and we wouldn't be able to stay on the regularly traveled roads. The bulk of our army was headed in the direction of Jetersville. General Gordon had told us he would be turning north just east of Jetersville and heading for Deatonville. He assumed General Longstreet would be going in the same general direction. That meant we could probably stay on the road, at least to Jetersville, without running into any Federals. But from there, we would have to cut out across the countryside, and be very careful not to encounter any enemy units. That would add to our time en route, but if everything went according to plan, we could still arrive in the Burkeville area just after nightfall.

The going wasn't easy after getting off the main road. Initially, we had to pick our way through some dense forest. Luckily, after only a mile or so of closely spaced trees, we hit open country. Crossing the south branch of West Creek didn't slow us since it hadn't reached flood stage. The heavy rains we had experienced the last few days hadn't affected this area, as yet.

"John, let's pull up over in that stand of oaks. We don't want to tire these horses out before we get to Burkeville. Looking at this map, I figure we should be just to the east of Jennings Ordinary."

"Yea, Mac, I agree. I think we will be crossing this road here," he pointed at the map I was holding. "It goes between Jennings Ordinary and Fergusonville. If this map is correct, that tall hill in the distance must be Mount Hall. See it over to the southeast?"

I nodded in the affirmative and said, "Seems odd we haven't seen hide nor hair of any Bluecoats. I think if we can cross over and get north of Burkeville, we'll stand a better chance of getting into the town unseen. Do you agree?" I wanted to make sure we were both of the same mind, particularly when we got close to town.

"Sounds good to me," John said, without hesitation. "There's a junction in the main road just a bit south of Jennings Ordinary. See it here?" He was motioning to the map again. "We can get a good view of it before we have to get out in the open. If the junction is clear, it may be the best place to cross both the main road and the railroad. Let's investigate it anyway."

We mounted the horses and moved slowly down the back of a sloping ridge for a mile or so. We were traveling along an old obscure trail, which wound its way in a large arc to the west. The overgrown pathway paralleled Deep Creek, as we got closer to the junction.

We stayed below the ridgeline until we were within a hundred yards of the junction. Tying the horses, we crawled up to the crest to get an unobstructed view. We felt we would be able to find a safe place to cross over the main road once we got a better idea of the lay of the land.

The entire area, including the small junction and the railroad, were clear in all directions and it looked like we would have no problem crossing undetected. Luck seemed to be with us. We were just turning to head back down to the horses when John said in a somewhat sarcastic tone of voice, "Mac, look what's coming down the road."

As we crouched behind the hill, a small group of Federal horsemen were headed for the junction at a gallop. I whispered, "They must have been up towards Jetersville on a scouting mission. They are too small a force for anything else."

"Hang on and let's see what they plan to do."

The squad, ten in total, pulled their mounts to a halt when they arrived at the crossroad. The officer or the NCO in charge, we couldn't tell the rank, motioned for two of them to dismount. He leaned over in his saddle and gestured in the direction of Jetersville. Then he pointed down the connecting road. It was evident the Federals were putting out pickets along the main road between Burkeville and Jetersville. We couldn't be sure just what that meant.

John said, "Maybe it means their main force is still south of here. Or, it could mean it's headed this way."

"Yea, we could be right in the middle of them if we get into Burkeville. But, we will still have to give it a look." Just as I finished my comment, the remaining eight horsemen galloped off towards Burkeville. I said, "Well, if we go a little further down the road, I think we'll be able to cross to the other side without those two pickets seeing our movements."

John was halfway down the slope towards the horses saying, "I think I have a plan. Come on, let's get going while the going is good." I was right behind him.

We started to the south and to my amazement; John wheeled his horse onto the road leading to the junction. I didn't have time to ask him what he had in mind. The Federals who had been left behind to guard the area saw us immediately. They weren't more than thirty yards away by the time John continued galloping toward their position. As John drew to within twenty yards of the two Yankees, they started to shoulder their muskets. At this movement, John brought his mount to a sliding halt and saluted. He then swept his hat off his head and waved vigorously in a friendly manner. At this unusual action, the two relaxed their cautioned stance and started their weapons back to the ground. The second John saw them relax; he spurred his horse forward while at the same time extracting his pistols from their holsters. Before the two men knew what was happening, flame belched forth from John's twin barrels. The two bullets hit their mark, dead center, killing both instantly with clean shots.

Reaching his position, I said, "That was a neat bit of action. Where did you come up with that maneuver?"

"It was something I learned from an old hunter who used to live near our farm. He always told me the unexpected would gain you the best advantage when in a tight spot. And, I considered us to be in a tight spot."

"Well, you surprised me almost as much as you did those two Yankees. Now, we need to get them out of sight and then move on. Here, hold my horse while I pull them over in those bushes. That should hide them enough unless someone comes back looking for them. By that time we should be pretty close to Burkeville."

The terrain north of Burkeville was mostly open fields with gullies running from north to south. There wasn't much cultivation, just some pastureland spotted with small groves of pine. Some of the gullies were large enough for us to travel in. They also gave us much needed cover, which made our journey a lot safer as we approached the town.

Darkness was falling as we made out the first silhouettes of buildings in the distance. A slight precipitation was beginning to fall again, although it was difficult to tell exactly what it was. The temperature was also dropping to a chilling degree we hadn't been exposed to in the last few days. It had certainly been wet, but not this cold.

We could see lights beginning to blink on in the town. By following alongside a small stand of trees, we moved towards the east end of town. The lights from the buildings at the railroad junction helped get us to a point just on the outskirts of the business area.

"My gosh, John, that's snow coming down. That just about does it; snow in Burkeville in April. I think I've seen everything now."

John, shaking his head disgustingly, said, "I hope it doesn't get deep enough to show our footprints. That's all we need now is to be found out by our tracks in the snow."

We continued along a thin row of trees, slowly walking our horses so we wouldn't make any noise and give our approach away. John said, "See that old barn over there?" He was pointing towards a darkened structure over to our left. "It should be a good place to leave our horses while we take a look around."

I nodded in agreement as we moved into the lee of the weather-beaten stable. Tying the horses, we took the pistols from their holsters and moved off towards two houses, which faced onto the main street of Burkeville. Or, at least I thought it was the main street. John seemed to know where we were and whispered, "The house on the left is where my cousin and her mother live. She may or may not be home. Why don't you stay here near this fence while I go up and check?"

"I'm willing to go with you, John, I don't think it would be wise for us to get separated."

"OK, suits me, Mac. Stay close and we'll get over to that back door."

John tapped lightly on the door. Nothing happened. He tapped again with a bit more vigor. Finally we heard someone rustling inside. It was a moment before we saw a light coming from under the door seal. A whispered voice said, "Who is it?"

"It's me, John. John Peebles. Is that you, Sarah?"

"My goodness, John, what on earth are you doing here in Burkeville?"

"Let me in and I'll tell you, but first turn off that light."

The light went out and the door opened slightly allowing us to slip into the kitchen. As soon as the door closed, Sarah lit the lamp again. John gave her a long hug and a kiss on each cheek. He stood back and said, "This is Mac McGrady, Sarah. He and I are on a scouting mission for General Gordon. We only plan to stay just a short time. Do you have anything to eat?"

Even in the flickering light of the lamp, it wasn't difficult to see that Sarah was a very pretty girl. Brownish hair, full-blown body, and quick dancing eyes which sparkled in the lantern's glow.

"Yes John, I have some cold beans and some corn bread left over from the meal my mother and I finished earlier. Also, there is a jug of buttermilk out on the porch. Will that be enough?" Her voice sounded a bit husky, but nevertheless feminine. Maybe she had a cold.

46

"It will be more than enough, Sarah," he said, as she put the food on the table. "This looks like a banquet to us. We haven't seen this much food in a long time. It will hold us for another day or two." John was almost bolting the food down as soon as she placed it on the table. But then, we were hungry.

I said, "Thank you, Miss Sarah, you don't know how good this tastes." I wasn't wasting any time getting the food off my plate either. As I sopped up the last trace of bean gravy with the final crumb of corn bread, I felt a bit guilty when I thought of our hungry comrades back in the battery. But, they weren't here and I was. It was nice to have a decent meal.

She looked at us in wonderment as we devoured the food in just a matter of minutes. "I'm sorry that's all we have cooked up right now. I could fix you some eggs, but we won't gather them until in the morning. I could cook up some more beans if you can wait until then." She was eager to please.

"No, no Sarah, this has been perfect. We just needed a little nourishment to keep us going. We only mean to stay until we can find out how many Federals are in town. Where is your mother?"

"She's upstairs in bed, she hasn't been feeling too well lately." Sarah appeared a bit worried as she spoke.

"Well, I hope she is better soon. I won't disturb her now, but tell her I asked about her." Sarah nodded as John continued, "We've seen a lot of camp fires, just how many Yankees are in Burkeville?"

"It seems to me like the entire Yankee army has descended upon us. Burkeville has them all over the place. Trainloads came in yesterday and they say more are coming tomorrow. They haven't hurt us any, but they have told us to stay off the streets unless we want to be arrested." Sarah's eyes got bigger the longer she explained about the Yankees in town.

"Well dear cousin, you have been more than kind to me and my friend. We best be getting out of your way, we wouldn't want the Yankees to find us here. We are going to slip out the way we came in. Maybe take a little look around before we start on our way back towards Farmville. Take care of yourself, and if this thing ever ends, I'll be back to see you." John hugged and kissed her a bit more passionately than one would expect cousins to embrace. But, maybe that's the way they did things around Burkeville.

Sarah went over to the sideboard and took out a piece of beef jerky. She handed it to John saying, "Maybe this will come in handy later on." He stuffed it in his jacket and gave her another embrace, which lingered even longer than the one before.

We slipped out the back door and crept silently alongside the house towards the main street. We could see more campfires burning all around the railroad yards. We ducked back into the darkness of the alley as a squad of Bluecoats came marching along the street.

I pulled John back and whispered, "I think we've seen enough to know there are more Yankees here than our army could handle. I think we need to get back to General Gordon and let him know what we've found out."

John said, "Not yet, Mac, I know the old man who runs the tavern just over on the next street. We can get there easily and he will know exactly what's going on in the town. Come on, let's cross this street and get between those buildings over there." His feet were crunching on the gravel before I could say a word, so I had no choice but to follow.

Luckily the street was empty as we dashed across. We were able to gain the shelter of two buildings before anyone saw us. We stopped for a moment to get our breath; we weren't in shape for those quick dashes. I said in a faint gasp, "John, just how close a cousin is Sarah to you? I know my cousins and I don't hug and kiss like you and Sarah."

"Thought you might have noticed that, Mac. Sarah and I plan to be married if and when this thing ever ends. She and I have known each other since we were very little. Her mother and my mother were friends before they were married. They went to school together. Sarah and I have been fortunate to live in the same town for the past twenty years. We have been close for the best part of our lives. I just say she is my cousin to keep the questions at a minimum until the right time comes. Didn't work with you though."

At least John has someone to come back to when this war ends. It is hard to comprehend how many young lovers' lives this war has interrupted. Luckily for some, there will just be a postponement; many others will be terminated forever.

In my case, I'm hoping Elizabeth will be waiting at my home. I wonder if she will know when the war ends? If not, I will for sure be spending more time over in New Glasgow when this thing is over. In fact, I hope to be going by her home when I head for Clifford. I'll stop in and surprise her.

I smiled at him as we moved along between the buildings. As we emerged into the open again, we approached the back of a long, low structure. It was about thirty yards across an open space. We made another short dash for its cover. When we got to the back of the building, John went down a small flight of stairs, which led to a basement door. Without waiting, he opened the door and entered a dark corridor. We followed it to another set of stairs, which went up into what must have been a back room of the tavern. He motioned for me to wait in the dark as he slowly inched open the door at the far end of the room. Light streamed in through the small crack. John peered through the small opening for a full minute before quietly entering, leaving me in darkness again.

It was difficult to make out anything in the room after the blinding shaft of light. I crept closer to the door where I could hear two voices in a whispered conversation. Footsteps approached the door, so I crouched back against the wall, readying my two pistols. The door reopened quickly and an older man, holding a lantern, accompanied John back into the room.

"Man, I is sure glad to see you two boys, I ain't seen nothing but Yankees for over a month," the old man said, as he came over and shook my hand.

John said, "Mac, this is Ike. He is my uncle by a second marriage, but he has been like a father to me for many years. He knows everything that's going on in Burkeville and where all the Bluecoats are camped. Pull out that map and let Ike mark it for us, then we'll really have some good information for General Gordon."

I put the map down by the lamp Ike had placed on the table and he started to move it around so he could orient it properly. "They is mostly down by the junction of the railroads," he said, as he pointed to that area of Burkeville. "They has been a coming in by the boxcar loads since yesterday. But from what I hear, they ain't staying long. They are moving out to the northwest, towards Appomattox Station so they can stop General Lee's attempt to get out to the west. Or, that's at

49

least what they are saying when they are drinking their fill here in the tavern."

"They must seem pretty cocky, if they are talking in public about what they are going to do to General Lee," I said. "They might be in for a surprise if they get too overconfident."

"They seem pretty sure they is gonna win this war, and it ain't gonna be too long in coming, according to them. They says they gonna be home in time for summer." Uncle Ike shrugged his shoulders as he pulled the map around for a better look.

"General Lee will see about whether they are right or not," John added, with some conviction in his voice.

I folded the map and shook hands with Ike. He had certainly been a great help in our attempt to gather information on the Yankees.

As John started for the back door fixing to leave he said, "Thanks, Uncle Ike, for giving us what information you had. It might help us out before this war ends. Do you have anything else to add before we leave?"

"Well, most of the Bluecoats who come in for a drink have been bragging about a General Ord. He must be heading up all the Yankees in this area. Hear tell, they all might be moving out come morning." Uncle Ike wiped his sleeve across his mouth after spitting into a can on the floor.

"We best be going ourselves if we intend to get back north of the Appomattox before tomorrow. Thanks again, hope to see you before too long." John was down the steps and out the door. I just waved and followed.

The eastern sky was just beginning to show streaks of red as we arrived back where we had left the horses. The light snow last night had long since melted. It hadn't amounted to much, but it was sure unusual for this time of year.

There wasn't any sign of Yankees in the surrounding area, so at least we hadn't been detected. John and I had agreed we would head directly north, staying well to the west of the Jetersville road. According to the map, if we could hit Ellis Creek and follow it to just south of Pride's Church, we might be able to stay clear of any Yankee troops.

We picked up a trace of a path as we headed out over open ground. After about a mile, the narrow trail dropped down to a small creek. We stopped to study the map and let the horses get water. The creek wasn't swollen with water like many in the area, so it wasn't difficult to ford. But, then the path on the far side rose steeply, climbing to a high point, which gave us a great view of the terrain ahead. It was amazing how clear the visibility was after such bad conditions the night before.

After getting a bit of rest to stave off sleep, we altered our plans. The landscape in front of us warranted a different approach than we first thought feasible. We felt it would be smarter to head in a northwesterly direction. It would give us a better chance of observing the road between Burkeville and Rice. The map showed that road and the Southside RR paralleling each other just a mile or so below Rice. If the Yankees were that far north, we should be able to see them and adjust accordingly. It meant going over more difficult terrain, but that was the least of our worries.

We headed down a steep grade to a small tributary which we thought to be Ellis Creek. Pine trees bordered its banks and the water was almost crystal clear as it cascaded over the rocky bottom. We crossed at a narrow spot and chose a well-worn path ascending to a bald knoll. We kept to the high ground staying just below the ridgeline so we weren't silhouetted against the skyline. Unfortunately, the open area petered out and we were forced to enter into an extremely dense forest, which sloped down the west side of the ridge. We had to weave our way through a variety of trees and bushes. It was getting on to noon when we stopped close by a small clear brook to rest the animals.

John pulled out the piece of jerky Sarah had given him last night, and handed me a part. It tasted good, anything tasted good when considering how little food we had consumed since before Petersburg. The cool water from the stream topped off our repast, however meager it was.

"Let me see that map a moment, Mac. There is something about this area that looks familiar to me." John intently scanned the map, finally pointing out a spot close to the road between Burkeville and Rice. "This little stream could be the beginning of Saylers Creek. It flows off to the north after it crosses the road east of Rice. Maybe it would be best to follow it until it crosses the road, then we can cut back into Rice to see what's going on."

"That sounds like a good idea as long as we don't run into any Yankees. If we find the area north of Rice clear, then we can stay close to the Southside RR until we reach High Bridge. Let's get moving."

The going was easier along the banks of the creek. We were making good time as we neared the point where the railroad and the road paralleled. In the distance we started to hear what sounded like artillery fire. Then as we got closer, we could hear muskets being fired in volley. The sounds had to be coming from just over the ridge to our left. We hobbled the horses and crept up to the ridgeline to have a look.

Suddenly, as if in a flash, we were spectators of a head to head engagement. We were surprised to say the least. West of the railroad in open ground was an entire brigade. They were in battle formation advancing forward in the direction of Rice. Their battle flags fluttered in the breeze. It was easy to see they were the Stars and Stripes. Several batteries of artillery were firing in their support. We could see the shells bursting and seconds later we heard the explosions.

There was movement past the shell burst, which appeared to be troops retreating in disorder. Through the smoke it was hard to make out our colors, but they had to be Confederate boys. However, there was some artillery fire being returned, because there were large explosions right on top of the advancing Bluecoats. It was slowing the long Blue Line's progress, but it hadn't stopped it. The return fire had the looks of a well-organized delaying action.

As we continued to watch the engagement, we were horrified to see Union cavalry closing in behind our boys. They were caught in a pincer maneuver, which offered little chance of escape. The Confederates fell in behind some earthworks, which must have been prepared in advance. This fortification gave them cover, however it was only going to allow them to be killed or captured as time wore on.

"Looks like some of our boys are trying to buy time for the major part of Lee's troops to get across the Appomattox. General Longstreet was going to go through Rice, it must be part of his rear guard trying to hold long enough for the rest to get on the way to Farmville."

John nodded his head in agreement and said, "Best we get out of here. I don't know how far we'll have to go to stay away from those Bluecoats. It's almost three o'clock, if we strike out for High Bridge, we may make it before the Yankees close it down."

We eased back down towards the horses, somewhat perplexed about our future.

We put those two horses to a severe test by galloping hard for a ways, then letting them walk for a spell to keep them from collapsing from fatigue. We were going to stay at it until we reached the river. It was a trial of endurance for both man and horse.

Chapter Four

Daylight was just beginning to fail when the sharp crack of breaking bone and the thud of a large body hitting the ground filled the air. It brought the quiet and shadowed glade alive. I reined in my horse and looked back just in time to see John tumbling head over heels. Luckily he had been thrown clear of his horse as the stead somersaulted through the underbrush.

We had been at a dead gallop through some scattered pines when the accident occurred. The rain had started again, large plopping droplets, but the ground hadn't gotten too slippery as yet. We had been attempting to put as much distance as possible between the head to head action we had witnessed near Rice and us. We had crossed the Rice/Pride's Church road just east of Rice, and were working our way back over to the Southside RR. We figured this would give us a straight shot to High Bridge. Also, we wanted to get there before it was set ablaze, and before the Yankees controlled both sides of the Appomattox. Now that possibility was extremely doubtful.

By the time I got back to John, he was in a sitting position, and shaking his head slowly trying to see if it was still attached to the rest of his body. I said, "Are you still alive, or is that fact in possible doubt?"

"I'm not real sure. Give me a hand, and I'll see if I can stand up." He steadied himself on my arm, and slowly rose to his feet. "I think I'm all in one piece, but it did knock the wind out of me for a second or two." John took a few steps without falling back to the ground.

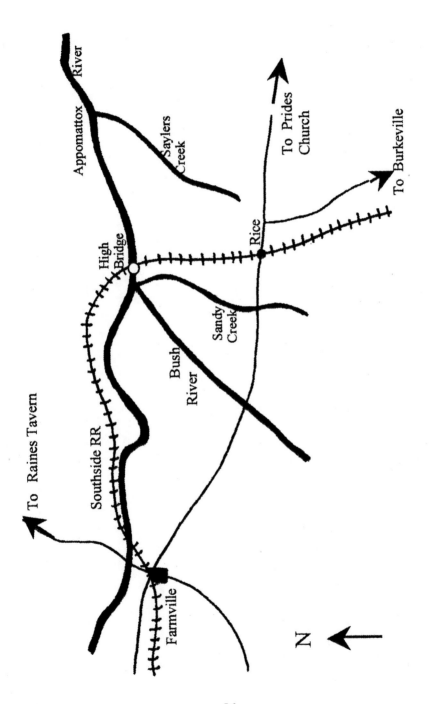

"I'm afraid your horse isn't in such good shape, looks like he has broken his right fore leg," I said as I stood by the fallen animal quivering there in pain. It was obvious he had stepped in a hole, which caused him to fall. Without hesitation, I pulled my revolver, and fired a shot into his head. Even with the possibility of having the gunshot heard by Yankees, there wasn't any way I was going to let that wonderful animal suffer any longer.

John spoke while leaning against a small pine, "Well, it looks like we may have a bit of trouble getting to High Bridge before midnight. Why don't you go on, and I will see if I can make it on foot."

"There is no way I'm going to leave you here. My horse will just have to carry us both. I think he can take the extra load, or one of us can walk while the other rides, at least for part of the way. That last sprint had just about done both horses in anyway. They can go just so far on little or nothing to eat."

"I could say the same for us. Where do you think we are?"

"I'm not sure, let me see." It took me a minute to get back to my saddlebags and get the map out. There was barely enough light to see by, but I was able to make out most of the details. "We are probably here," I said, pointing to a spot just to the north of Rice. "It isn't too much further to High Bridge, at least as the crow flies. However, I'm pretty sure we won't be able to travel in a straight line like a bird."

"Yes, it all depends on what's between us and the river. If it's Yankees, then we are going to have a tough time joining up with General Gordon. We had best get started or we'll never get there. Let me get the revolvers and whatever else I can from my saddle bags." John took a few steps forward and immediately fell to the ground.

I retrieved his essentials, and said, "OK, you get on the horse, and I will lead it." He balked at that comment, but I continued, "At least until you can get all the cobwebs out of your head. Then we'll take turns riding."

"OK, but I should be clear headed in a little while. My back is starting to ache a bit, and my left arm is feeling a bit numb." He was going over his body with his hands, touching all the major areas in self-examination. "I can't feel any broken bones, so I guess I'm lucky to be able to get on a horse again." John reluctantly got up in the saddle, and we started towards High Bridge.

John's horse had fallen while we were on a slight down slope, so we continued down the slope until we came to a shallow creek. It wasn't much more than a trickle, but the water in it was beginning to rise from the heavy rains. We followed it for several yards, finally crossing it and going up the far side. The trees were very thick on this upper slope, and the rain continued to increase, making conditions worse. The steady downpour forced John to get off the horse and walk along with me. Circumstances were making it difficult to keep a firm footing for both man and horse. We were almost at a snail's pace as we reached the top of the ridge.

Just as we topped the crest we literally came face to face with a caboodle of Federals. Not fifty yards down the hill were at least two squads of infantry. They were just in the process of putting out sentries and preparing to camp for the night. Both of us being on foot was one of the luckiest moves we ever made. Otherwise, if one of us had been on the horse, we would have been silhouetted in the fading light. Either way, we suddenly had a real problem.

We slowly backtracked to a position just short of the crest. Unfortunately, in backing up, the horse shied, and began to whinny. We heard one of the sentries yell out, "There's a horse up there somewhere."

We quickly pulled the bridle and saddle off the horse and threw them into the underbrush. John hit the horse on its hindquarters, causing the surprised steed to bolt over the crest and down towards the Yankee encampment. There were a couple of shots fired as the horse ran through their bivouac, luckily for the horse the shots missed. In the confusion, John and I moved off to the northeast keeping the ridgeline between the bewildered Yankees and us. We could hear the shouting and hollering for at least half a mile. Finally the noise diminished, so we stopped to catch our breath.

John had expended about all his reserve energy with our rapid departure from the ridgeline. His breathing was raspy, like a man gasping for air after almost drowning. His chest heaved and he said, "What now my friend? I'm afraid we've just about used up all our luck these past few days. I don't think we'll ever make it back to join up with General Gordon."

"Don't give up hope just yet," I said, trying to keep my voice as calm as possible. "We couldn't be more than five miles from the river. If we take our time and are lucky, we should get there a little after midnight. Depending on where we hit the river, we can try to use the bridge if it hasn't been fired, or we can swim for it. We just need to stay clear of the Bluecoats until we get to the other side."

"Well, let me rest a little longer, then maybe I'll be able to go for at least another mile or two. I can't remember the last time I was so tuckered out. You would think I was getting old." John tried to chuckle but his heavy breathing only produced a cough.

After resting for a good twenty minutes and having heard nothing from the direction of the Yankee bivouac, we moved out in what we hoped was the direction of High Bridge and the Appomattox River.

It seemed there were nothing but ridgelines between our destination and us. No sooner did we go up one slope than we were down another. We had traversed two ridgelines; as we approached the crest of the third, we stopped.

The third ridgeline formed the edge of a small clearing, which dropped off sharply. The lack of trees gave us a clear view down to a road below, which ran from east to west. An eerie glow in the sky to the north reflected light off the cloud bottoms, creating a respectable amount of illumination.

I said, "Of course, John, that glow is coming from the fires on High Bridge. They've set it ablaze already. Once we cross that road down there, we'll at least know the direction to the trestle."

"There must have been some heavy fighting down there," John said pointing to the road. "Look at all the broken and abandoned equipment, both ours and theirs. I guess most of our boys have gotten north of the Appomattox by now; I hope so anyway."

The road appeared well rutted from what must have been some heavy wheeled traffic. In the distance we caught a glimpse of several wagons disappearing off to the west. We hung back, staying in the edge of the woods, watching for additional traffic.

It was only a matter of seconds before a company size cavalry unit, heading west, went by at a gallop. Three batteries of artillery followed it immediately. The guns looked like twelve pound howitzers to me, or something of an equivalent bore. They were all Yankees.

As the howitzers passed, John said, "Let's get down close to the road so when there's a break in traffic, we can dash across. I think we'll be safe enough in this eerie glow. It sure is casting some weird shadows."

We moved out of our sanctuary, walking quickly down the slope. We stayed in a crouch, ducking behind what little cover we could find, mostly broken wagon parts and other gear. We were still a hundred feet or so from the edge of the road when we saw a large body of infantry approaching. We had no choice but to flatten ourselves into the wet, muddy ground. We banked everything on blending into the surrounding slop and gore.

We couldn't see them as they passed our position for we had our faces all but buried in the mud. But we could keep track of their progress by the din they created. Each step produced a variety of sounds ranging from clanging canteens and muskets, to clamorous sabres and cartridge belts. As the cavernous jangle diminished, we were finally able to get our faces out of the mud. It took what must have been the best part of thirty minutes for that entire unit to pass us by.

The way was clear once more, but we weren't sure for how long. We pulled ourselves out of the mire and made a mad dash across the road, diving into the underbrush on the other side. High Bridge couldn't be much further away, let's hope the rest of the way is clear.

From our vantage point overlooking the trestle area, it wasn't difficult to tell who was winning the battle. Bluecoats were firing volley after volley across the expanse of the railroad trestle known as High Bridge. But only a few rounds were being returned by a small handful of Confederates that had been left behind to slow down the Yankee advance. We could see that only a portion of the trestle was on fire, while the wagon bridge below appeared to be still intact. Apparently, the plan to fire both bridges had failed. The Yankees definitely had the advantage and would soon be in control of this important crossing point.

It was also obvious to both John and me that the possibility of us crossing the Appomattox River at High Bridge was out of the question. We would have to seek other means.

I said, "Well, John, it looks like it would be best to move up stream if we plan on getting to the north side of this river. And, we'd better move fast, or the Yankees will block that avenue."

"Mac, I think we will be wasting our time. This war is lost, and I don't think us getting back to General Gordon is going to make any difference, either way. I'm about ready to call it quits, and head for home." John's voice projected extreme disgust as he spoke.

"Well, that's easy for you to say. You're on the correct side of the river. My home is north of the Appomattox, and I still have to cross this river to get there. Also, regardless of what you say, I'm going to try my darnest to get back to General Gordon. But I certainly won't hold it against you if you want to leave. If my home was on this side of the river, I just might feel the same way."

I said it, but deep down I didn't believe it. I would never take off from a duty I had sworn to keep. I was going to get back to General Gordon, or die trying. It wasn't going to be an easy task, but I felt it was possible.

If John wanted to leave me at this juncture, that was his choice. I could see his point, but I was hoping he would stick it out to the bitter end. In a few more minutes I would know for sure.

We moved up the river, staying in the woods, hoping to avoid any enemy troops. Most of the action was centered near the trestle, and the wagon bridge. That made it easier for us to escape from the area without being detected. I guess the majority of Federal forces were too busy trying to capture the bridges, rather than looking for Rebel stragglers.

In my earlier study of the map, I had noted a junction of the Bush and Sandy rivers, both tributaries to the Appomattox. That junction was to the west of High Bridge. I felt if we moved further on to a point where the Appomattox turned north, and then back to the west, we would find a reasonable crossing place. If we entered the river just before it turned southward, the current should force us into the eastern bank before the course of the river turned for High Bridge. It would give us our best chance to cross for miles in either direction.

John was still with me as we headed for the junction of the Bush and Sandy. It wasn't difficult to find in the eerie half darkness. As we approached, we could hear the rushing waters several hundred yards before we got there. Their confluence was near flood conditions. I was sure the water would be just as high and swift along the Appomattox.

With our bearings still intact, we moved off to the north, going through some heavy underbrush along the river's edge. It took us at least a half hour to reach the point that I had picked out to enter the river. I thought launching into the river from this location would give us our best opportunity to safely set foot on the north shore.

I said, "John, I'm going to give it a try. If I make it to the other side I'll give you a whistle to let you know I'm safe. Then you can do whatever you want."

"You won't have to whistle, Mac, cause I'll either be with you, or drowned. I'm not going to have you being forced to make up some cockeyed story about what happened to me. As you say, we've been at this war long enough not to quit at this point. We can all probably go home with our tails between our legs in a few more days anyway. Provided, of course, we are still alive."

"Your optimism outshines your good looks, John. But regardless, I'm happy you will still be with me. Let's go for it."

The words almost choked in my throat as I hit the swift and icy water. April really wasn't a good time to go swimming in Virginia. However, I wasn't doing much swimming, instead I was being swept along by the swift current. There was a large amount of garbage in the water along with broken branches and some larger logs. The rushing waters were collecting any and all pieces that were normally higher up on the banks. Luckily the flow pattern in that part of the river rapidly moved me towards the opposite shore. I was able to avoid any debris, which enabled me to cross in only a matter of a hundred or so yards. That flow pattern also kept me well to the west of the High Bridge area.

As I crawled onto the muddy bank, I looked down at bare feet. It was evident the swift water had taken my shoes for a second time. At least the rest of me had come through all right.

I looked around for John, and there he was only a few yards further up the bank from me. I don't know how he did it. He was all smiles, "I wouldn't want to do that everyday of my life, but it was sure fun for a minute or so. Where to now?"

We were still wet when we made contact with a small company size group of Confederates moving along the road towards Farmville. Their Lieutenant said they were some of the last leaving the High Bridge area, and that the Yankees were right behind them.

I said, "Sir, do you know where General Gordon's headquarters might be? We are on a special assignment for him, and must report to him as soon as possible."

"The last I heard, Sergeant, was that he had camped just this side of Farmville. I understand there are some supplies there. I hope they aren't all gone by the time we arrive."

We thanked him and set off down the road in an attempt to find General Gordon.

"Do you think we will find any food when we get to Farmville, Mac?" John whispered, as we trotted down the road.

"I sure hope so John. It seems like a week since we had those beans and bread in Burkeville. Getting in that cold water sure takes the energy out of you."

I was amazed to see so little traffic on the road. Only a few scattered units, most of them barely able to move along at a decent pace. Looked like some of our boys had already called it quits, from the way they were acting. Most were laying along side the road, while others were barely shuffling their feet in the direction of Farmville. No one seemed to be in command, and even if you could have gathered them all together, only a very few appeared in condition to fight.

We hadn't traveled more than three miles when we saw a large group of our cavalry moving into a stand of trees. There was a tent, and some activity, which would suggest a headquarters of some type. We moved towards the grouping and were soon challenged by two alert sentries.

"What business do you two stragglers have here?" The question came from a big redheaded soldier who used the tip of his bayonet to enforce his overbearing authority.

"Is this General Gordon's headquarters? We were sent on a special mission by him, and we are reporting back to give him some important information. If this is his headquarters, would you please let him know Sergeant McGrady and Corporal Peebles are here to see him?"

"Stay here and let me check," his words were clipped. "Keep an eye on these two while I check out their story, Ted."

"OK, Seth, they ain't getting past me."

We slumped down in utter exhaustion, leaning against a tree while the remaining sentry turned away from us like we had the plague or something. I guess we did look a bit bedraggled; we hadn't been the sharpest before we went into the water west of High Bridge.

General Gordon greeted us with, "I wasn't sure I would ever see you boys again after what has happened at High Bridge. The order to fire both bridges was never executed properly, and now the Yankees have crossed to the north side. They are trying to cut us off and prevent us from moving towards Lynchburg. What did you find out on your visit to Burkeville?"

I straightened as I said, "Sir, it doesn't appear to us there is any possibility of General Lee heading back that way. The entire area is full of Yankees. We didn't see any of our boys until we got back north of the Appomattox. Sorry we didn't make it back to you sooner. We are lucky to have gotten back at all, what with the bridges being in the hands of the Yankees."

"Were the Yankees in full strength south of the river? How many do you estimate near Burkeville?"

"Yes sir, there were at least two corps of infantry coming into Burkeville by rail. We were told a large majority of them would be moving in a westerly direction in an attempt to cut General Lee off from the south. On our way towards High Bridge, we saw nothing but Yankees. We were lucky to get through without being captured."

"You both did your best, and I'm sorry you had such a difficult time. As it is, the situation is changing hourly. Longstreet has moved through Farmville. The Yankees are approaching New Cumberland Church, and I have been ordered to move through the woods to protect the wagons. If I'm successful, I will be heading for Appomattox Court House, then on to Lynchburg to spearhead Lee's breakout to the west. Longstreet will take up the rear guard position. General Lee and what's left of the main army are heading along the

Lynchburg Stage Road, as we speak. He will eventually go through Appomattox Court House.

Major Sandiege's artillery unit is just over the next hill. Earlier, I instructed him to reassign the Napoleon and the three-inch rifle back to your command. That was, of course, if you, and Peebles showed up again. I never lost faith in you boys. I knew you would make it back with your report, regardless of the situation. Now, I need you to perform one more special mission for me." We both nodded our heads a bit tentatively.

"You are to take the guns over the shortest route possible to cover this ford here on the Appomattox." He opened a map and pointed to the spot. "I need you to control that ford, and keep any Yankees you might come in contact with south of the river."

"That looks like where Vanghans Creek comes into the Appomattox. That could be a main crossing point if the Yankees decide to come up that way." The general was nodding his head in the affirmative as I spoke. "How long do you want us to defend the ford?" General Gordon didn't answer immediately, so I continued, "I would think the Yankees would follow the railroad if they are trying to cut General Lee off near Appomattox Court House."

"You may be correct Sergeant, but we need to ensure this crossing is covered, just in case. If there is no activity, you might venture south of the ford a ways to make certain where they are concentrating their forces. Either way, get to Appomattox Court House no later than the ninth, and meet me where the Lynchburg road crosses the North Fork of the Appomattox." He pointed again to the map. I indicated with a nod that I understood most of his instructions; even though they were somewhat vague due to the rapid way he was waving his hand over the map.

You could tell he was in a hurry, so I was reluctant to waste any more of his time asking him to explain again about the ford. I felt sure John and I could carry out his orders.

"We'll do our best, General. Are there any rations in Farmville?"

"I'm afraid only a very few of the troops were able to get rations before the trains were forced out towards Lynchburg. Some of the units in my Corps received two days' rations and ate them all at once. Maybe you can catch up with the commissaries along the Southside RR."

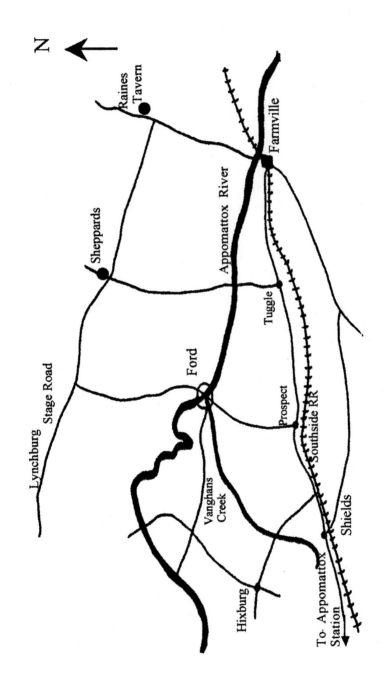

"I doubt that, sir. If they haven't been captured by the Bluecoats, they've already gotten a good jump towards Lynchburg. I think we'll be staying north of the Appomattox, at least until we reach the ford at Vanghans Creek." John and I saluted the general, and headed out towards Major Sandiege's position.

It was like homecoming to be reunited with all the boys. Ben Anderson, David Hubert, William Sands, Trevor Crawford, and all the others came over to welcome us back. They looked a bit wearier than when we had left them but nothing that would keep them from fighting a good battle, if we ran into one.

Both the Napoleon, and the three-inch rifle appeared no worse for wear. They looked ready for action. Even the supply wagon still had four wheels on it.

Major Sandiege greeted us warmly and didn't seem upset with me for removing part of his firepower. In fact, he wished us well. I hadn't seen him when the guns were turned over to him near Jetersville, but I had visualized him to be along the lines of Captain Ball. As it turned out, he was quite different. His receding hairline made him appear somewhat older than most Majors. He reminded me of a portly schoolteacher I once knew in Clifford.

"You've got some good men there sergeant," his voice was soft, but clear. "We'll look to join up with you again near Appomattox Court House. Did you and John get anything to eat?" When I shook my head in the negative, he said, "Too bad, the rest of us got a few rations before the commissary wagons pulled out, but we were only able to cook and eat on the run. It wasn't much, just a bit better than nothing. Maybe you can find something on the way. At least the horses got their share of oats. Too bad we didn't have feed bags like they did, that would have given us a bit more consumption, as we were moving. Well good luck, see you in a day or two."

Steady rain was falling again as we crossed a well-traveled road connecting Tuggle and Sheppards. We were at least four miles south of Sheppards, which was on the Lynchburg Stage Road. We had been moving mostly in open but rolling country; however, we could see heavy woods ahead of us. The rolling terrain combined with the rain made passage difficult, causing the guns and wagon to slide, and slip as we went up and down the changing grades.

I figured the ford was still five or so miles ahead of us, and the map bore that out as we descended into a hollow with a raging creek. A check of the map told us we were at Horsepen Creek. It was usually just a gentle stream, but the crashing water gave it all the characteristics of a rampaging river as it headed pell-mell for its junction with the Appomattox. Crossing was going to be a problem.

I called to Ben Anderson, and said, "Ben, do you think you can get over to the other side and secure a rope to a tree? We could then use it as a safety line to get the guns and wagon across."

"Give me a strong horse and I think I can make it. If I can get the rope secured, then we should be able to winch the guns and wagon across." Ben was one of the most positive individuals I had ever encountered. He would attempt anything he felt would help the cause.

As he and the horse entered the stream the current immediately caught them. Ben's head bobbed up and down more than once during the trip across. As for the horse, he seemed to falter from the time his feet went under water. They made it, but for a time I wasn't sure they wouldn't be swept downstream to destruction. I could only hope that a strong safety line would make it easier for the rest of us. Boy, was I ever wrong.

First off, one of the safety lines attached to the supply wagon broke while the wagon was only halfway across. It was only by chance the other line held, and we were able to swing the wagon to the correct side of the creek. Two boxes of ammunition spilled into the raging waters, and we only retrieved one of them. I guess we were lucky there wasn't any food aboard, or we would have certainly lost it, too.

As for the guns, the three-inch rifle made the crossing without a hitch. The trouble came when the Napoleon first entered the water. One of its wheels came off, and we had to pull the gun back out of the water to repair it. By this time it was getting dark, so we had to work fast before the light failed. In our attempt to rush, we missed tying off the rear safety line, which almost cost us the gun. But, luck was with us again. The horses on the far side of the stream strained to their limits, and had just enough strength to haul the Napoleon through the raging water to safety.

We were all wet and tired. Ben, who had worked the hardest, said, "Mac, let's hope we don't run into many more of these small creeks. I don't think the horses or I can take much more."

"Well said, Ben," Trevor chimed in, as did most of our crew. We had been successful, but none of us knew what was ahead as we moved on towards the ford at Vanghans Creek. There was a lot of slipping, sliding, and more than one oath filled the cool, wet, night air. But these men who had risked their lives more than once were always ready to proceed with the task ahead. Onward went our progress, however slow.

It was close to midnight when we reached the overlook above the ford. The rain was still falling, but had lightened up a lot since darkness had set in. William Sands and Trevor Crawford went down to the ford to establish a location that would alert us if any Bluecoats attempted to cross the ford.

We were amazed that the water level at the ford was only moderate. We had expected it to be raging like most of the previous ones east of this location. Maybe the rains were easing to the west. Let's hope so, for it was our intended direction of march once we finished here. We had had our fill of crossing raging and swollen streams.

We, in the meantime, positioned the guns in what we hoped would provide the best coverage if a Yankee crossing attempt was made. By the time we completed spotting the guns, we were fatigued to the point of exhaustion.

John and I made one final inspection of our location before trying to get a few moments of sleep. John said, "Mac, we aren't really in a very defensible position. We could probably hold out against a small force, but if any sizeable unit charges us, I'm afraid we would be overrun."

"You might be correct, John, but if we can put part of our men in those trees over there, we just might have a flanking action that would be in our favor. Let's take a look at the possibilities when the light is better. For now, I need some shut eye." With that, we tucked in with the rest of the boys trying to get a few winks and keep as dry as possible in the process.

Most of the squad slept fitfully on empty stomachs wondering when, if ever, we would eat a decent meal again. The morning of the eighth dawned to overcast skies. The absence of rain was a welcomed sight.

It was near mid-morning when Trevor came running up the slope. He almost collapsed as he reached the guns. Panting deeply, he squeaked out, "Mac, there's a squad of Union cavalry approaching the ford. Looks like they intend to cross and scout out this area. William is hiding upstream and will be out of our firing pattern if, and when, we start to fire."

"Good for you, Trevor. See if you can work your way back to William without being seen. We will get in position up here and commence firing when the situation warrants. See you after we put those Yankees to rout." He disappeared over the knoll before I could hardly finish my words. He must have gotten a second wind.

Hearing Trevor's words, the men were immediately in motion to their assigned tasks. John took ten men and moved over on our flank under cover of the wooded area we had discussed. The cannons were ready, only the order to fire was needed to put them into action.

Through my binoculars I could see the squad of cavalry stop on the far side of the ford. They seemed hesitant to cross, although the depth of the water certainly wasn't a problem for them. The officer in charge was waving his sword about, and gesturing wildly in an attempt to move his unit across the ford. I let them get halfway across when I shouted, "FIRE."

The effect was devastating. The water erupted violently amidst horses and men. The horses reared, throwing their riders in every direction. Those riders still astride were attempting to get their mounts under enough control to return to the south side of the river. Several of their comrades would never make it or see another day. Our rounds had been dead on target.

Our second volley furiously churned the water and convinced those still alive to begin a rapid departure to the south. I'm sure those survivors would make it clear to whomever they reported to that it would take more than one small squad of cavalry to cross at this ford.

It always bothered me to be the instrument by which other men died. I had only been in this war for two years, and in that short period of time I must have aged twenty. Would I ever get over these horrible times? That is a question only time could tell me the answer to. That is, of course, if I didn't fall to the same fate I had just rendered on those poor men in the water.

How many more days could we endure in this senseless conflict? How many more days could these men around me tolerate? These are the questions I don't know if I will ever be able to answer. But, I must go on regardless.

Lord, please give me the strength to proceed.

We had accomplished our mission at this site as far as I was concerned. Now it was time to advance on to join General Gordon again. If a stand was to be made at Appomattox Court House, I'm sure our two guns would have some added effect to the overall diminishing Confederate force.

John came up as the unit was preparing to depart and said, "What looks like our best route to Appomattox Court House?"

"You have a good question there. Let's look at the map again." As I pulled the map out of my saddlebag, it had a threadbare look from the continued folding and unfolding it had endured. At least the area of our interest was still legible. "It appears we have two choices. We can either go along this route," I traced my finger along the north side of the Appomattox River, "or, we can cross the ford here and head directly for Appomattox Court House along the north fork of the river. It will mean we have to cross the main river again somewhere north of Hixburg. The waters seem to be lower the further west we go, so crossing might be easier than we have experienced before. What do you think?"

"We could run into more Yankees than we want to by going across this ford. That squad of cavalry had to come from some place down that way." John pointed along Vanghans Creek as it ran southwest towards Pamplin.

"Yes, but it is my guess the Yankee's main force is following the Southside RR in the direction of Appomattox Station. Another point is I'm not sure just how long we can last by going the greater distance up towards the Lynchburg Stage Road. I'm for going the most direct way, and if we are lucky, there might be some forage we can find along a less traveled route. Let's put it to the boys, we all need to be together in this."

"Suits me either way, but I agree, we all should have a voice in the decision." John got up from the map and turned towards the group. "Mac has a few words for you. Listen carefully, for this might mean the difference between any further success or failure."

"Men, these are our choices to complete our mission and rejoin with General Gordon." I outlined the alternatives John and I had discussed, trying to paint both the positives and negatives to each possibility. "I want your input to this decision; it could mean life or death to us."

There was a deep murmur from the group, and then in almost one voice, they said, "Mac, you have brought us this far without our input. Whatever you decide is good enough for us. Lead on."

Chapter Five

The jangle of our equipment was beginning to sound like a locomotive without oil. The wheels on the gun carriages hadn't been greased since we left Petersburg, and the water crossings had taken their toll on the bearings. Our supply wagon clattered and clanged since the springs were all but shot. If there were any Yankees near-by they would certainly think an entire host of pots and pans peddlers were coming their way. Regardless of the noise, we were on our way to Appomattox Court House to meet General Gordon and be a part of what could be the final hours of our Confederacy.

We crossed the ford headed south and immediately turned west on what could only be called a fraction of a road. The trail wasn't more than one hundred and fifty yards south of the river and difficult to see because of the heavy growth surrounding the intersection. Initially it ran along a ridgeline, which was mostly pine covered, interspersed with some budding hard woods. Scattered fields were dotted amongst the trees as we moved farther along the ridge. None of the fields appeared to have been planted for several years. They must have been cleared sometime in the past and left as is. The path meandered a bit but was, for all practical purposes, a direct course for Appomattox Court House. The direction served our needs well, provided we didn't run into trouble before we came to the main river again. If we were forced to deviate, it could cause us undue delays in arriving at our destination. I wanted to join up with our main fighting force as soon as possible; that way I felt we would stand a much better chance of survival.

It was apparent our selected course hadn't been traveled much in the past few days. This reinforced our belief that the Yankee cavalry unit we rebuffed at the ford hadn't come from this direction. We assumed them to be part of a major size enemy unit. Hopefully they were scouting for an easy place to cross the Appomattox, which could get them to the southern flank of Lee's army. I hoped we were correct in our thinking, because we were basing our continuing existence on it. Our deduction was that the unit had come from the Prospect area, and its main body was following the Southside RR to Appomattox Station. If this were true, then the cavalry unit had in fact been just a probe to the north as the main force moved along the railroad.

The skies were still overcast, but the lack of rain was a break in our favor, enabling us to move along at a fair clip. The roadway most generally stayed along the ridgeline with only a few gullies to cross. This more than eased some of the strain on both horses and men. However, there was still a lot of energy being expended. If we could keep up at the present rate, we would certainly be able to arrive at our rendezvous with General Gordon on the morrow. Maintaining the speed would depend on finding food somewhere before we arrived at Appomattox Court House. The lack of food was beginning to take its toll on every man and horse.

John was slightly ahead of me as I hailed him to wait. "Don't you think we had better put a little more effort in scavenging for something to eat? Those horses on the Napoleon look like they are ready to drop any minute, and the others don't appear any better. If we don't find something soon, I'm not sure we'll make it to Appomattox Court House."

"I agree," John nodded. "What do you want me to do?"

"Why don't you pick up Ben on "Point" and range farther out ahead. Hopefully with both of you covering our front you will run across something."

John quickened his pace as he headed for Ben's position, which was well out to our front. He didn't even wait for me to say - Go Ahead. I yelled, "If you don't find anything in an hour, meet us on this road, and we'll try to figure some other way to sustain ourselves. For sure, don't cross over the Appomattox before we are all formed up together again." He threw a salute back in my direction and was out of sight in a matter of seconds.

David turned to me and said, "Vee, it may be a good idea to give the rest of us a break before we continue towards the river."

"Excellent suggestion, David." I hurried to the front of the procession and yelled out, "OK men, let's take a five minute rest break."

It was like I had shot them. They dropped dead still in their tracks, hardly taking the extra time to move off the road. I did insist that William and Trevor, still our rear guards, move back a ways. I wasn't going to be surprised just because we were running out of energy. David moved up as "Point" to cover what was ahead, while Ben and John foraged ahead.

The break lasted at least fifteen minutes longer than planned. I had dropped off to sleep for the first time in days. As I slowly awoke, my mind remained in a pleasant state of euphoria.

I could hear birds chirping for the first time in months. It was springtime in Virginia, and there were signs of buds on many of the plants, which always brought a renewed sense of beginning to me. I could faintly see the fields around the farm in Clifford starting to green up. It would soon be time to get the fields ready for planting. It was always a joy to me to start the cycle, which would mean another beginning of our yearly toils and chores. To reap the rewards from the earth made life worthwhile for me.

The war should be over, but it wasn't. We were hardly fighting for anything more than our "Pride" now. These people, and particularly this land, had suffered enough. Now it was time to let it heal from all the scars inflicted upon its grandeur.

Clifford, my Clifford, I longed to be home. If I expected to make it home, I'd better remain solid and focused. The sand in my time glass was running low, and I wasn't sure how much longer I could take this terrible ordeal.

"Vee, Vee, wake up, it's time we were moving out again." David had come back from up ahead when the rest period had exceeded ten minutes. He was shaking me back into this world. It took just a matter of seconds before my mind snapped back to the reality around me. The short nap had helped revive me; I hope it had done as well for the others. Now it was time to get back to the business at hand.

"OK men, let's get this equipment on the move, there's not a lot of this day left. We need to get some miles behind us before the sun sets."

The groan of the wheels renewed their serenade to the surrounding countryside. Both guns and the wagon continued to squeak and cry as we moved them up a slight incline and down another. I felt we should be nearing the junction just north of Hixburg before long. At that point, we would have less than a mile before we reached the banks of the Appomattox again. We were making better time than I had originally thought we would, but our pace would certainly slow if we couldn't find food.

For a while, the sky brightened in spots, and I thought the sun might break through. We hadn't seen it for what seemed like days. But alas, in just a matter of minutes, the brightness faded slowly back into the solid gray overcast we had come to expect. We would have to live with this dreary and gloomy weather for another day. To make things worse, it also looked like more rain clouds were forming up in the west.

I sent David ahead to scout out the junction since Ben and John hadn't returned.

The eighth of April was drawing to a close, so we needed to get at least to the river before we bedded down for the night. Our plan was to cross the river at first light and then make a dash for the rendezvous with General Gordon on the ninth.

We were on a slight down grade flanked by heavy pine trees on both sides. The lighting was a bit eerie, for the darkening overcast caused visibility to decrease and the air to cool by several degrees.

Suddenly John appeared out of the woods on our right. He was beaming, and it wasn't difficult to tell he had news that would be to our liking.

"Mac, you've got to see what we found. It isn't more than three quarters of a mile through this forest. If you go to the cross roads, and turn north, it will only be a stone's throw to the cabin."

"Whose cabin are you talking about, John?"

"It belongs to Ned and Martha Jones. They have a small farm, which is just over the ridge. They call themselves lowly dirt farmers,

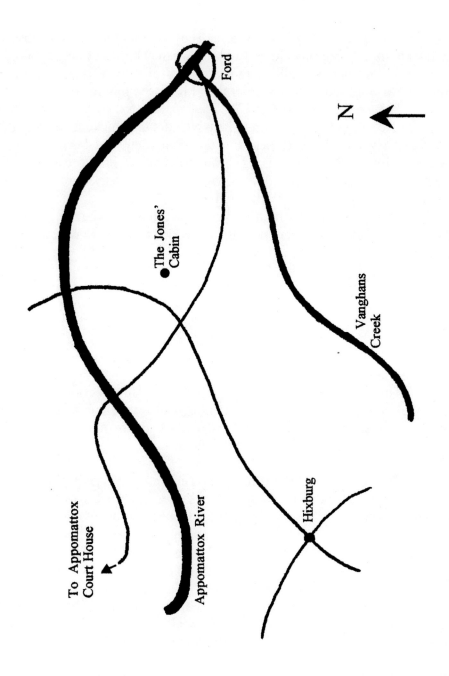

but to me they are the salt of the earth. They support the South's cause and want to help our boys in any way they can. They have some food, not much, but they are willing to share most of it with us. Come on, times a wasting." John was happier than I had seen him in weeks.

"Where is Ben? Is he OK?"

"He's fine. He stayed on to help Ned get the chickens ready for frying. They only have fifteen, but they said they had been saving them for just such a cause as us. From what we've had to eat in the past few days, it will seem like a banquet. I'll cut back through the woods and tell them you will be coming soon."

"Are you sure it isn't a trap or something? Maybe we should keep most of our equipment near the crossroads, that way we can fall back if it is a trap."

"For goodness sake, Mac, this isn't any kind of trap. These are good people who want to help us, and for sure, we can use all we can get." John was shaking his head as if to indicate I had gone a little daft.

"OK, we should be there within the hour. There's still a few hours of daylight left before nightfall. It will be nice to have some food before we bed down."

The pace quickened. The men had heard John's conversation, and the mere mention of food was enough to revive the weariest of warriors. Even the horses must have sensed nourishment of some sort, for they seemed to strain harder at the harness.

The hiss and sizzle of hot grease in an open frying pan, plus the aroma of chicken cooking, were senses not many of us had experienced in many, many days. It was wonderful just to enjoy these simple pleasures we had only been dreaming of for weeks.

Ned and Martha Jones's etched faces showed the character one would expect to see in some hard working people. They were people who had scratched a meager living out of a small homestead. There were no slaves here, only they could be in bondage to themselves. This couple had accomplished every small advantage they had by doing it the hard way with their own hands. They had cleared their land and planted the few crops they raised. It hadn't been easy for them and the crush of four years of war had only made it worse.

It was then that I noticed Ned's limp. He said he had been badly wounded in both legs during the early stages of the war at Bull Run, and that as far as he was concerned, it had been a blessing. He had survived the terrible days in the hospital and had been able to return home. He had been declared unfit for further duty. If not, he was sure Martha wouldn't have been able to keep the place going. Talk about a positive attitude when the world around them was all but falling apart.

They were bustling around the outdoor fireplace, preparing to share what little they had with a group of bedraggled warriors. Most of our boys were trying to help in any possible way. Some cut wood to keep the fire going. Others had picked and gutted the chickens to prepare them for frying. Even the horses had been given some oats, which should sustain them for a day or two. It was a case of Virginians helping Virginians. It brought tears to more than one eye that evening.

"How much longer do you think this war will go on?" Ned asked, while we were sucking the last chicken bones dry.

"Not much longer, Ned," I replied. "If General Lee can't break out to the west in the next few days, the war will be over before the end of April. We are headed to Appomattox Court House, and it could be the Confederate States of America's last stand unless some miracle comes our way."

"Well, Martha and I are ready for it to end. We have been lucky not to have had the Yankees overrun us. We don't have much, just the one cow, a few pigs, and the chickens. But, we wouldn't have that if they ever came through this way."

"You might just be in luck. I think most of the Yankees are southwest of here. At least that's what I'm hoping. There are also a bunch of them north of the Appomattox, right on General Lee's heels, but I don't expect they will be moving down your way." I tried to sound as confident as possible. These were good people who didn't need to be upset by various possibilities of where, and if, the Yankees would be moving. Particularly at this late date in the conflict.

"Well, we are just going to stay put. If those Yankees come this way, we hope they miss us in our small valley. I was really surprised when your man Ben came out of the woods earlier today. It was kind of nice seeing a stranger after such a long time. Especially a Southerner like you boys."

"Ned, you and your wife have been more than hospitable, but we best be going. You will never know how much your generosity has meant to this group. I wish you and your wife well. If I ever get back this way I will be sure to stop in." There were tears in my eyes when I shook his hand. These people had come close to saving our lives.

It took a minute to get all our troops moving. Many were reluctant to leave, and I wasn't sure we wouldn't lose a few. However, to a man, they all departed with a much livelier step than I had seen for several days. I'm sure they would remember this small, but sweet repast for years to come, plus the people who had shared their meager larder with them.

The crystal clear water in the river was calmer than it had been much farther to the east. So much so, that we crossed with very little problem just before dusk descended on the land. We were able to camp on the far side, which aided in using the river as partial protection for our rear during the night. We didn't light any campfires, for we had nothing to cook, and we didn't want to give our location away in case Yankees were close by. That had been the case many of the nights before, but this time at least our bellies weren't growling from the total lack of food.

We put out sentries to our west and north, and I left William and Trevor on the far bank for the night. This way they could provide us with early warning in case Bluecoats attempted to close up behind us.

As we hunched in around the guns and the supply wagon, I said to John, "Running into Ned and Martha was a stroke of good luck for us. I've never known people like that to be so friendly. What was theirs was ours, as far as they were concerned. I hope I can get back by their place some day and repay them for their generosity."

"I agree, Mac. When Ben and I found their cabin, I thought we would have to insist they give us some food. But instead, when they learned we were Confederates, they were the ones who insisted we share some of their larder." John closed his eyes as if to remember more clearly. "Ben was the one who, just by chance, stumbled into that little valley, which sheltered their homestead. I was on the other side of the ridge and would have missed it altogether if I had been by myself. I guess that's part of the reason they've never been bothered by the Yankees. Their little dell certainly isn't on the main track."

"Well I hope our luck holds out for tomorrow. No telling what we will run into between here and Appomattox Court House. Guess we'd better get a little shuteye while we can. I'm going to take a short stroll around to check on the sentries. Don't want them to get too lonely or go to sleep now that they have a bit of food in their bellies. Good night, John."

"Good night, Mac. Tell Ben he did good work finding that cabin. See you in the morning bright and early."

We were on the move before the first streaks of light came through the trees. It had gotten colder during the night, and most of us were chilled when we awoke. The departure activity helped to warm us as we bustled about, getting the equipment on the road. For some strange reason, I felt a sense of urgency as we prepared to move out.

The road took a slight jog to the south, going down a shallow slope to a small tributary, which flowed into the Appomattox a few yards farther on. The water rippled as we crossed, its level still low enough not to cause a problem. The guns and wagon hardly got their wheels wet. We were getting to be experts on fording rivers and creeks.

John spoke out as we exited the water, "What are your plans for getting us to the court house from here, Mac?"

Once again I pulled out the tattered map and pointed to our location. "I estimate us to be less than two miles from the Hixburg/Rose Bower road. While this isn't the main thoroughfare headed northwest, it has the possibility of being used by Yankees if they were looking for a less difficult path in that direction. I think we'd better avoid it if possible."

"I agree. Our best chance might be to proceed down to this little valley short of the river and use it for cover as we go northwest." John traced the route with his finger.

"Looks good to me. If we go this way, we should be running into some of General Gordon's rear guards before too long. Hopefully it will be us Confederates, instead of the Yankees, trying to link up with General Lee." I looked around at the waiting group and said, "OK men, let's move these guns out of here. We don't have far to go now." The creaking wheels were almost beginning to sound like music to my ears.

We were following the North Fork of the Appomattox and were approaching an open stretch of high ground bordered by heavy trees on both the north and south sides. The rain had started again, and large drops were beginning to spatter our path. If this brutal weather kept up, our way would soon become muddy again. I guess the last few days with only an overcast sky had spoiled me. Would we ever see sunshine again? We could only hope so.

The distant roar of artillery from a northwesterly direction started to reach our ears. It was intermittent at first but, as we progressed towards the courthouse, the din became a steady rumble. Somewhere ahead of us troops were engaged.

Suddenly John yelled out, "We've got Bluecoats to our left." I wheeled around, at the same time grabbing my binoculars. Sure enough, a small unit of Federal cavalry had abruptly appeared out of the woods to our south, not more than a half mile away. They didn't spot us instantly, which gave us a fraction of extra time to veer nearer the trees off to our right. This wasn't the occasion, nor did we have time to put our guns into action. The only course available to us was to make a run for it.

The Federal cavalry quickly formed into an attack formation, and spurred their horses into a fast gallop. We could hear their yells as they commenced their charge. It was only going to be a matter of seconds before they would close on our position.

We had just reached a point where the creek forked, and a covering of pines spread to the north. Quickly we swerved the Napoleon and the three-inch rifle into the trees, attempting to put as much distance between the guns and the Federal cavalry as possible. I grabbed five men with muskets and deployed into a stand of tall pine trees on the far side of the gun's departure route. John took five more and spread out to cover the other side of the escape path. We used the time well to get into a proper defensive position before the screaming horde came pounding down upon us.

The amount of time before the charging herd of cavalry reached us seemed like an eternity; it was probably only scant minutes. The small Federal cavalry unit was coming full tilt with their sabres flashing in the air. Really a foolhardy thing for them to do, as far as I was concerned. The low tree branches in the area would certainly hinder any sabre attack.

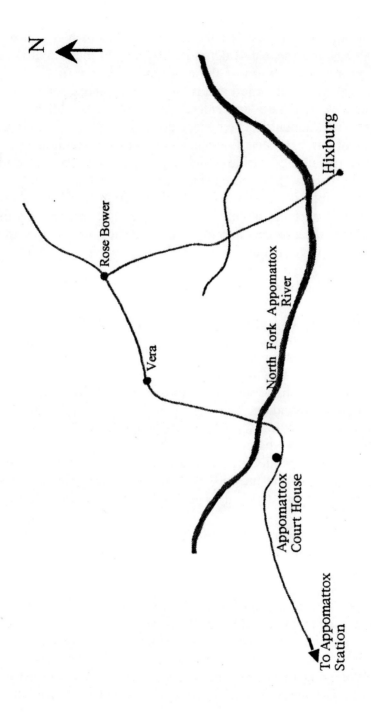

In the instant we realized the moment of truth had arrived, they were abreast our makeshift defenses. We caught them in a cross fire, downing a major portion of the attackers with our first volley. Horses and men were falling left and right. Screams and shrieks filled the air. Horses reared, throwing riders who hadn't been hit by our musket fire. Their standard bearer went down propelling his guidon into the trunk of a tree. It was more than enough to deter their effort.

Those remaining astride quickly turned their mounts and broke off their charge. They veered sharply in all directions with their main purpose being to return southward. The action had been short lived. They made no more attempts to reengage. The last we saw of them was as they disappeared into the woods on the south side of the clearing. We had once again saved the guns - another small victory for our side.

However, the tranquil period following the attack lasted only minutes. We rapidly moved forward to join up with our guns, which had halted several yards from our defense position. As we closed on the guns, a Confederate rider was coming full tilt towards our waiting caissons. He was almost breathless as he hauled his mount to a stop. He claimed to have been trying to locate us for over an hour. When he heard the musket fire, he knew we should be close by. He carried a message from Major Sandiege.

His words were almost a whisper as he gasped out, "We are in one hell-of-a-battle near the court house. The Major needs you. You are to fill a gap in General Gordon's artillery line." There were more words, but the crux of the message was that we were to proceed as quickly as possible to an area only a few miles away, and the courier would lead us.

Now we knew where the artillery sounds we had heard earlier were coming from. This just might be the battle, which could seal the fate of our Confederacy.

The smoke from the artillery formed a pall over the countryside as far as one could see. With the steady rain, the scene was that of a dark cloak cast over the entire battlefield. Lines of Yankee infantry could be seen on the far ridge facing our position. They were volleying their fire. Small puffs of smoke blossomed on both flanks as they systematically fired and reloaded. Their battle streamers and the Stars and Stripes could be seen interspersed amongst the long wavering blue lines.

Our boys were returning fire with a vengeance. Our Stars and Bars were evident, but they somehow appeared more tattered from the devastating bombardment. What trees left standing had been threaded clean of branches and leaves. The area was strewn with broken equipment, horses lay dying, and men were in various stages of despair. The stench of death was heavy in the air. The scene recalled the many previous battles, which had gone before to make up these gruesome four years.

However, none had been so pivotal as this one could be. It was evident that General Grant had forced General Lee to this juncture at Appomattox Court House. There wasn't any way for him to proceed in a westerly direction and join General Johnston without defeating these superior forces facing us. The future fate of the Confederacy surely would hinge on this battle's outcome.

The dash through the woods to this point had all but done in our horses, let alone the men. As we wheeled the guns around to a firing position, the horses were just short of collapsing in their harness. The men, bless them, were still performing at near peak efficiency. Surprising with what they had been through.

It was only minutes before our first salvo joined the intense barrage already underway against the Union forces massed to our west. From that moment on it was load and fire, load and fire, just as fast as possible. We would keep at it until either the men fell or we ran out of ammunition. We were locked into what appeared to be a relentless hostile action.

"John, how much ammunition do we have left?" I had to yell at the top of my lungs to be heard.

"Only enough for about three more volleys. If we don't get more shells, we will have to abandon our guns. Want me to see if I can find any more in the vicinity?"

"Yes, by all means. You and David check those broken wagons over there behind us. They look like ammo wagons. Could be they broke down coming up that grade because of the weight they were carrying."

John signaled for David to follow him. They were only seconds away from the three-inch rifle when the area surrounding it exploded. A Yankee shell had burst squarely on top of the gun, eradicating it and the people around it. John and David were thrown to the ground from the concussion, but Trevor and William, plus three others, hadn't fared so well. They were all but vaporized by the explosion.

Half our assets and five good men had just gone up in fire and smoke. After all the hard times we had endured, our little force was reduced to one small gun. It seemed useless to continue.

"Keep that Napoleon firing. We'll get you more ammunition in a minute." Major Sandiege was screaming at the top of his lungs as he rode by. "We need every piece of artillery firing that we can muster. McGrady, do what you can for those wounded. We may be too late to do any of them any good, but whatever happens, keep that gun firing."

"OK men, you heard the Major. Ben, see if anyone around the three-incher is still alive. Josh, you and the others keep that Napoleon firing until we run out of shells. I'll check on John and David to see how they are doing."

Time seemed to stand still. The din of cannon fire almost forced the brain into limbo. Concussion after concussion endlessly punctured the rain soaked air. The pounding and throbbing seemed to penetrate deep into the body. How much longer could this be endured? Something had to give before we all went mad.

I caught up with John and David just as they were coming back up the hill with extra ammunition. They were moving it box by box from those broken wagons, which had been carrying ammunition. What they found would keep us active for at least another hour. After that we would have to depend on Major Sandiege for supplies.

Those long blue lines opposite our gun had begun to falter a bit. Maybe after all the intensive exchange of artillery there would be a chance for General Lee to break through to the west. "Keep that gun firing boys, we may be victorious before the day is done."

Then suddenly, all went quiet. It was like the entire world had stopped in mid-orbit.

Out there in front, what was it? A rider with a white flag was galloping across in front of our lines. He would certainly be shot if he didn't take cover. But no, he was riding on, and the shooting and shelling was ceasing as he passed. Could it be a flag of truce? The courier who had led us to this spot had mentioned something about the war being almost over. To me, that was a foregone fact, but maybe in a week or so. I wasn't expecting it to occur in the middle of one of the most intense artillery exchanges I had ever witnessed.

There had been other rumors of a truce as we came on line. General Lee and General Grant were supposed to be meeting to discuss terms of a surrender. But surely General Lee wasn't going to quit while there was still a chance to join up with General Johnston. We were right in the middle of General Gordon's breakout to the west. This barrage must be the beginning of the attack, which would turn the Yankee lines blocking our way towards Lynchburg. Then our forces would have clear sailing up the Southside RR.

"Better see to it that we have more ammunition available when the firing starts again. John, you and David check again to see if there were any more cannon balls remaining in those broken down wagons. We need to move everything close to the guns."

"We'll check again, Mac, but I think we got it all." John was laying down the last box he had brought forward.

"Clear your weapons, men," Major Sandiege was riding by again. "We are going to pull back to the ridge behind us. The order has been given to silence our guns. As soon as the guns are repositioned, we are to leave them standing and move back into bivouac in the trees to the south. We are to wait for further orders. This may be the end."

I was in a stupor as we wrestled the starving horses into harness. I wasn't sure they were capable of moving the Napoleon back to the desired position. John was coming up on our left when I said, "Is it over, John? It certainly sounds like it is."

"I believe you're right, Mac. Everyone I've seen says it's over. General Lee is supposed to have agreed to the terms of surrender set down by General Grant. I wonder if we will all be locked up? If that's the way it's going to be, I'm for taking off right now. They will have to catch me."

"Let's wait for a little bit to determine just what the terms are before we rush off and get in trouble. Too bad the news didn't come sooner, Trevor and William would have still been with us. I guess timing is everything, and theirs was poor today. They were good people. Where is David?"

"He's OK, he should be along any minute. He was hauling the last of that ammunition we found. Guess we won't need it now."

To my surprise, the horses moved the Napoleon to the designated position with what appeared to be little effort. Somehow they seemed to know this would be their last haul. John and I unhitched them and then collapsed on the wet muddy ground. We leaned exhausted against the wheel of the Napoleon and just stared at each other. It felt like all the air had gone out of my balloon. I looked at my hands as if to say, I'm amazed you are still attached to my arms. I was amazed that any part of me was still attached. The fact I was alive was wonderment enough to fill my mind for days to come.

David approached us saying, "I think I'll sleep good tonight." He plopped down with a thud and joined the rest of the group, which had gathered. There wasn't any conversation, only the drained faces of men peering into the distance at some unforeseen visionary.

Looking back towards the ridgeline we had just vacated, the pall of artillery smoke was still visible over the battlefield. It was hard to imagine that only minutes before we were fighting for our very existence. Now all was quiet.

Our small unit had seen more than its share of fighting, and we were glad it was over.

Chapter Six

The smoke from the fire stung my eyes so much it was hard to see through the tears. Even when your hands were being used as fans, the smoke continued to curl around, causing most everyone to cough. The only firewood we could find was soaked through from the recent rainy weather, which produced more smoke than heat.

The bivouac we had set up was in the woods about a half-mile from where we had left the Napoleon after the truce had been called. We found the location by moving through an open stretch of fields after crossing the small river just east of the Court House. John, David, Ben, and I, along with a few of the other boys, had selected as dry a spot as could be found. General Gordon's entire corps had pulled back across the small river to this general location, so the area was full of ragged, tired, wet, and hungry people.

We had brought the horses with us; most of them weren't much more than skin and bones. We found them some grazing in amongst the pines, not much, but more than they had the previous few days. Seems like they had been in harness constantly since we left Petersburg. They couldn't have lasted very much longer.

It was still raining hard, but luckily we found some tent material, which we used to make lean-tos. The partial shelter kept most of the water off us; however, we had to continually add wood to keep the fires from being snuffed out by the downpour. It was surely a cold, wet night, which would be a long one for us if we didn't find something to eat. Also, there was the question of what was going to happen now that the war was over. Would we be hauled off to a prison camp, or would they make us march back to Richmond for sentencing? That had been one of the rumors, and if true, there wouldn't be many left to sentence. I believe very few would be able to march all the way back to Richmond. More than half would die of starvation or exhaustion on the journey.

Our officers had said we would learn our fate in the morning, and had left us to fend for ourselves. All of them went off before sunset to we didn't know where. Major Sandiege told me to take charge of our boys, but he didn't say anything else about finding food or exactly what was going to happen tomorrow. He did say to make camp and not to move around. He didn't want anyone to get hurt now that the musket fire and shelling had ended.

The incessant spatter of rain was like the continual throbbing of a distant drummer. I tried to close my eyes to keep them clear of the smoke, but my efforts were useless. The smoke kept blowing into the lean-tos. So, it was either stay dry and have the smoke, or get wet and be somewhat smoke free.

John turned to the group and said, "At least while the war was going on we were mostly on the move. We didn't have time to think about how hungry we were. Now all we can do is hunch down together, trying to stay warm and dry by the fire."

"I agree with you, John, we would have been better off if we hadn't arrived so early here at Appomattox Court House. If we had been late, maybe we could've gotten away before the surrender became official. Now we are stuck with whatever is decided by the Yankees. We could all be going to jail for a long time." David spoke as he drew back into the shadows. He appeared to be trying to hide under the cover of the lean-to.

"I don't think General Lee would agree to any surrender terms that would allow the Yankees to put his army in jail. Even though we are a shattered bunch, he would have let us fight on before he would concur with such a fate. Many of us would have continued to fight for that fine old gentleman, and he knew it."

"Well, I hope you're right, Mac, but I won't be surprised at anything that happens to us tomorrow. I hear those Yankee prisons are really bad places to spend any time in. I've seen what our prisons are like for the Yankees, and it would make you sick to see the sight. I don't think many of us could survive for any lengthy period of time."

Ben shrugged as he edged closer to the fire, and added some branches to keep the flames at full strength.

The steady downpour and the growling of our bellies were so loud we didn't hear the rustle of wagons coming through the trees to our rear. A herd of buffalo could have come up behind us before any of us would have heard them. The soft ground had long since passed its saturation point, so there was no alert from snapping underbrush. Before we knew it, a ghostly procession was upon us. Where had it come from, and what were its intentions? We reached for our rifles, but realized we didn't have any since they had all been stacked as ordered back by the caissons.

All we could do was watch as the wagons turned slightly, stopping with their tailgates towards the fires. Suddenly, Bluecoats jumped down from the wagons and pulled open the tailgates. We thought they were here to take us away. Some of our boys started to bolt for cover.

"HOLD IT REBS," came the call. "We've just come to bring you some bread. Ain't you hungry?"

I had seen some mighty strange things since being in this army, but this topped them all. Our former enemies were bringing us food. It made you wonder why we had been fighting each other when all the time we were brothers under the skin.

We would have done the same thing for them had the circumstances been reversed. Or, at least I sure hope we would have. This gesture of friendship was overwhelming, beyond belief. Over and above any dream I had ever contemplated. Smoke wasn't the only thing causing the tears in my eyes this night.

They made sure each man got a loaf of bread before they latched up the tailgate and headed back for their lines. Their parting comment was, "We'll see you tomorrow; maybe we can find some meat to go with that bread."

Words of thanks were voiced by almost everyone. Maybe a few were too choked up to utter a sound; at least that is what I told myself. Surely everyone had to be grateful to have something to put in their bellies. It had been a long time since a freshly baked loaf of bread had been consumed by anyone in this crew.

The downpour hadn't abated with the coming of a new day. Our grey world continued as the tenth of April dawned, which only exaggerated the deplorable thoughts of most of our crew. What wasn't wet was going to get wet. The tenth of April surely wasn't going to be much improvement over the previous few days as far as the weather was concerned.

Ben, John, and David were standing by our small fire trying to warm their hands as I walked up. "I'm going to find Major Sandiege. We need to get some information from him about what is going to happen with us now that the surrender is final."

"Well, if they don't do something soon, I'm heading out of here for the Williamsburg area and home." Ben was stomping around the fire trying to keep warm and sound tough at the same time. I hadn't known he was from the Williamsburg area. Also, we hadn't been far from his home when we were fighting near Petersburg. Luckily for us he hadn't taken off for home then.

"I'm asking you to wait until I can get some news. If we all start going in different directions, it's for certain the Yankees will put us in jail. There's got to be some rhyme or reason to what they plan to do. Now stay here, I'll be back as soon as I can." My words were met with grunts and groans, but everyone seemed to agree to wait around.

In my mind, the primary thought among the men was their relief at being alive. With time to think, we began to go over all the terrifying moments where our life could have ended. We start to remember the many friends who didn't make it, and a cold chill enters the spinal area. A chill that makes a person shudder deep down inside. I'm sure that must be the case with most everyone here, for it certainly is the situation with me.

If I were back on the farm there would be enough work to keep both my body and mind busy. Hopefully, I will be back there before this month is over. Sometimes those faces at the farm have gone dim, but other times they are the strongest things in my mind.

Just hanging around with nothing to do gives me too much time to think. Activity will pick up soon, I hope.

Major Sandiege was standing near a group of tents, which were serving as General Gordon's headquarters. People were hustling around, seemingly doing important things, while at the same time trying to stay out of the rain. Without any fighting going on, it looked to me like there were more people than were needed. They were probably having the same problem everyone else was having, so used to the rigors of warfare; they didn't know what to do when it wasn't happening.

Catching his eye, I walked over to the major. He was using a tree to ward off some of the rain, but it wasn't doing a very good job. Water was dripping from the brim of his hat, and he looked like he was just as wet as the rest of us. I saluted saying, "Sir, we need to get some information on what's going to happen so I can pass it on to the men. With nothing to do, they have too much time on their hands. All they can do is wonder about their future. If we don't learn something soon, it may be difficult keeping them from taking off."

"Sergeant, I don't know what's going to happen any more than you do. If I did, I would have told you earlier this morning. I do know General Gordon, along with Generals Longstreet and Pendleton; have been designated by General Lee to arrange the details of the surrender. He left about an hour ago to do just that."

"Major, is it possible we are going to be put into prison camps by the Yankees?"

"No, not to my knowledge. I think we are all to be paroled, and it will be put in writing. But, just how it will work, I don't know. However, I did overhear them say there would be a formal surrender with every man laying down his musket and cartridge boxes. They are to be deposited and stacked in front of the Yankees in a day or two. So until then, it is your job to keep the men in good order without causing any trouble. As soon as I get the final arrangements, I'll contact you. Any questions?"

"No sir. We were given some bread by the Bluecoats last night. Said they would be back today with more. Sure was a surprise. Have you heard what will happen to the horses?"

"I'll check about the horses and get over to you this afternoon. Just stay calm sergeant, I think this whole thing will be over in a day or two, and we can get on our way home." The major was headed for the tents as he said that last part about going home. I sure hoped he was right.

I lingered for a while under the tree trying to pick up any additional information about what might happen to us. However, the tree didn't offer me any more protection from the rain than it had for Major Sandiege. Plus, there wasn't any further information to be gleaned from the few people in the area. So I headed back to our bivouac area and the semi-dryness of the make shift lean-tos.

"Come and get it boys." Two older men who looked like seasoned veterans in glistening rain slickers were passing out more bread and some dried meat from the back of their wagon. They looked like they had seen a fair part of the fighting but were glad it had finally ended. They went about their task with efficiency and without fanfare.

The food looked like a banquet to most of us. It was received with thanks just as it was the night before. I planned to put a little of mine away for the trip home, just in case they let us go in a day or two. I was still awed by the fact that the Yankees were sharing rations with us. I would remember it for a long time. Brother helping brother would stick in my head for years to come.

"Hey Yanks, what's going to happen to us?" The question was asked more than once as they went about distributing the food. Their only answer was a shrug of the shoulders. I'm sure they didn't know any more than we did. One decent thing, they certainly didn't heckle or ridicule us for losing the war. I guess they were just as happy not to be getting shot at as we were. They were here to deliver food, not taunt us.

As they were putting up the tailgate on the wagon, one of our boys said, "How much longer do you expect to be hanging around these parts."

The older of the two turned his head and said, "We heard there's supposed to be some sort of ceremonies tomorrow or the next day. Then we'uns are supposed to pull out for home. Hope I don't see as much rain in Pennsylvania as I've seen around here in this muddy hole."

"Well, it's our mud Yank, and we like it." John's voice was up an octave or so, as he stepped forward to be seen.

"Sorry about that Reb, didn't mean to rile you. It's just I've had about all the rain and mud as I can stand. Didn't mean no offense about your part of the country." He held up his hand in a sign of peace. "We gotta be going. Good luck to you boys. Hope the next time we meet it's in some tavern somewhere. If you ever get up in northern Pennsylvania, look us up. I'll do more than give you food, I'll buy you the tallest, coolest beer you've ever seen." They tapped the horses on their rumps and were off through the trees.

A voice from the back rang out with, "We may take you up on that Yank. Thanks for the offer."

John turned to head back to the lean-to and said, "Got to admire them for giving us food. I'm sure he meant no insult about Virginia. I'm more than tired about this rain and mud myself."

No one disagreed with him.

The fire in front of the lean-to had died down a bit, but there was plenty of firewood to keep it stoked throughout the night. We didn't want to get it too low because it was going to require a hot fire to burn that damp wood. And, gathering it did give some of the boys something to occupy their time.

John was standing near the fire when he turned to me and said, "Did you find out anything, Mac?"

"Not much, but Major Sandiege said he would let us know as soon as he heard anything final. He did say General Gordon and two other generals were ordered by General Lee to help arrange the details of the surrender. He also said there was to be some sort of ceremony consisting of laying down our weapons to the Yankees. After that, there is to be a formal pardon in writing, but I'm not sure exactly what that is all about, or precisely when it will happen."

"Well, they'd better do something quick. I'm not about to stay around here waiting much longer." David seemed to be getting a bit edgy. "We should have kept on fighting if all they are going to do is make us stay here in this wet and miserable place." He shifted around so not all could hear and said, "Vee, John and I would like to speak to you alone later tonight. We've run across some people who might have an idea, which will benefit some of us who want more than being humiliated by the Yankees at some surrender ceremony. Right now, we've got to meet with them again, they are over in another bivouac." With that, they got up and headed south towards the other camp areas.

"Get back before dark, you don't want to get yourself killed walking around in the dark." My warning didn't seem to slow down their pace as they disappeared into the trees.

"Untie those horses, and get them over towards the Court House. The Yankees got fodder for all of them. They want to round up all these starving animals and get them back to their proper strength. They've got a lot of wagons that need pulling all the way back to the North. After you get them fed, bring two of them back so that when we are ordered to move the Napoleon, we'll have the means to relocate it." Major Sandiege was astride his own horse, which was in pretty good shape.

"How about your horse, Major?"

"General Grant is allowing any officers who own their horse to keep them. He might have done it for everyone, but I'm sure he was afraid none of them would have lived to get back to the farm. And, he may be right."

One of the boys in the back of the crowd said, "Well, if we ever get home, it sure ain't going to be easy getting a crop in. I hope my old lady has already scratched out a little garden, or we may starve when winter comes again."

Ben spoke up, "Let's just worry about getting home before we go off about getting a crop in. Our folks been living on something all these years, I'm sure we can survive a little longer until things get back to normal."

"I'm sure you will all make it." The Major looked around at me and motioned for me to come over to him. He leaned down from his saddle and whispered in my ear saying, "McGrady, I should hear something about what will be occurring later on this afternoon. Come over to the headquarters area and see me at five."

"Yes sir, but why are you whispering?"

"I'm not prepared to answer any questions from the men at this point. But I do know there will be some sort of surrender ceremony either tomorrow or the next day. They wouldn't let us have those two horses back to move the Napoleon if something wasn't afoot. Now get those horses over to the Yankees." I saluted as he rode off.

"Ain't that something? The officers get to keep their horse, we don't get nothing." Josh, one of the older cannoneers standing in the back of the group, was trying to get a disagreement going.

"I won't stand for bad talking our officers at this point. You didn't come in here with a horse, did you? No! Then there is no reason for you to be leaving with one. As the Major said, some of these horses who have been pulling our guns will be lucky to make it over to the court house. Now come on and give me a hand with them, or they will die before we can get them to the Yankees."

Josh and Ben went to get the horses. I turned to the others huddled around the fire and said, "Tell John and David I need to see them when they get back. This trip to the court house shouldn't take more than an hour or two."

A voice from one of the wagoners standing in back of the fire raised as I started to leave, "Think we should know something by evening, Mac?"

"I sure hope so, Ted. I'm to go over and see Major Sandiege at five. You can tell that to John and David when they return."

There must have been well over fifty of the poorest looking horses I had ever seen at the Yankee gathering point. Not a one of them could have pulled their own weight for more than a mile. Most had their haunches and ribs nearly poking through their hides. Their heads hung low, and their eyes were like doleful pits of sadness. They had plum been worked close to death. Ours were some of the best looking of the bunch.

"I sure hope you're gonna be able to bring all these critters back to life, Yank. I'm afraid most of them have been worked well beyond their limits."

The Yank looked at me and said, "I'm sure with some of this here feed, they'll come back to normal fore long. Understand you need feed for these two so you can move your artillery piece when the order comes down."

I nodded, and he gave me two feedbags for our two best. Then he said, "You look like you and your boys here could stand a little extra feeding yourselves."

"Well, thanks to some of your compatriots, we got our first real meal in several days last night and this morning."

"Look over in that wagon yonder. There's some extra jerky you are welcome to. Might be just the thing to tide you over until you can get out of this place, or until you are on your way home. How far you got to go to get to home from here?"

"Not rightly sure of the exact distance, but it will take a few days. It's a little crossroads called Clifford. Shouldn't be such a bad walk this time of year. That is, if General Grant plans to let us go."

"I'm sure he will be letting you go, we've got all we can do to get ourselves back to Pennsylvania. That's why we need to get these critters back in shape. We've got a lot of expensive equipment and goods to haul." He paused, looking down at my feet while he wiped his brow. "But, you'd better get yourself some shoes if you plan to walk very far."

"My feet are pretty tough. Been with and without shoes for a week or so now. I'll make it if and when they let us go."

Finally he coughed a bit and said, "Well, thanks for delivering those horses, they look as good as any we received yet. I think the two you're keeping will make it once they get some more oats. We'll see to that tomorrow after you move your gun. Nice talking to you, but I've got to get back to these oats and feed. Good luck to you and your buddies, Reb. Hope the next time we meet it's at a social."

"I'll hope so too, and thanks, Yank. Have a safe trip home yourself." We pocketed some of the jerky he offered, it would come in handy somewhere down the line. I looked back, and waved as we led our two animals back towards our bivouac with the feedbags hung over their noses.

John and David still hadn't returned when we got back to the bivouac area. It was closing on four thirty, and there wouldn't be much daylight left. I also needed to get over to see Major Sandiege; I didn't want to be late for our five o'clock meeting.

"Ben, be sure to tell John and David I need to see them when I get back. Don't let them go wandering off again. I should return not later than six, so be sure to keep them here."

"I'll do my best, Mac, but those two sometimes have a mind of their own. Sure hope the Major is able to tell us something. We will be awaiting to hear the news." Ben waved as I departed for the headquarters area.

Major Sandiege was leaning against a big old oak as I approached the tent area. A curl of smoke wafted from his pipe, and he seemed to be at ease with the world. He motioned me over and straightened as I saluted. "Here as you ordered, Sir."

"Be at ease, Sergeant. I would offer you some tobacco, but this is my last pipe full. How are your men holding up?"

98

"They are getting very skittish; I sure hope you got some news for me to take back."

"Well, I have. At first light on the twelfth, that's day after tomorrow, General Lee's army will be forming for the last time. Tomorrow, the eleventh, you and your men will take the Napoleon to a gathering point just south of the Court House. The Yanks will take the gun and the horses. You will then go back and get your men ready for the activity on the twelfth. It will consist of forming up to march down past the Court House where you will turn over your muskets, cartridge belts, and any flags or banners you might have. General Gordon's corps will be the second unit to turn in their weapons. After completing your part in the formal surrender, you and your men will return to your bivouac area. You will be awarded paroles, which I will sign as your commanding officer. The paroles should be here from Lynchburg where they are being printed. These signed parchments will be evidence that you are paroled prisoners of war and that you have the right to return to your homes unmolested."

"You mean we have to wait around for two more days to get the paroles because they haven't been printed yet?"

"That's what I'm saying sergeant, but this piece of paper is very important to each and everyone of us. Without it you could be shot or put in prison as a deserter. We've gone too far for that to happen. I feel sure we will have the copies we need by noon on the twelfth. So tell the men we should all be free to head out for our homes sometime after all the weapons are turned in and the paroles have been distributed."

"I sure hope you're right, Major. I'll stop by to see you tomorrow after we deliver the Napoleon. I sure hope I can keep the men from bolting. I never thought it would take us three days to get out of here. Fighting was one thing, but just hanging around is much more difficult to take." I saluted and headed back to our bivouac with some doubts in my mind.

It didn't take me long to tell the men what the plans were for the next two days. There were lots of questions, very few that I had complete answers for. The biggest contention was having to stay in this place for another day. The next was about the parole paper. Comments ranged from: "I just might take off and leave", "It is bad enough to lose, but to have to hang around is cruelty beyond limits";

to: "What happens if I lose mine?" "You don't expect me to carry around a silly piece of paper the rest of my life, do you?"; and finally: "Well, I guess it's certainly better than going to some Yankee jail."

Everyone would have plenty of time to get their belongings together for the day after tomorrow. We certainly didn't have much, and it would be even less after we turned in the cartridge belts. I think one of the boys had a battle flag, but I wasn't sure if he would toss it in when the time came. I noticed he was starting to fold it to go under his shirt. I couldn't blame him, and I certainly wasn't going to tell him not to keep it.

Deep down, I felt that most were pleased with the conditions of our surrender. It wasn't going to be easy going back to our homes after experiencing the horrors of war, but time should heal a lot of the mental wounds.

I wondered if my father or brother is someplace near here. Of course, they could already be home since they were wounded well before the Petersburg battle. It is very unlikely that they would be here. However, if I could run into one of them, we could head for home together. I will look around tomorrow, but if I don't run into either of them, I will be on my way alone.

There will be more than one person from our unit who will be heading in my direction. I'll probably have more company than I can handle.

John and David had listened with the rest, neither coming up with any questions. They had appeared to be satisfied with the way things would unfold. They had busied themselves with getting what little they had together. But after all the conversation had died down, they came over to me and pulled me behind our lean-to.

David said, "Vee, we have something to tell you, but if you don't agree, you've got to promise to hear us out. You can't tell another soul, or this entire scheme could be jeopardized."

"I'm not sure just what you have in mind, but at this point I don't plan to say too much to anybody about anything. I just want to get my parole and head for Clifford."

"We've been in contact with about ten men from one of General Gordon's other artillery units. We've talked with them at great length. We think they might have a pretty good plan to alter the outcome of this war as far as a few of us are concerned."

"What in the daylights are you talking about by furthering the outcome of this war? I'm through fighting."

"Now, hear us out before you get your dander up. You promised to listen." I shook my head in the affirmative as they continued. "They are planning to join up with another group who will be gathering over near where the road from Appomattox Court House intersects with the Richmond/Amherst turnpike. There is supposed to be a rendezvous just to the west of Mount Rush. Their scheme is to attack and ambush small Yankee units headed back up the turnpike on their way north. They know where they can get all the guns and ammunition needed for such an operation. They also feel we can get rich by capturing their commissary wagons and selling the products off to the various stores along the route. John and I are planning to join up with them. We want you to come along."

Their faces were brighter than I had ever seen them before. Their excitement could hardly be contained. But, when they saw the expression on my face, their enthusiasm faded a bit.

"I've been with you two for what seems like a lifetime, but actually it has only been a matter of weeks. However, we've been through a lot in that short period of time, and I thought I knew you both. But apparently I don't.

John, what about that pretty little girl we saw in Burkesville? The way you two embraced and you vowing you would be with her as soon this thing ended. Have you forgotten that?

And you, David, you were so hot to light out towards Williamsburg. I thought for a while you were going to leave us at Petersburg. I admired you for staying on until the end. Why change those wonderful ideas? What has changed you both?"

"We are just as tired of the fighting as you, Vee. But look at us; we are going to come away from this thing without the means to make a restart. We haven't been paid in weeks, and even if we had been, Confederate dollars aren't going to be any good for us. We won't be able to resurrect a life if and when we get home. We feel that by fighting just a bit longer we can get a grubstake that will enable us to have a new beginning when we do get home." David was almost getting red in the face trying to make his point.

"John, you haven't said much. Do you really feel like David?"

101

"Mac, these guys have figured out a way for us to get even with the Yankees, and at the same time enable us to go home with something in our pockets. This won't last for long. We plan to hit them for about a week, then we'll scatter and be on our individual ways home. What could go wrong with such a scheme?"

"Plenty could go wrong. Do you think for one minute the Yankees will stand for some renegade hostiles ambushing their units without immediate retaliation? They will be down on you so fast; you will be lucky to get away with your lives, much less money. I wish you two would think this over; you aren't the kind to be traitors to our cause."

"Well, it might be easy for you to say we are traitors, but we've almost given our lives more than once. We've fought for the cause, and we have nothing to show for it. Now we have a chance to reap a few benefits." David seemed to be the most adamant of the two. "Shucks, you don't even have shoes to walk home in, Vee. I can't live with nothing, and I think I will be able to get what's due me with this band of warriors."

"Mac, I sure wish you would join us. If you were with us, I feel we would have a better chance to accomplish what we are setting out to do. Some of these guys are a bit hot headed, and your calming approach would keep us on the right path." John was almost pleading as I turned to go back by the fire.

"I'm afraid you two will have to do this without me. When our part in the surrender is complete and I get my parole, I plan to head out for Vera. I'll spend the first night there if I can get that far, then I'm going to head straight north towards the James River."

"Vee, don't make up your mind so fast. We have a full day before we will be leaving. We will also be heading the same way as you with a few of the boys who will be joining the group. Maybe we could go over and see the leaders of this plan tomorrow while we are just killing time. They might add some additional points we haven't covered, which could change your mind. Anyway, don't say for sure you won't give it some more thought."

"OK David, I'll give it some more thought, but regardless of what your new friends say, I don't think I will be joining you. I will look forward to your company on the first leg of my journey home, after that I wish you both well. Let's get back to the fire. I need to keep the rest of these men from wandering off. As you say, we have another full day to kill. I also need to get the Napoleon turned over in the morning."

The fire was still going, but it was mostly smoke blocking out the first rays of daylight. A bit of heat sneaked through but not enough to warm the innards of your body. The firewood was just too damp to give off the heat needed to dry out our wet and soggy clothes. Unfortunately the rain hadn't slacked off, we would be moving the Napoleon through the mud for one last time. The eleventh of April wasn't much different from the previous days. At this point they all seemed to run together.

Our two horses had perked up considerably after getting those oats and grain. The short trek to the turnover point didn't take near the effort we had previously expended when we were moving the guns those last few miles into Appomattox Court House.

The Yankees had over seventy artillery pieces all lined up when we arrived. There didn't seem to be any attempt to separate the various guns from one another. Seems they were more interested in getting the horses back so they could get them ready for their trip north.

The Lieutenant in charge said, "OK Rebs, get that gun over there by those two." He pointed in the direction of two three-inch rifles. "Once you get it set, unhitch those horses, and lead them to the corral up there on the far side of the road. After you turn the horses in, you are free to return to your unit. I'll see you tomorrow morning over near the Court House at the formal surrender ceremony."

"Yes sir, we'll get on with it. We'll be out of your way as soon as we can." It wasn't difficult to notice the fresh uniforms being worn by all the Bluecoats handling the guns and horses. Either they had just been issued, or these soldiers hadn't seen much action before they arrived here.

John and David were waiting for me when I returned to the bivouac area. "Mac, come with us, we have someone we want you to meet."

"John, I don't need to meet anyone. My mind didn't change over night. I'm still planning on heading straight for Clifford after the weapon turn-in tomorrow."

"Oh, come on. You don't have anything to do for the rest of the day. Take a little walk with us, we'll get you back before dark."

The distance to the other bivouac area wasn't more than a half-mile through a small pine grove. The ground was almost swampy as we mushed through the undergrowth, now beaten down by many feet. A large barrel-chested man with a shock of red hair was talking quietly with at least nine other individuals as we approached. He went silent as John, David, and I walked up.

"Hello, Seth, this is Vee, the man we told you about." John shook hands with Seth as he spoke.

"So you're Vee. Now I remember you from the day you and John wanted to see General Gordon. Mighty important, weren't you? I understand John and David have given you some idea of what we have in mind after we move out of here. I don't rightly know if we would want the likes of you with us. But, if John and David want you, I'll make an exception. There won't be another opportunity like this again."

"Seth, I've heard all I want to know about your scheme. I've told both John and David I wasn't interested. They insisted I come over to meet you, and that is the only reason I'm here."

"Maybe John and David made a big mistake by telling you anything. I would hate to think you might spill our plan to the wrong people. You might run to your buddy Gordon; you seemed so close with him." Seth stepped towards me in a menacing manner but stopped short. He turned to the rest of his gang and added in as venomous voice as possible, "We'll be better off without this kind of righteous loser."

Not moving an inch I said, "No need to threaten me, Seth. I'm not the telling kind, and I certainly don't take kindly to being pushed one way or the other."

He turned to look at John. "Guess Vee don't need any money when he gets back home. Maybe he's got something already stashed away." His voice was gravelly, and the sneer on his face left me with a chilling feeling. "Well, the heck with him. Are you two still with us?"

"I think I speak for John when I say we will be with you. We plan on meeting you at Mount Rush in a day or two. That is where you will be, isn't it?" David looked at John as he spoke, getting John's nod of agreement.

"Mount Rush may or may not be the place we will meet. I'll let you know before we move out. Can't be too careful about letting everybody know our plans." Seth stared in my direction as he said "everybody."

"I'll make my own way back. You can make any plans you want, and you won't have to worry about me knowing any of them. I will expect to see both of you back before nightfall. I plan for all of us to be in that final formation tomorrow. Don't let me down at this late date." They both nodded in a sheepish way. As a parting shot I said, "I won't say it was a pleasure meeting you, Seth." With that I turned on my heels and headed for our camp.

It really stuck in my craw to meet people like Seth. His type of hatred could become infectious when dealing with people who were tired and hungry. They could unwittingly be led into more problems than they faced with the present circumstances. I would like to think he was in the minority, but this war had changed many people in a lot of different ways. Maybe there would be a chance to talk John and David out of joining up with the likes of Seth and his kind. I would for sure give it another try tomorrow.

There was a serene mood prevailing the group around the fire for this last evening together. Maybe everyone had made their peace with the way things had turned out. Maybe the relief was so great that words weren't available to describe one's true feelings. Whatever the case, this would be the last time any of us would be together again for a long time, if ever.

I cleared my throat and said, "Let's kneel and give thanks we've made it this far. And pray that our future will bring better times."

To a man, we all kneeled, and bent our heads in our own silent prayers. This terrible war was finally over.

Chapter Seven

The rain had stopped, but the sun didn't have a chance of getting through the heavy clouds hovering over the rolling countryside that surrounded Appomattox Court House. The air was heavy, almost like the feeling of moving through swampland. If we had been near the ocean, the moanful sound of foghorns would have been expected. Here, it was the non-sound of sadness as grey-clad men moved about in eerie silence.

This day, the twelfth of April, marked the end of the Army of Northern Virginia.

Major Sandiege had come over to our bivouac early. He wanted to be sure we were ready to meet the requirements of the surrender agreement. He wasn't greeted with much enthusiasm as he rode up to our fire. I don't think he expected a very rousing welcome, and his expression showed it.

Staying on his horse he looked down on the small gathering and spoke in a nasal voice, "Men, today isn't a happy one for any of us. We've had difficult times and this will surely be one of the most difficult. We will march over to where we stacked our muskets and retrieve them. We will then fall in line behind the men of the Stonewall Brigade and march to the appointed place to surrender our weapons, cartridge belts, and flags. After we meet the demands set down by General Grant, we will return here so that I can issue the parole documents to each of you. I'm sure Sergeant McGrady has told you of the importance of this document. Put it in a safe place and keep it there. It is your safe ticket home and something that will be important to you until our country's unification has once again become fact."

There was some shuffling of feet, a few groans, and many downcast eyes. When I looked around at our small group, I felt I was seeing it for the first time. The tattered clothes, the bandaged arms and legs, the gaunt faces, and the bent shoulders stood out above all else. We looked like a defeated army. It was almost more than I could stand. I looked to Major Sandiege, hoping he would say something more, but he was trying to steady his horse and really wasn't paying any attention to the mood of the men.

Someone spoke from the back of the group, bringing Major Sandiege's gaze back to the men. "Why do we have to march all the way over to the Court House and give them our guns? As far as I'm concerned, those Yankees can pick up the muskets where we left them."

"I feel that General Grant has been very fair in what he has requested for our surrender. It is my intention to have the men of this battery follow those guidelines to the letter, or there won't be any paroles." His horse spun with him as he said 'paroles', almost tossing him to the ground. That didn't improve his disposition any from what it had been when he first arrived.

Before any further comments were voiced from the ranks, causing a greater void between the Major and the men, I stepped forward. "Men, we don't have anything to hang our heads about. We have fought long and hard. We haven't always had the proper means with which to win, especially these last few months. But we fought for the things we thought were right and now we have been defeated by a superior force. Maybe this is the way it was supposed to end. Maybe there was some great devise, which brought about this conclusion. Whatever, we are now one nation again and it's time to get on with consolidating and welding that nation torn apart by strife and misunderstanding.

We will be marching together for the last time today. Let's hold our heads high and let our brothers from the North know we may have been defeated materially but never spiritually."

It was rewarding for me to see a few heads raise and some backs straighten. "Fall in. It's time to show them we are men of valor."

Major Sandiege didn't utter another word. He turned his horse and rode off towards our rendezvous point.

There were no drums. The line of men was certainly shorter than it should have been as the ragged column plodded down the slope leading to the small river below the Court House area. As we approached the rise just south of the Court House, we were greeted by two long rows of Yankees clad in what must have been their best blue uniforms. There were at least two brigades or more. They bordered each side of the road leading to the surrender point. As we drew abreast, their commanding officer, a general, brought his sword to his shoulder, saluting our group. His troops shifted their muskets from order arms to carry arms, the marching salute.

I could see Major Sandiege as he swung his horse towards the assembled officers and returned the salute. There was dead silence, not a spoken word passed between either side.

We continued on until our unit was abeam the Yankee forces on our left. We halted and an order to face south was given. Major Sandiege inspected our line and then gave the order to fix bayonets. Then his final order came in almost a whisper, "Step forward and stack arms."

We hung our cartridge boxes on the muskets. Our lone shredded battle flag was folded by tender hands and laid on the stack of weapons. We returned to the road and resumed our formation. Without another word, we turned to the west and marched as one until we passed the Court House.

The finality of the moment was like a heavy weight pressing on your chest. It was more than difficult to hold our heads high, to keep our backs straight, and our shoulders squared. We had been beaten.

To me, the eyes told the story. No one could make eye contact. Almost every head was bent, not really in shame, but in a type of despair, which was hard to understand if you weren't there.

What could the future hold? I was going to be on my way home to Clifford before this day was over. Because of that, I felt a sense of beginning that more than offset the frustration of the last few months. Somehow, everything was going to be better. I wasn't fooling myself that there wouldn't be difficult times for the immediate future.

But after what we had been through, how much worse could things get?

It was now time to take each day in turn. The trek to Clifford would give me time to unwind. Would I find Elizabeth at home? Only time could answer my questions. I knew for certain, what I had experienced so far in this short life had added a maturity that wouldn't have been gained by staying home. Since I'm alive, I'll say it was worth it for me.

However, the expense for many others will always be too high. Those many men who paid the extreme sacrifice have left a void that won't be filled for several more generations. Some of the cream has disappeared.

Major Sandiege was busy signing the paroles for each individual. He was taking time to lecture each man about the importance of the document even though he had said it all before. I guess there was some benefit in the fact that our unit wasn't at full strength. If we had still been at full muster, we could spend a few extra days listening to the major.

Finally, the last in our group, I stepped before him. "Sergeant McGrady, I want to thank you for all you have done for this unit and the cause. If I can be of assistance to you at some future date, I will do so with pleasure. I can't help but repeat your words again and again about how important it is to get on with life now that the fighting has ended. We are again one nation, and it's going to take all of us to see that we stay united. I pray that we will never again have to fight our brothers.

You have done a good job and I wish you well. If you ever get to Richmond, look me up and we can have a stein together."

"Thank you, Major, for the kind words. Don't know when or if I will ever be down Richmond way, but if I do, I'll try to look in." I saluted for the last time and started towards the lean-to to gather up my few belongings.

Major Sandiege mounted his horse, hardly acknowledging the few men still around the camp. He rode off towards the Court House without a look back. He probably was thinking about home, too.

David, John, and Ben were already at the lean-to preparing to move out. Being the last in line to receive a parole, plus all the conversation between the major and each man, had allowed the time to grow late in the afternoon. I needed to be on the road to Vera soon or I certainly wouldn't get there by nightfall.

"Well, Mac, it's time to move along. You do want some company as far as Vera?" John's words were clipped a bit, like he was not really asking a question, more like making a statement of fact.

"Certainly I want your company, I'll be with you in a minute." I took some pains to put that extra piece of bread and the little bit of jerky I had gotten from the Yankee when I turned in the horses, into my blanket roll. I put my parole into my pants pocket, it was the driest place on me and I didn't want it to get wet. I said, "Let's take down the lean-to and make sure the fire is out. We should try to leave this place as we found it."

"There is no way this part of the country will ever be like we found it, even if we stayed here another month trying to spruce it up. Plus, there isn't any way this fire will hurt anything. It was only dying embers even before we left to turn in our weapons. But, I will take some of that lean-to canvas. It might come in handy on our way to Mount Rush. Anybody want some of it?" David was beginning to tear the material into smaller strips. "Come on, Vee, times a wasting."

The distance from Appomattox Court House to Vera wasn't more than four to five miles, however, the heavy traffic on the road made travel difficult and slow. The Yankees were already moving equipment so they were taking the right of way. Unit after unit went by with artillery and commissary wagons. Occasionally, wagons carrying wounded would take priority over everything on the road, thus slowing the flow even more.

Our straggling group had to give way or get run over. Since the road was still muddy and spotted with deep water holes, we were constantly getting splashed. To avoid as much of that as possible, we moved several yards off the road, which made travel a bit more difficult since the ground under foot didn't allow for a fast pace. It isn't easy to walk through mud and make good time too.

Shortly after crossing the Appomattox one last time, it wasn't much more than creek size this far west, we proceeded up the hill past General Lee's headquarters. At least it had been his headquarters before the surrender. There was still activity around a few scattered tents, but for the most part, things had been packed up and shipped out days before. General Lee had long since departed. After signing the surrender with General Grant, he had headed for the Lexington area. I assumed that to be true, for it was the story we heard while we were waiting for the ceremony earlier today.

I stopped momentarily and saluted the memory of a man who did his duty for a cause, which may or may not have been his total choice. He honored his Virginia just like so many others. In my mind, he would never be forgotten.

We had journeyed on for about a mile when we ran across some men digging graves. Seemed some of the men in Jackson's old brigade had left the burying of their fallen comrades until they had completed the surrender ceremony. These men hadn't been killed during the fighting, instead they had died of exposure and starvation after the truce had been declared. We were lucky not more had met the same fate. Those Yankees delivering bread must have missed a few units, although they would have probably been too late for these poor souls. The diggers still had some work left to accomplish so I, along with several others, pitched in to help.

After the bodies were put to rest, one of the older men of the group put his hat over his heart and started to say a few words. "Lord, these men made it through one of the worst conflicts in the history of our country, only to fall to the exhaustion faced by many of us. We ask you to accept these warriors into your heavens and keep them safe from further harm. We thank you for sparing us who remain here this day and hope that at some future date we will be able to meet you with the bravery shown by these few. May God have mercy on their souls."

The few of us who had stopped to help slowly moved away. Only a nod of thanks came from the main burial group, nothing more was expected as far as most of us were concerned. It could have been our problem; we just felt lucky it wasn't.

I had been somewhat aware that a few of our weaker men had died after the truce; I just hadn't seen it firsthand. None of our small group had expired, maybe because of the food given us by the Yankees. Maybe because we were younger and had better stood the waste and ruin of the last few weeks of conflict.

But now it hit me that even though the killing had stopped, the dying hadn't. And it probably wouldn't for many months to come.

How many of us would die on the way home? There was no certainty that just because we had survived one of the bloodiest wars we had ever known, that we would be granted the privilege to continue to live. There was no unwritten rule to allow us free passage. The conflict may have ended, but the struggle continued.

We faced a new and perhaps as deadly a foe, 'Survival.' It didn't shoot at you, but it was just as deadly if you let your guard down.

I must be ever alert if I expected to see Clifford again.

Even though the terrain was mostly open fields interspersed with scattered groves of pine, making our way across the land was slow. The fields were soggy and mushy from the continual rains of the last few days, and the inevitable ridgelines presented natural barriers that sapped one's strength. It wasn't easy going up the inclines, and coming down the slopes was almost as difficult. A small creek, Rocky Run, presented more than the usual problems. It was running swift and it forced us back to the road in order to cross. Again, traffic was our dilemma. We went single file across the small bridge, nearly getting knocked into the water more than once by the never-ending line of wagons.

Daylight would be beginning to fail soon, so I took one last check of the map I had sketched from the one I had seen in Major Sandiege's tent. I had been particularly interested in the area between Appomattox Court House and the James River, because it was all unfamiliar territory to me. I had made note of some of the major terrain features that would be prominent during my trek. Once I could get across the James, I felt I would be in an area of some familiarization. I had been down to Bent Creek with my daddy on several occasions before the war. I had been younger then, but I hoped I could remember a part of the land once I was on it again.

The sketch showed forest just short of Vera. If it was correct, the woods we were entering should open onto cut fields, making the rest of the way easier. However, the woods were thick, and it wasn't easy weaving our way through the trees.

John and David had stopped not too far from me and as I approached their position, David said, "Vee, why don't we rest for a minute or two? There should still be enough light for us to reach Vera before dark."

"I don't know, David, the light will fail fast once the sun sets, and that shouldn't be more than an hour from now. Best we press on if we expect to get to Vera in the daylight." I stopped with them as they shifted from one foot to the other.

"This is probably the last time we will be together, Vee. I hate to have you not go with us, but I can understand your reasons for staying clear of the likes of Seth and his crew. If I had as sure a place to go home to as you, I wouldn't be going with them either."

I listened to David for only a second or two more, but I couldn't think of any words I cared to answer with. I just nodded my head and moved on my winding way through the trees. As I glanced back, both John and David were underway again, staying a couple of yards to my rear.

Finally, we burst out into the open area I was hoping for. Being in open country was a welcomed relief, plus the open ground turned out to be firmer, permitting us to quicken our pace.

It was dark by the time we saw lights twinkling from what must be Vera. The crossroads that comprised Vera couldn't have had more than four or five houses, and maybe a store or two. It was surprising to me that lights were coming from any of them. Both armies had passed this way more than once. While I'm sure the word of the surrender had gotten to them, it was a time to lay low.

There was plenty of space for camping after reaching Vera. We picked a small glade near a rippling stream whose water tasted cool and sweet. Each man prepared his own spot for the night. Most had something to eat. I ate the remaining part of the bread and a piece of the jerky I had saved. There was very little conversation, however, John eased over and spoke in low tones to me.

"Mac, is there any chance you could have changed your mind about coming with us? I'm only going to be with this group for a few days, then I'm taking off and heading for home. We could have some money in our hands which I'm sure will come in handy when we do get home."

"John, as I've told David, I haven't changed my thinking a bit from the other day. And I wish you wouldn't get involved in this either. As far as that is concerned, I wish you, David, and Ben would head in the other direction, and let these madmen go on their fiendish way."

Suddenly a loud clatter of banging arose from the direction of the crossroads. One of the sounds was that of a musket being fired. Something was amiss, but none of us were willing to venture forward to find out the cause.

John continued to talk, "Wonder what that was all about? Must be somebody upset with something." He paused and stared at me for a moment, then said, "Well, I wish you well and hope our paths will someday cross again. We have been through some tough times these last few weeks. Ever since you selected David and me to accompany you on that scouting mission, I have respected your judgment and enjoyed being in your company. Too bad it will have to end now. Take care of yourself, Mac, I won't forget you." He moved away and went into low conversation with David and Ben. I guess they had written me off.

I must have been asleep for an hour when shouting and yelling brought me out of my deep fog. As I looked over towards the sound, I could see Seth and a few of his crew talking loudly with John and the others. They were waving bottles of whiskey around and hollering at the same time.

I couldn't help but overhear part of the conversation. Seth was the loudest and was saying, "Well, we've got a start. That storekeeper wasn't going to give us any whiskey, but we showed him. After we took what we wanted, we banged him on the head to let him know we meant business. He won't be giving anyone else any problem for a few days. Come on guys, have a pull on this jug; it will give you a new outlook on life. There will be more and better of this once we swing into full operation."

"Seems like we shouldn't be beating up on our own kind. I thought we were going to do this sort of thing to the Yankees, not the people who had supported our cause." John's voice wasn't as loud as the others, but it still carried in the night.

"What makes you so sure these people supported our cause? You sound like that yellow-bellied friend of yours. By the way, where is he? I might want to give him a little drink of this whiskey. It might put some starch into his backbone." Seth was looking around, but luckily I was far enough back in the dark not to be easily seen. With

115

his continuing intake of alcohol, I could have been standing next to him and he might have had trouble seeing me.

Just to make sure I wouldn't be forced into some type of confrontation with Seth, I decided to move further down along the creek. I pulled my few belongings together and moved along the waterway distancing myself from most of the people I had traveled with from the Court House.

In doing so, I bumped into two men who were strangers to me. They said, "Come on and join us. We don't blame you for not getting involved with the likes of that crew. That whiskey is going to cause them more problems when they wake up in the morning. You can bed down over there."

"Thanks guys, I don't think I'll have any problem with those people. After what's happened today, it will be nice just to get some sleep in peace. See you in the morning." I placed my knapsack by a small tree and rolled myself in the thin blanket I was using for a bedroll. I had thought about starting a fire earlier, but there hadn't been any real need for one. I didn't have anything to cook and it really wasn't that cold. The night sounds and the racket from the boisterous crew seemed to blend together allowing sleep to wash over me once again.

It was a bit past first light when I awoke, much later than I was used to rising. The leaden sky was foreboding, but at least there wasn't any rain. There were a few streaks of light but no real signs of sunshine in the immediate future. I realized the hike from the Court House had been more tiring than I had expected, and it felt good to have a genuine night's sleep without any interruptions.

The cool water from the stream was a refreshing jolt to my face as I splashed it on by cupping both hands. I dried my face with the sleeve of my right arm and as I brought the arm down, I looked to the base of the tree where I had put my knapsack. IT WAS GONE. As a matter of fact, there wasn't a soul in sight.

I was alone by the cascading water. The only other sound was my stomach growling over the loss of that last piece of jerky I had been planning to use as breakfast. My camp mates of the previous evening apparently hadn't been as friendly as they seemed last night. I guess I had just learned my first lesson in survival: Be Wary of

Strangers. It was going to be a hard lesson to learn, for that was surely not my way of approaching people.

Looking around to get my bearings, I spied the remnants of the paper I had wrapped the jerky in. I could only guess that it had been someone else's breakfast; at least it hadn't gone to waste. However, there weren't any signs of my knapsack or the few other belongings I had stored in it.

Then I remembered my parole. Frantically I reached for my pocket and was immediately relieved to feel it was still safely secured. Thank goodness I had placed it in my pants pocket and not in my knapsack. I may lose food and what few belongings I had, but I would never let my parole leave my body.

There wasn't any reason to hang around this locale any longer, so I slung my bedroll over my shoulder and started out for the road leading north out of Vera.

Approaching the few buildings, which comprised Vera, I noticed a commotion near the country store. Several people were milling about on the porch and a man with a bandaged head was holding court. As I moved closer I could hear some of the conversation.

"If I'd had a gun I would have given that crew what they deserved. What really galls me is that they were Rebs. Never thought any of our boys would be robbing their own people."

"Must have been some renegades who don't want the war to end. You would think they would be happy to still be alive."

"What did they take from your store, Ebb?"

"Mostly whiskey and some bacon and beans. I was surprised they had guns, especially when I thought the Yankees had made all our boys turn in their weapons before they were released. Guess this crew must have slipped off without turning theirs in."

"Well, you were lucky they only hit you in the head rather than shoot you. I'm sure they'll come to no good before too long. I sure hope so anyway."

I was just turning away when they spotted me and yelled, "Hey there, Reb, where you headed?"

"I'm headed north towards the James. That trail yonder is the best way, isn't it?"

117

"Yeah, but you sure you're not part of those renegades who caused all the trouble last night? They beat this storekeeper in the head and stole some of his goods."

"I heard them. I was sleeping down by the creek and I was glad they didn't come my way. Don't know who they were, but they sure made a racket. My knapsack got stolen by a couple of other men who were sleeping near me. They took what little food I had saved for the trip north."

The man speaking turned to his friends and said, "Maybe we'd better hold this fellow until we make sure he ain't one of that crew from last night."

"Yeah," said another. "Can't let him get away. Quick, grab him."

Before I could turn to run, two men whom I hadn't seen grabbed me from the back and pinned my arms to my sides. They dragged me into the center of the group in front of the store. There they released my arms and spun me around to face the growing crowd.

"Well young fellow, what do you have to say for yourself?" The man with the bandaged head spoke from the top of the store steps.

"I didn't have anything to do with the commotion here last night. I'm on my way home after fighting a war, which should never have been fought. We not only lost, but way too many of our brothers will never be around to see their folks again or their families grow. I've had enough of fighting, but if you people try to railroad me into something I've never been a part of, then I guess I ain't seen the last of my fighting days. Cause, you are going to have one very upset ex-confederate on your hands."

"Well now, don't get too riled up. We just wanted to make certain you didn't have any part of last night's affair. Do you have any idea who these people might have been?"

"I know they are some of the most misdirected people I have ever seen. Several days ago they were trying to get people to join them in their efforts to continue the fight against the Yankees. Not many of the people I fought with were having anything to do with them." I didn't add anything about John, David, and Ben joining up with them. "I guess they broadened their field when they hit you over the head last night and stole some goods from your store."

118

"Well, I hope they get their deserves before too long." The storekeeper was slowly rubbing the bandage on his head. "It sure leaves folks like us with a bad taste for any strangers like yourself who might be asking for help. With people like that running around the countryside, you sure can't expect us to help anyone on their way through."

Their small group began to loosen up around me and I sensed I wasn't a suspect any longer. Easing my way towards the outskirts of the crowd while keeping an eye on the two who had grabbed me, I said, "Unless you can help me out with something to eat, I'd best be getting on my way home. I hope you find out who those renegades were and give them what they deserve."

"Wish we could help you but we are almost as strapped as you. We're sorry we suspected you, but you can see why we grabbed onto the first person we saw who might know something. I hope we won't be as jumpy the next time. Try not to hold it against us. If you take that trail over by that stand of pines it will take you north towards the Liberty Baptist Church. From there you can head over towards the turnpike and then on to Bent Creek. That'll get you to the James. Good luck."

I waved cautiously and headed towards the pines, glad to be away from what could have easily turned into a hanging mob. It seems another lesson could be added to my list: Stay Away From Disgruntled Groups and Unknown Things. I sure didn't need to be involved with other people's problems; I had enough of my own.

I could have pressed them for something to eat, but they were more concerned about the robbery at the store and the wounded head of the storekeeper. I could have given them Seth's name, but it wouldn't have done them any good. He and his crew were long gone and without any guns to go after them, they didn't have a chance of bringing them back to face the consequences of their crime.

By now, that crew should be almost to Mount Rush or someplace near. It shouldn't be many days before they start to rob the Yankee wagons headed north. I reckon most of their work will be along the turnpike between Mount Rush and Bent Creek. I'll avoid that area for sure, particularly the section closest to Mount Rush.

There are enough of those Yankee wagons moving north to keep them busy for a good period of time. I wondered how much protection the Yankees will be providing for their wagons? Probably not as much as they should.

If Seth and his crew are successful, it is certain there will be news about before too long. Maybe when I get to Bent Creek there will be some word.

There were a few breaks in the cloud cover allowing the sun to come through in hazy beams. The shafts of light reminded me of the light streaming through the windows in the church at Clifford on a hazy Sunday, in what now seemed like ages ago.

The delay with the folks at the store had used up part of the day, and I wasn't sure how much further up the road I would get before darkness caught me again. The road I was on wasn't much more than an overgrown path. However, the going wasn't too bad, a lot easier than the hike from the Court House to Vera. Also, all of the Yankee wagon traffic had continued on towards Mount Rush instead of turning north along my route. In all probability they would connect with the turnpike there for their movement on north.

Piney Mountain was supposed to be directly north, and sure enough, there it was. I could see it off to my left even though the visibility wasn't the best. I knew I shouldn't head directly towards it for that would put me more north than I wanted to be. If the road didn't turn towards the east soon, I would have to take off across country to stay to the right of the mountain.

I was just coming up to a ridgeline when out of the corner of my eye I saw something move in the distance across a small field off to my left. It appeared to be human and making some attempt to stay hidden. I wondered if any of those renegades were attempting to work this route?

I scurried off the trail and ducked behind a tree. Keeping low to the ground, I moved as close as I dared to the location where I had seen the movement. I wasn't positive it was a person; it could have been an animal. I froze, waiting for something to happen. Nothing moved.

Three minutes must have passed before I slowly rose to a standing position. I moved as quietly as possible towards a large group of cypress that covered a small depression in the ridgeline. Here I was, in less than a day, breaking my resolve of lesson number two - Stay Away from Disgruntled Groups and Unknown Things.

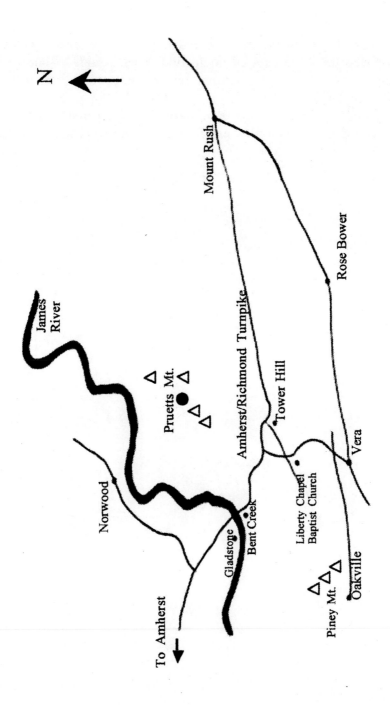

Again, movement from behind the cypress. I reached down and grabbed the largest rock I could find. Then I said, "Whoever or whatever is in that cypress grove better come out before I start throwing rocks."

A quiet voice with fear laced through it whispered, "Boss man, I ain't no slave, I's been a free-man for more than two years."

Chapter Eight

One of the largest black men I had ever seen rose from behind the cypress trees. He stood at least six foot five and weighed somewhere near 270 pounds. He was dressed in gunnysack material, neatly sewn, and warm enough for this time of year. He was barefoot and his feet looked like they had been that way for a long time. He slowly brushed off some loose straw from his pants leg while grabbing his hat and knapsack. He was about fifteen yards from my position and seemed to cover the distance in a minimum number of strides. He stopped short and said in his low but solid voice, "Boss man, my name is Jethro, what's yours?"

Not flinching from the onrush I said, "My name is Valerius, but most of my friends call me Vee or Mac. My last name is McGrady."

"Well, Mister Vee, you must have just finished fightin' for the South. From the looks of that uniform, you must of fought hard. They is sure some tattered clothes you got on there and you's wearin' the same kind of shoes as I has. Had anything to eat lately?"

"I've had a little, but not much in the last twenty-four hours or so. Food was mighty scarce those last few weeks of the war. If I had anything I would be more than willing to share some with you, but the last bit of jerky I had was stolen from me just last night."

"Wasn't goin' to be askin' you for anything Mister Vee, I's got a little bit of rabbit left and thought you might like a taste." He reached in his knapsack and pulled out the last remnants of a carcass. Quickly pulling it in two, he extended part to me.

123

Even though it was cold, it tasted good. I devoured it in a matter of seconds, licking the leg bone dry to ensure there was nothing left. Jethro gazed at me and then extended the other piece.

"Looks like you could need this more than me, Mister Vee. I done had the larger part earlier this mornin'. Go on and have it."

"Thank you anyway, Jethro, you are more than kind, but I can't take it. That one piece will keep me going 'til I can fend for myself."

"Where is you headed, Mister Vee? I was on my way up to the North, where I was hopin' they would accept a free black man like me. However, I was unfortunate to come through this part of the country where all the fightin' was goin' on. I been holed up in these parts for a couple of weeks now, a feared I would be picked up as an escaped slave. But I's got papers sayin' I is been set free. See here."

He rummaged in his knapsack a minute and produced a legitimate looking piece of paper saying he was a free man. It appeared legal to me, but, of course, I wasn't a lawyer. It was signed by a plantation owner in South Carolina, a William K. Morrison, Jr. whose signature was very graceful. It had been witnessed and co-signed by a lawyer from the same location.

"It sure looks like a legal document to me, Jethro. You shouldn't have any trouble getting through to the northern states with this piece of paper."

"Yas sir, but lots of time I hear some of these folk who sell people don't take no time to look at pieces of paper. They just truss you up and peddle you off as if you hadn't been set free. Don't seem right, but I hears they just do it anyway. That's why I's been laying low until things settled down. Now I hear the big white-haired general done surrendered to the Yankees, so things might start to gettin' a little less bad. Anyways, I is about to head out north."

"Well, I'm heading that way myself, at least some of the way. Would you like to go along with me?"

"I sure would, Mister Vee. I would be good company and I can trap us some more rabbits so we won't go hungry." Jethro was ready to move out, but it was getting dark.

"Why don't we stay here for the night? It's almost dark and we couldn't get much further anyway. I had planned to head up towards a place called the Liberty Chapel Baptist Church. Shouldn't be more than six or seven miles. However, when you are traveling across country like we are, it could take more than the best part of a day, what with the creeks in these parts running high. Do you know of any place nearby where we could camp?"

"Sho do, Mister Vee. I's been stayin just over that knoll yonder. It's well concealed and I ain't seen nobody come around the whole time I's been there 'ceptin an old man on his way to the east. He'uns the one who told me about the surrender. He kept agoin', hardly took time to say hello. The place has good water close by and some of the traps I set out may have somethin' in them. I can check in a minute." He grabbed up his knapsack and was off before I could swing my bedroll over my shoulder. Looked like I had just gained a companion for at least a part of the way home.

Trees surrounded the campsite so it was almost impossible to observe until you walked right up to it. There was a small nook back in some rocks, which concealed any glare from the small fireplace Jethro had constructed out of river rocks. From the looks of the area, it was evident Jethro had made the place as comfortable as possible. He had constructed a lean-to and cleared a small piece of ground where he had put the rocks for the fireplace. The trees provided a canopy over the lean-to, which killed any smoke from the fire. I doubt if many people would have any reason to wander this far from the path I had been on. No wonder he had been able to stay so secure for two weeks.

"Pretty neat little hideout you have here, Jethro."

"Well sir, I didn't know how long I'd be holed up, so I tried to make myself as comfortable as possible. I was gettin' ready to leave when I saw you on the path headed north. I had been watchin' it for bout an hour just to see how many folks might pass by that way. Must of got a little careless when I moved a bit and you saw me."

"I was lucky to see the movement, I just happened to glance over that way. Anybody else might have missed it." Jethro just shrugged at my comment. "Looks like we could use some firewood. I'll go round up some."

"Yas sir, I used all I had last night since I was headin' out. I'll go check the traps I left and see if we got anythin'. Here's some flint in case you need somethin' to get a fire goin' before I get back."

It was getting dark by the time I got back to the camp. The shadows were deep and the sky, what you could see of it, had started to threaten rain. It took me a minute before I could get a fire going. The flint Jethro gave me made a good spark on some dry kindling I found near the fireplace. The flames had just reached a decent height when Jethro came walking back in, swinging a rabbit in his left hand.

"Boy, that looks good. I didn't know the country around here had so much game. It sure was lacking down around the Court House while we were holed up there waiting for the surrender. Of course, there was a bunch of hungry people looking for anything they could find to eat. Any respectable rabbit wouldn't have come close to that place or he would have been in a pot so fast his fur would've still been on him."

"Well, I'll skin this one and we will roast him over that fire you got goin' there. See if'n you can find something to make a spit out of and I'll get him ready to put on it."

It didn't take me long to get the spit ready and we had the rabbit cooking in his own juices before you could count to ten.

"Don't know if'n you saw the creek while you were gettin' firewood, but it's over there about twenty yards or so. The water is mighty sweet and cool. You might want to get you some before we eat."

"Good idea, Jethro. Come to think of it, I haven't had too much to drink since I started out this morning. The canteen I had was in my knapsack that those fellows carried away sometime early this morning. Luckily there are enough streams between here and Clifford so I won't go without water on my way home. I'll be back in a minute."

As I walked away from the camp I heard Jethro humming a tune as he turned the rabbit. It was going to be nice to have some company at least part of the way to Clifford.

I had never thought much about Blacks, one way or the other. We never had any slaves nor did our neighbors, so I really hadn't seen too many of them except on an occasional trip into Amherst Court House with my daddy. Most had seemed friendly and honest, and Jethro certainly fit the friendly and honest part. He also seemed industrious and resourceful, traits, which would get him a long way in life.

I know the Bible spoke a lot about men being treated the same and our Constitution said something about all men being created equal. So when they said we were fighting to continue slavery in the South, I never did think too much of that as a valid reason.

For me, I fought because my daddy and brothers did. If anything, the rights of our state to make the laws as it pleased without interference from others made as good a reason as any. Of course, I guess if the state of Virginia wanted to legalize slavery, that wouldn't be too good. There had been a lot of slaves in Virginia, especially down in the Tidewater area where peanuts and cotton were farmed. Now slavery had been abolished so that wasn't a factor anymore.

Now that I was older and had been through a war, I had better find out just what was fair for everyone. Maybe I would make that one of my main goals when I got home.

The rabbit was plenty for the both of us and my belly felt full for the first time in a long period. We let the fire die down and rolled into our bedding for the night.

"Jethro, I think it is a good omen, me running into you. It should make the trip more enjoyable having someone to talk with. It will pass the time which seems to drag out when you are traveling alone."

"You don't know how much it means to me, Mister Vee. Fate sure has a way of makin' things get together. I'll make one quick round of the traps in the mornin' so as we can have somethin' to eat as we goes along."

"That'll be just fine, Jethro. It sure is different for me to eat regular meals. We went far too long without something to eat those last few weeks before the surrender."

"Let's hope that don't happen again for you. Good night, Mister Vee. I see you in the mornin'."

"Good night, Jethro."

The morning sky was lighter than it had been for the last few weeks. There seemed to be several layers of clouds with the lower one moving fast towards the east. Hopefully that would mean clearing skies, for this part of Virginia was due to have a spell of good weather. It would be nice to see the sun for a change after all the rain that had been evident the past several weeks.

Jethro had ensured the ashes from the fire wouldn't cause any problem and was standing at the edge of the small clearing ready to travel. It didn't take me anytime to roll up my sleeping blanket and throw it over my shoulder. We were on our way.

"Mister Vee, is we goin' back to the trail or is we headin' directly north from here?"

"Let's head north from here, Jethro, and work our way back to the trail if in fact it exists further along the way. On a piece of high ground back near Vera I was able to see a hill called Piney Mountain. I was hoping to be able to see it from here, but the trees are too thick. It should come into view a bit further along; when it does we will have a better idea of a good heading to travel on. According to my map, we should come to a clearing up ahead pretty soon, hope we can see it from there. The clearing should be just north of here. Also, my map shows a road crossing our path from east to west. When we get to it we'll know our position for sure."

We had traveled nearly half a mile when we broke out of the trees and there directly, in our path, was Piney Mountain. We had been heading a bit too much on a northerly course. We could see the trail heading west just short of the mountain. It was the one, which went to Oakville. From my sketch, Oakville was west of the mountain and we didn't want to go that way. A fairly good-sized creek flowing in a northwesterly direction was visible in the small valley below. It should give us some idea of a proper course to follow. We needed to move a little more to the east of the mountain, which would cause us to cross the creek before getting to Liberty Chapel Baptist Church.

"Jethro, from the sketch I have of this part of the country, we need to head a little more in that direction." I pointed northeasterly. "We'll get along a little further and cross that creek you can see down yonder. Hopefully we can find a safe place to cross. It appears to be still running pretty swift for us to just wade across."

"Ah, Mister Vee, we shouldn't have any trouble gettin' across. Why, I bet I kin almost jump it when we get there."

"Hope you are right, we don't want to get wet at this point in our journey. Let's move down that slope there and stay west of the creek as long as possible. Going should be easier that way."

"Suits me boss, you lead the way."

"Watch your step, the downgrade could be slippery. If your feet go out from under you, you might slide all the way to the creek." Jethro just grinned.

The land was rolling and mostly wooded. The ground smelled of early dew and the moisture brushed off on our feet as we made our way across the land. There was a mixture of pine, oak, and cypress. Occasionally there were small-cultivated areas, which appeared not to have been worked for many months. We had climbed back up a slight incline and were moving along a ridgeline that looked down on the creek. We could see a fork in the creek where a feeder stream entered.

"Jethro, this might be as good a place as any to get to the east side. Let's go down this slope and take a look. Appears that the creek gets wider as it goes off to the northwest."

"Suits me, boss. Looks like as good a place as any."

He was off down the slope towards the creek before I could hardly get going. Good thing I had been leading us or he would be out of my sight before we had traveled a mile.

"Well sir, this here creek is a bit wider than it looked from up on that ridgeline. And it shore is runnin' swift." Jethro had sat down on a fallen tree while he stared down at the raging water.

"I was afraid it might be this way. Looks like it may be difficult to find a good place to cross. If we split up we stand a better chance of finding a narrow part where it will be easier for us to cross. You look up stream and I'll look down stream. First one to find a good place, yell out."

"Suits me, boss," Jethro said, as he stood up and stretched. "Should be somethin' near here for sure. I thought I might of seen a spot as we were coming down the slope back a ways. If'n I find it, you'll know for sure when I yells out."

It had been near fifteen minutes since we started looking for a place to get to the other side and I hadn't seen anywhere I wanted to attempt a crossing. I was about ready to return to the point where we had split up when I heard a scream coming from up stream. I assumed it must be coming from Jethro, but it certainly wasn't the sound I was expecting to hear from him. It was more like a screech that would come from someone who had been hurt bad. I started off at a trot toward its origin.

I almost passed him by. He was down below the level of the bank, with one of his legs partly in the water. It was wedged between two rocks and part of it didn't look just right to me. I could see where the bank had given way, causing him to fall. It had to have been a nasty spill.

"Jethro, can you move at all? Can you get loose from that rock?"

"Boss, Jethro done got hisself in a bad fix. Don't know exactly what's wrong with my leg, but it shore don't feel right."

"Just hang on a minute and let me try to figure a way to get you out of there. I saw some vines hanging in some trees back up a piece, maybe we can use them to rig up some type of hoist."

"I ain't goin' nowheres Boss, but that leg do hurt a bit."

I eased down next to him and slowly extracted the leg from its wedged position. It was evident that he wouldn't be walking very far anytime soon. "Looks like you got a break in your right leg just above the ankle." I turned so he couldn't see my hands and quickly twisted the leg back into its original position. There was a loud grunt; I had expected a scream. "Luckily it wasn't a compound fracture, at least the bone didn't break the skin."

"I guess that's good. It shore did smart though when you pulled on it."

"Sorry about that, Jethro, but we had to get it set back straight or you might never have been able to walk right again."

"OK, boss, but what we'uns gonna do now?"

"Well, let me get back up and see if those vines I saw back there are strong enough to haul you out of here. Then we will see what choices we have after that."

The vines were just the thing. I was able to loop them around Jethro's body and by using a stout tree as a fulcrum; I got him back up on firm ground. He was panting hard and I knew the pain to that leg had to be something terrible. I found a straight limb and was able to make a satisfactory splint. It wasn't anywhere near what a medic could do, but it would have to hold him until we could get him to some proper care.

Looking around I found a forked limb, which Jethro could use for a crutch. He tried it and was able to move in a jerky manner. He grimaced with pain at each step.

"This isn't going to do, Jethro. We've got to find some other means to move you along other than letting you try to make it on that crutch."

"It do hurt a bit every time I take a step. But if'n it's the only way for me to travel, I guess I can stand it. I knows it will be slow though."

"There's got to be a better way. What could we use?"

"With this here leg the way it is, I's gonna hold you up from gettin' home. You go on, Mister Vee, and I'll stay here till my leg gets some better. I'll be just fine, you go on now. Old Jethro can take care of hisself."

"I'm sure you could, Jethro, but I'm not leaving you, so just don't suggest it again. If you could stand the pain, I think we could at least get to the other side of this creek. I saw a place while I was getting those vines where it is narrow enough for us to cross without too much problem. Don't know why we didn't notice it before. There are some rocks nearby we might be able to use. I'll build us a little walkway by adding rocks to the ones already there. Do you think you can stand the pain long enough for you to make it across?"

"I can do anythin' you wants, Mister Vee. Let's get started. Can you give me a hand?"

"All right, but you rest a bit until I can move those rocks. It may take me a bit of time to get enough to do us any good."

"I ain't goin' nowhere. Old Jethro gonna wait right here."

It didn't take me as long as I thought it would to carry enough rocks to the edge of the creek. I was able to place them in the water so we would have some place to step as we crossed. Also, I found the water a bit shallower at this point which would aid our attempt to get to the other side.

It took longer than expected to get Jethro down to the crossing point. But, with me under one arm and him using the makeshift crutch, we made it without too much pain on his part.

Panting heavily, and with sweat popping up on his brow, Jethro spoke softly, "Well sir, boss, here we is. Now what?"

"I'm going to string this vine across from one side to the other, and anchor it to that big tree over there. It should give you something to hang on to as you inch your way across. I'm going to tie this other piece around your waist so, in case you should slip, I can haul you out of the water before you drown. You willing to give it a try?"

"I's ready if'n you is."

"I'll go first. Here, let me get this vine tight around you, we want it as snug as you can stand it." It took a minute to secure the vine around his waist. "Does it feel too tight?"

"No sir, seems just right."

"I'm off, wish us luck."

Sliding down the bank to the creek was easy, but it did take me a few minutes to negotiate the rocks crossing the creek. I didn't want to fall into the water, which would have defeated all our plans. I scrambled up the bank on the other side, happy to be there. The footing hadn't been bad. The rocks I had placed in the creek were more secure than I had expected. Jethro might have a chance to make it if the pain didn't get too bad and the vines held.

Securing the vines to the tree was more difficult than I'd first thought it would be. I ended up looping the vines around and around the trunk hoping they would hold if all of Jethro's weight fell on them. If they didn't, we would be in bad trouble. I would have the one tied around his waist as the only hope of saving him from the swift waters. Deep down, I wasn't sure I could haul all his two hundred plus pounds out of danger. But, I wasn't about to say this to him. We both needed to be on the east side of the creek if we were going to have any chance of continuing on towards the Liberty Chapel Baptist Church.

"Jethro, you ready?"

"Yas sir, Mister Vee. I's as ready as I will ever be."

"OK, ease yourself down to the edge of the creek and give that vine a good tug. If it holds, we'll be ready for you to cross."

It looked like slow motion as he slid down to the creek's edge. I could see him grimace as he stopped his slide. But he didn't hesitate; he used his crutch to raise himself up to the level of the handhold, bracing it against the creek bank to maintain his balance. He pulled on the vine with more strength than I thought he had. It held.

"OK, Jethro, rest a bit and let me know when you are ready to start across. We want you to get over the water part as quickly as possible; you can rest on this side after you make it."

He didn't waver as he moved out along the stones. Amazingly, he used the crutch and vine in a balancing act from stone to stone. I could see the pain on his face as he moved, but he didn't falter as he inched his way across. There was one point in midstream where he almost slipped but the vine gave him enough leverage to keep from falling. A good fifteen minutes must have passed when he finally collapsed on the east bank. He was gasping for air as I slid down by his side, but he had a smile on his face, which showed his pleasure at having accomplished such a difficult task.

Looking at me with his big brown eyes, which showed just how much strain he had gone through, he said, "Well sir, Mister Vee, where is we headed to now?"

"We can go anywhere we want to after that ordeal, but maybe we should rest before we do. We need to figure out someway for you to move that won't cause you so much pain." I slapped him on his shoulder and grinned at his big, toothy smile.

It had taken the best part of an hour to get Jethro up from the creek's edge. We took our time because of the pain it caused him to move. By mutual consent, we felt it best to stay in this area for the night. Tomorrow we would decide just how we would continue on our journey.

I was able to make a partial camp by using some fallen trees as shelter. I started a fire and things seemed to brighten up. Even Jethro seemed more comfortable leaning back against the large log backing our shelter.

"Boss, I wish I could go out and get us a rabbit, but it don't look like Jethro is gonna be of any use for a while."

"Don't worry about that. We had enough to eat last night, don't want our bellies too full of food. My stomach couldn't stand the change."

"Well, you might'n not be used to eatin', but I is. Reckon there's any fish in that there creek?"

"Don't know, but I'll give it a look in a bit. Right now I've got an idea of how we are going to travel."

"And how's that. It do hurt to walk and I's too heavy for you to carry me."

"You ever see an old Indian drag? Well, I think I can put one together. That way you can lie flat and I can pull it along. It sure beats you having to walk and it should get us to the church since it's mostly downhill from here. Maybe there we can get some help for your leg. Somebody around these parts should have some medical knowledge."

The two small fish netted from the creek weren't the meal the rabbit had been, but they quelled our hunger pangs for the night. We had plenty of water, the fire warmed the cool night air, and Jethro's pain had eased a bit since the creek-crossing ordeal.

Jethro watched as the drag began to take shape. Two long poles were fastened together at one end to form a point. The other ends were spread apart to allow room to fashion a pallet. The vines used in our crossing were interlaced about midway of the poles to make a platform. It was double laced to ensure it would hold the weight of a big man. The remaining vines were used to loop a harness for the puller at the pointed end.

"Does you think you can pull me in that rig, Mister Vee? It don't look none too sturdy to me."

"I think it will do the job. Now, I don't intend to break any records, but if you will lie still and not roll around, I think we'll be able to move towards the church. It might take us an extra day or so to get there, but we'll make it."

"I don't doubt you, Mister Vee. I just don't wants you to run yourself into the ground tryin' to take care of Old Jethro. You done more'n enough for me as is."

"We'll take it easy as we go. Now get some sleep and we'll start off first thing in the morning. Need anything before I let the fire die down?"

My question was answered with a snore.

The effort was more than expected. The dead weight seemed to double as we inched our way forward. The trees made straight-line travel impossible. The vines cut into my shoulders, especially when the grade steepened. Downhill wasn't any easier, trying to hold a two-hundred-plus pound sled from sliding over me took all the strength I could muster. Wasn't there any flat ground in Virginia?

"How far do you think it is to the church, Mister Vee? You beginnin' to look plum tuckered out. Let me try to use this here crutch so's you can rest a spell."

135

"Stay where you are, Jethro. We'll go just a bit farther and then rest. I'm not sure, but it shouldn't be much over two miles from here. I think if we can just get to the top of this rise in front of us, it should be all downhill from there. We might even be able to see the church from the crest." I pointed ahead to the prominent ridge directly in our path.

"Mister Vee, rest here for at least a minute. Your legs is shakin' like two saplins in a strong wind."

"All right Jethro. I could stand a short break before we start up this hill."

The damp ground felt cool against my face as I laid flat out on the forest floor. I closed my eyes in an attempt to stop the throbbing of the blood pounding in the veins of my head. Even as my breathing returned too normal, the pounding was still there. Then I raised my head.

"Jethro, listen. What I thought to be the blood pounding in my head sounds like someone chopping wood. Do you hear it?"

"Yas sir, I hears it too. Must be somebody not far from here doin' that chopin'."

"You stay here and I'll see if I can find out who it is. Maybe they can give us a hand in getting to the church. Shouldn't take long to find them as long as they keep chopping."

"You go on, Mister Vee. Jethro ain't goin' no place."

The ridgeline was heavily wooded along its crest, but the minute I started down the slope, the trees thinned to small clumps. It appeared some of the land had been planted recently while other open spaces were left to scrub grass. Couldn't tell what the crop would be, it would be a while before anything broke ground.

The chopping sound continued and before long I spotted the woodcutter. He was off to the left about a hundred yards or so swinging his axe in a perfect rhythm. He must have been at his work for some time since he had almost a cord cut and stacked. He was stacking the wood on a sled with wooden runners. Nearby I spotted an old swayback horse tethered to a stump. It had to be the power to get that wood back to where it could be of use.

It took the axe swinger a minute to realize someone was approaching his position. He didn't seem unduly disturbed about having unexpected company. He just laid his axe down beside the log he was working on and wiped the sweat from his brow with a big old, red kerchief.

"Howdy, stranger, where you headed?"

"Well sir, eventually I'm headed back to my home in Clifford, but I've been delayed with a chore I took on. My friend, who is traveling with me, broke his leg back a ways when we were trying to cross a creek. It took us a time to get him up on even ground. Since then I've been trying to haul him to find some help. I was hoping to get to Liberty Chapel Baptist Church, but the drag I made is about more than I can handle, specially going uphill. We stopped to rest back over the ridge there and heard the chopping. We were hoping we might get some help from you."

"Well, you've come to the right place. My name is Peter Johnson; I'm the minister at the Liberty Chapel Baptist Church. What's your name?"

"Valerius McGrady, but mostly I'm called Vee or Mac. My traveling companion is a freed slave by the name of Jethro. He's on his way up North so he can get away from the life he had to live before. He has what looks like the proper papers testifying to his freedom. We ran into each other as I was coming from Appomattox Court House."

"Sounds like you are one who helps his fellow man. That's my trade, too. Let's take old Ned," he motioned to the swayback, "and see if we can get your friend to my place across from the church. My wife and a girl who works for us should be able to help. The girl is a freed slave herself, so they might have something in common. I'll come back for the wood after we see what can be done for your friend."

"I'll come back with you and give you a hand with the wood. Two of us should be able to make quick work of it."

"That would be mighty nice. I've been working on this stack for most of the day. Don't have to do it but once a week, but it's a chore I always put off until the last minute. Guess I'd rather preach to my flock than cut wood."

"I'll be happy to be getting back to any chores that have to do with farming. These past two years have surely shown me enough of killing to last me the rest of my life."

"You mustn't be more than nineteen. Mighty young to have been put in such terrible places."

"Well sir, I'm eighteen, but I feel like I must have aged more in the last two years than the normal person. Don't want to do it again. You ready to go?"

"I am. Let me get the horse and we'll be on the way."

Old Ned had been munching on some dry grass and seemed indifferent on whether he stayed or went. I'm sure he hadn't been worked too hard in the past few years. He had to be ten or twelve years old and had seen better days, probably the reason neither army had tried to put him into service.

I couldn't tell if I was living right or just lucky. In only a matter of days I had seen a variety of situations. A war had stopped and the killing had supposedly subsided. I had been victimized by what I thought to be friends, only to find them my enemies. I had met a man who really knew the true meaning of freedom only to have him become a victim of fate. And now I meet a person whose business is helping his fellow man.

I guess deep down there are really more good people in this world than bad. I certainly hope so anyway. Just a short while back there near Vera, I was thinking the bad were getting the upper hand.

Maybe peace will truly come over this land again and things will get back to what I knew before I left home. People didn't want for another man's property or worry about what others were doing that they didn't like. People worked hard and enjoyed life. They helped their neighbors and believed in God. It was a good life.

Would the rest of this journey change my thinking? I hoped not, for right now the good certainly was having the upper hand.

Jethro was waving madly as we came into his view. He had climbed from the drag and worked his way over to a stout maple stump, which propped up his back. He must have experienced some pain in the move, but his face didn't show it. He was all smiles when he saw the horse.

"Jethro, this is Preacher Johnson. He's gonna help us get you to some relief. Old Ned here is gonna supply the power to pull this drag."

"Here, Jethro, let me take a look at that leg. I've had a little experience with broken bones before I started preaching. Always thought it might come in handy around these parts." Peter Johnson bent over Jethro's leg and started to examine it.

"It don't hurt too much unless I moves it. Did pain me some to get over to this here tree stump, but I couldn't lay on those vines much longer."

"You've done a right fair job of setting this leg, Vee. We might replace these vines you used to brace it with when we get home. But, otherwise it should be healing in two or three weeks. Might be a month or so before you gonna be able to put a lot of weight on it, Jethro, but you should be good as new then."

Preacher Johnson and Old Ned had been our saviors; otherwise it might have been days before I could have gotten Jethro to the parsonage. The minister had put Jethro in a small shed out away from the house. It had bunk beds in one corner and a small potbellied stove not too far from the door. There were a few tools hanging on the opposite wall and a small storage bin below the tool rack.

Mrs. Johnson, Katie by name, had given Jethro some cool lemonade. It helped ease the slight fever he was running from the inflammation caused by the leg. She had also provided some cake-like bread to go with it. It had probably been a long time since he had eaten anything so delicate.

The girl, Bessie, seemed to hover around Jethro like a butterfly securing nectar from a flower. By the time Preacher Johnson and I returned with the wood, she had cleaned Jethro up and had replaced the vines holding his leg. He looked downright pleasant bedded down in the bunk bed in the corner of the little shack.

"Jethro done died and gone to heaven, Mister Vee. These is some of the nicest people I's ever met. I don't know how I's gonna be able to repay them for all this kindness."

"I'm sure you'll find a way. The minister was talking to me on the way out and back to get the wood, and he told me he could sure use someone like you around here when your leg heals. Wanted me to ask you if you was willing to stay on. I'm sure he will let you work off any debt you have with him. Also, that Bessie sure seems to be taking a shine to you. You might just have found a home without going way up North."

"You could be some right, Mister Vee. I'd be more of a mind to stay." He shook his head back and forth and said, "The good Lord done smiled on us today."

"Well Jethro, I need to be getting on my way if I expect to get back to Clifford before all the spring planting is done. I think you will be in good hands here and I'm sorry we won't be continuing our journey together. But as you just said, 'The good Lord done smiled today.' If I wait for you, I may forget my way home."

"Oh, Mister Vee, Jethro don't expect for you to wait. It has been nice to have spent the time we has together. I sure hopes we run into each other again someplace along...."

Before Jethro completed his words, Bessie came through the door with a tray of steaming food. The aroma was enough to make my mouth water. There were beans, pone, and a slab of bacon - plus coffee made from real beans. Something I hadn't seen in months and months.

"Mister Vee, the minister would like to talk to you when you finish eatin'. I'll stay here with Jethro so's he don't get lonesome."

"Fine, tell him I'll be there in a minute. I'll come and get you when I finish eating."

I stopped by the door as Bessie was fussing around Jethro, making sure he was comfortable. They looked good together, it wasn't a certainty, but Jethro, to my mind, had found himself a home.

She saw me and said to Jethro, "I'll see you in the morning. Have a good night. I's sure glad your journey made you pass this way."

"I's just as glad. Thank you for all you's done for me."

She tittered as she passed me on the way to the house. "Glad you is here, too, Mister Vee. See's you in the morning."

Jethro watched me as I came into the shack. He wasn't going to say anything until I did, so I made him wait until I added some wood to the stove. It crackled and spit for a full minute.

When it had settled in with the rest of the fire I said, "Well, I talked with the minister and he is mighty glad you plan to stay on. He says he has plenty of work for you and also there's a piece of land you might want to look at when you can start moving around. And knowing you, that will probably be sooner than normal."

"I's goin' to take him up on his offer. I was headed up North because that was the only place I thought I would be treated like a man. But I's seen the difference right here in less than a day. Bessie done asked me to stay on, too. I guess there's not too many black people around these parts. So for us'uns to find each other is truly a blessin'."

"In my mind Jethro, you are making the right decision. I would wish my life could fall into such a nice pattern when I get home. There's a little girl I knew before I left home that I'm hoping is still around when I return. I plan to stop by her place before I get to Clifford."

"I's sure she will still be there, Mister Vee."

I couldn't say anymore, I just went back to the door and looked out into the night. Jethro seemed to understand.

The vision of Elizabeth's face flashed into my mind more vividly than since I'd been gone. Don't know if seeing Bessie and Jethro together made our image together appear even stronger. She was there just as plain as if she was standing beside me now. And, she was pretty as ever.

She had always been in my subconscious even during the fiercest part of the fighting. Wonder if mental images travel between two individuals?

The time we had spent together had been golden for me. There was always a spark when our eyes met. She was there at the farm the last day before I left for Richmond and she had said, "Vee, come home to me, please."

And I said, 'I would'.

I will plan to stop by New Glasgow before I go home. It is less than half a day's travel from Clifford. I just hope she will be there.

We have some years to make up for.

The morning came with a bright glow, which was almost strange to us. I wasn't positive when was the last time I saw the sun so early in the morning. The dew was heavy and the dampness felt good between my toes. My feet were itching to be on the move. The preacher was standing on the back porch with a couple of mugs of coffee. The steam was curling up from the heated brew. He offered me one and sat down on the steps.

140

He reached behind him and pushed a neatly tied checkered napkin toward me. "Here's some little something Mrs. Johnson put together for you. It's some jerky and bread to tide you over until you get to the James River."

I tucked it in my bedroll and said, "Thank her for me. You've been mighty kind."

"Vee, are you headed for Bent Creek? That's the only bridge across the James near round these parts."

"Yes sir, that's where I'm headed, I was there a long time ago with my daddy. He took me down there when I was pretty small. Place must have changed a lot by now."

"It has. That bridge is the main thoroughfare between Richmond and Western Virginia. You could go directly north from here, but there's a pretty rugged ridge between here and there. If I were you, I'd head over towards Tower Hill and hit the turnpike. You would make better time that way."

"Sounds like you are right. I could probably get my bearings on Pruetts Mountain from the high ground there. That way I would be sure to know that I was headed in the right direction."

"Only one thing though. I heard there have been some renegades attacking Yankee wagons in that area. Hear tell the Yankees gonna wipe them out. You need to watch out for any of that, don't want to get caught up with those types."

"Thanks for the warning. I'll plan to stay well clear of any such problems. Also, thanks again for all your help. I'm sure Jethro will be more help than you ever thought. He is one of the best Black men I've ever seen. Believe you might have gained a new neighbor when all is said and done. If I ever get back this way I'll be sure to look in."

"You do that for sure. Have a safe trip home."

I looked in on Jethro to say my good-byes. Bessie was there by his side. It was hard to leave, but I had to be on my way.

"I knows that little girl you told me about, gonna be there awaiting for you, Mr. Vee."

"I hope you're right, Jethro. I know she's been in my thoughts for a long time now. Seeing how things are turning out for you, I'm ready to have some companionship, too." Bessie turned her head towards Jethro and smiled.

141

I shook both their hands and headed out the door. Too bad he wouldn't be going with me all the way to Clifford. He was my kind of person, but I felt almost certain I would run into some other companionship before I reached home.

Chapter Nine

The view from Tower Hill was spectacular. You could see Pruett's Mountain slightly to the northeast. Its domed ridge was spotted with a greenish tint from the new buds of the season. Other prominent peaks were visible, but I wasn't sure of their names. It was nice to take in the view and to realize the war had ended. Peace could be seen lying over the land, and the future was straight ahead. The twitter of birds filled the forest, a sound that hadn't been heard by me for a long time. It was a sure sign Spring was on its way.

Keeping my bearing off of Pruett's Mountain on the way to Bent Creek would ensure an accurate course. The turnpike was only a mile or so away; I would try to stay on the roadway as much as possible. However, traffic along the turnpike could become very heavy. It was a certainty the Yankees were still moving their equipment North. They had pushed us off the road between Appomattox and Vera, it would probably be worse along this well-traveled road. If I was forced off the turnpike and lost sight of the peak, I could head for high ground to reaffirm my location.

It had been an up and down journey through heavily wooded countryside getting to Tower Hill. Just before the summit, I had crossed a rushing creek which seemed a good place to make camp, so rather than continue on to the turnpike, I backtracked a bit and bedded down for the night.

The nighttime was cool, and a fire felt good. The jerky and bread Mrs. Johnson had so kindly fixed for me filled my stomach. I consumed all the bread, but saved some of the jerky for a later meal. I did miss the wonderful coffee she brewed, but water from the creek sufficed to keep my throat from becoming dry. Maybe I should have stayed longer with the Johnsons, seeing how well they were living life together. But their happiness only spurred me to be on my way home.

The same togetherness was true for Jethro and Bessie. They appeared to be a perfect match. Both had known the despair and pain of slavery. Their new freedom had given them a choice, which Bessie seemed to have made instantaneously. It might take Jethro a bit longer, but from what I had seen of the couple, the light would dawn for him before he was able to move around again. I would be very surprised if Jethro continued his journey north, but if so, certainly not by himself.

Sleep was deep, but it was abruptly shattered by spasmodic musket fire coming from someplace not too far away. The din died down momentarily, but in only a matter of minutes the sounds of a full pitched battle rumbled through the night. At first I thought I was dreaming, but it was evident the sounds were real. I rolled out of my bedding, trying to locate the direction of the sounds. The uproar was coming from the area of the turnpike which couldn't have been more than a mile or so away. Suddenly the clamor died just as quickly as it had begun.

I listened. The rustling of the trees attested to a slight breeze, which had come up even before I had dozed off. The chirp of crickets echoed from the creek, and the hoot of an owl pierced the dark. Otherwise, there was silence. I returned to my bedroll, but getting back to sleep was out of the question. I rolled and tossed until the first streaks of light entered the eastern sky.

The clouds were scattered, and it appeared to be the beginning of another good day. I ate most of the jerky, saving one very small piece. I was like a squirrel saving a small bit of food for later. It could be my last nourishment before I arrived in Bent Creek. Since I had become used to eating on a regular basis and it was at least a day's walk to the James River, I would have to find some food someplace.

Approaching the turnpike by the trail leading from Tower Hill didn't seem to be the best idea. I didn't want to run into what could be a difficult situation so I made a wide arc to intersect the road well south of the junction. The way through a heavily wooded section took a bit of time since I couldn't find any distinct path to follow.

The roadway was quiet as I approached, no traffic in either direction. I inched my way out from cover. I could see some broken wagons about two hundred yards up from my position. One was on its side, the other had wheels missing. Quickly I dashed to the east side of the roadway and moved along the tree line towards the wreckage.

The wagons belonged to the Union forces, the US being clearly visible along the sides. No cargo was in evidence; it had either been stolen or transferred to some other means of transportation. A dead horse lay over in the ditch, but there were no other signs of people or animals in the area. Skid marks could be seen where one of the wagons had been hauled part way into the woods, only to have been dragged back to the turnpike. Just as I turned to peer into the woods, a glint caught my eye. There was something shiny several yards into the woods. Slowly, I advanced towards the glitter, not being sure what I was approaching. Could be only a piece of metal which had caught the sun, but I wasn't certain.

David had his back to a tree, and seemed to be bending over a fallen branch. His musket was propped into the fork of the branch, and the glitter I had seen had come from the bayonet on his gun. One arm was dangling at an odd angle; a volley of rounds from several muskets must have broken it. He had been peppered by more than one hit; his death must have been instantaneous. Two other men that I didn't recognize were lying in the same vicinity, seemingly hit by the same barrage of fire.

It took me awhile to bury them. I scratched David's name into the small cross I made to put over his grave. The other two I left as unknown. One of them had shoes that fit. I borrowed them; I was sure he wouldn't mind.

As I was finishing up with the graves I heard the rumble of traffic. I eased my way back to the tree line overlooking the turnpike and observed wagon after wagon moving at a very rapid pace. They were headed north and interspersed were Yankee cavalrymen, their muskets at ready. Their eyes were scanning along the woods as they passed. I crouched even lower so as not to be seen. Finally, when there was a break in traffic, I went further into the woods and started to move parallel to the turnpike.

I hadn't advanced more than a few hundred yards when I came upon what must have been the main fight I heard earlier this morning. At least fifteen bodies were unevenly spaced along a small trail. The entire group were boys who had gone along with Seth and his scheme for riches at the expense of the Yankees.

John and Ben were about in the middle of the stench that was beginning to rise from the debacle. They were face down so it took me awhile to find them among all the others. With David back in the woods a ways, I felt sure they would all probably be in the same vicinity. As I started to move their bodies, John groaned.

"Can you hear me, John? How bad have you been hit? Let me get you over near those trees, and I'll see if anything can be done for your wound."

His voice was so low and raspy I could hardly hear what he was trying to say. "Is that you, Mac? We were wrong to have gone with Seth. He is a bad man, and we should have left him when you did near Vera. Are David and Ben all right?"

"No, John, they're both dead."

He coughed as I tried to see where he was wounded. There was so much blood on his shirt it was difficult to see where the musket ball had entered his body. Finally I was able to see the wound. The bullet had entered near his rib cage on the left side of his chest. The ball had shattered one of his rib bones, and had devastated the inside. I was amazed he was still alive.

"I don't think there is much you can do for me, Mac. I'm burning up," he wheezed. The whistling sound of his voice made my skin crawl.

"I'll do what I can, John. Hang on while I get you some water. It should cool you down a bit." I looked around trying to find a discarded canteen nearby.

He tugged at my sleeve, pulling me closer so I could hear him. "Listen to me, Mac. I haven't got much time. Seth and two of his cohorts set us up in this trap." His words were coming with great effort now, and I wasn't sure how much longer he would last. "He was supposed to be paying us off for the two raids we had made. They were to be the last, then we would be on our way home. But instead, he must have told the Yankees where we were, and they ambushed us. It was a massacre."

146

"I figured Seth would do something along that line. Too bad I couldn't get through to you, David, and Ben."

"Mac, if you ever go to Burkeville and run into Sarah, please don't tell her how I ended up. Tell her I was killed at High Bridge, or something. I know it's a lot to ask, but please, please do that for me." His words were hardly audible.

"Don't worry, John, she will never know about this from me. Let me get you some water. Stay calm for a minute." I spied a canteen and reached over for it. As I turned back to him, his head slowly dropped over sideways. His upper body rolled to the ground. He had stayed alive longer than anyone would have thought. His suffering had ended here in the deep woods of Virginia.

I went back and got Ben's body, pulling both him and John deeper into the woods. I buried them in shallow graves. The crosses were fashioned from some pieces of wood I found nearby. Their names were scratched into the soft wood, similar to what I had done for David. I placed their hats at the head end of the graves. Those two battered, worn, and sweat stained fedoras bore the CSA emblem they had fought so hard to support. They had been proud of those hats and had worn them with pride. Too bad they hadn't stopped their conflict when the war ended in Appomattox.

Why, oh why, had their fine endeavor for the Confederate cause during years of strife come to such a poor end? In my mind, it was impossible that they couldn't see the fallacy of their ways. Seth and his companions were what we didn't fight for. We had been beaten; it was time to accept our fate and go on to build a better world we could live in without conflict.

I should have tried harder to convince them it was wrong. Maybe if I had been more adamant to Seth to show how wrong he was, they would still be with us.

My tears were the first I could remember since I was a little boy. Oh Lord, show me the way to do better if the opportunity occurs again. Give me another chance even though it is too late for my friends.

After searching for the best part of an hour, it was evident to me that Seth wasn't with the dead. What John had told me must be true. He hadn't been there when the carnage occurred. He had been some place else, I'm sure by design.

I found what was left of my knapsack, but it had been trampled and torn and was useless. Little else was worth salvaging. I sure didn't want or need any broken muskets; however, I did find a hunting knife, which could come in handy during the rest of my journey.

Counting the corpses, it seemed the Yankees had put an end to their renegade problem. I wasn't sure they were aware of it, but unless there were other bands I didn't know about, they wouldn't be having any more difficulties. I was sure the Yankees would still be on alert; so traveling along the turnpike might be dangerous. With the trouble they had had, they might be shooting first and talking afterwards.

I had used up the best part of the day burying my friends, and night would be falling before I could get much further along. There was no way I could get to Bent Creek before midnight so it was sensible to stop rather than trying to move on in the dark. My hunger would be at a peak when I arrived in the village, but at least I should feel fresher after a good night's sleep.

I made camp near a small stream, which was only a half-mile from the massacre. Some fresh pine boughs made a soft bed, and an overhanging rock provided shelter in case of rain. There was ample wood so a warm fire kept the chill away for the night. I ate the one small piece of jerky I had saved, which had to do for my supper. It didn't begin to fill the void. The cool water from the fast running creek quenched my thirst; the wonderful coffee at the Johnson's was now just a faint memory. Water had kept me going the many days before getting to Appomattox; it would have to suffice again until I got to Bent Creek.

There was no telling what would be going on there. For sure, Yankees would abound.

What day is it anyway? The war ended on the ninth. We were paroled on the twelfth. I was one night on the road to Vera. I met Jethro and spent two nights with him. Another night at Liberty Chapel Baptist Church which would make it the seventeenth of April. Now two more nights and I'm still in the woods short of Bent Creek.

Tomorrow will be either the nineteenth or twentieth and I haven't made it to the James River yet. I'll have to ask someone what date it is when I get there.

I best get on the move, or my Mother and Elizabeth might think I'm never coming home.

The morning near the creek was crisp and clear. A bit of fog lingered in the low places but it would burn off within the hour. I wish I had saved more of the jerky from Liberty Baptist, for my stomach was growling loud enough to be heard all the way to Bent Creek. I would have to find some type of grub when I arrived there, or I wouldn't be able to go on much further.

The trees thinned out as I made my way down through the forest. A small trail enabled me to make good time. I encountered only one tiny creek, which didn't cause me any problem in crossing. Along the north side of the creek, I followed a well-worn path, which headed back towards the turnpike. The going got even easier as I approached the roadway. There were no sounds of wagons or horses to be heard, only the pleasant chirping of birds flitting in the trees.

I eased through some low bushes, which put me on a slight rise overlooking the road. The vantage point gave me visibility in both directions. Just as I was preparing to cross, two horsemen approached from the south traveling at a hard gallop. I ducked back into the woods. As they passed I could make out their rank. One appeared to be a Yankee colonel, the other his captain aide. I had no idea what their business was, but they were sure in an all fired hurry.

After their passing, the way was clear so I crossed quickly to the west side putting me south of the main part of the village. I could see the first buildings of Bent Creek just up the way. I worked my way along a small creek, which flowed into the James River west of the town. Three or four houses comprised the residential section with the rest of the build-up being stores, taverns, and one lone blacksmith stable. The bridge crossing the James was a bit further on, although there didn't seem to be much traffic activity moving across. Guards were stationed at the approach end, and a lot of stirring action was going on in what must have been a holding area for people and wagons waiting to cross.

Must be some sort of problem, either with the bridge, or the Yankees were holding up traffic for some other reason.

The general store at the center of town appeared empty when I walked in. I hadn't seen an older woman behind the counter dusting something on the lower shelves until she stood up. I had to clear my throat to get her attention.

"What can I do for you, Reb?" Her voice was gentle and quiet, it reminded me of my mother.

"I need to work for some food. I'm headed north towards Amherst, and I don't think I can make it without eating. Got any chores around here you need done or things you need fixing?"

"Well, Sonny, don't think there's much needs fixing here, but I do have a plate of beans I was going to throw out. You interested? My boys ain't come home yet so there's some extra food in the kitchen. I'm hoping they will be coming home any day now. So, if'n someone what's done fought for the Confederacy passes by, he's gonna get some food from me for as long as I'm alive. These Yankees and some of their kind are driving me plum out of my mind."

"That's mighty kind of you ma'am, but I would like to do something for you."

"You's already done it boy. I's just sorry you weren't able to beat them because now there's gonna be tough times in the South for a longtime. Come on with me back to the kitchen."

Her kitchen was spick-and-span and true to her word, there was a plate of beans and some corn bread on the table. It didn't take me long to clean up both. It was like home cooking, and she could tell how much I enjoyed it.

"You planning on heading north soon?"

"Yes ma'am. I've spent all the time I need south of the James."

"Well, you ain't gonna be crossing that bridge for a while. Seems someone done shot and killed Mr. Lincoln the other day, and they's looking high and low for him. The Yankees ain't allowing nobody north or south until they catch whoever done it."

"Well, that is some real bad news. I heard General Lee spoke highly of President Lincoln. He was reported to have said Lincoln was a fair-minded man, and that he would treat the South proper. Now, no telling what we can expect."

"You are more than right. Already we got some arrogant northerners and southerners acting like they is God Almighty. If you stay around Bent Creek long you will see what I mean."

"I don't plan to stay long. I can always swim across the river."

"Watch out for yourself then. The Yankees have boats patrolling the river day and night. Your best possibility would be to go up the river a couple of miles. You should be able to see some lights from Gladstone, which will be directly across the river. If you plan it correctly, there is an island or two, which would give you a chance to rest if you were to get tired on the way across. Some tells that the river has some queer currents in places. Best you be careful, so use those islands."

"You have been most kind. If I get back this way I'll be sure to look in on you and your boys. I know they will be coming along any day now."

"I hope you're right. Wait a minute; I've got a little something for you to take with you. This bit of bacon and some pone might come in handy when you get hungry again. Let me wrap it in this heavy paper, it may keep it dry on your swim across the James."

I gave her a hug and left out the back way. She gave me a wave as I rounded the corner headed for the river. I would be waiting for nightfall before trying to cross. With all the patrols she talked about, I wouldn't have a chance during the day.

It was still early in the afternoon as I headed down towards the bridge. I wanted to get a feel for how many guards they had posted and to see if the patrolling boats were on any kind of schedule. I wasn't planning on waiting until they opened the bridge for traffic that could be days or even weeks. I hoped they caught the assassin soon, but even if they did it would be a while before the word got down this far.

Nearing the pier just west of the bridge, I stopped short in my tracks and ducked behind a parked wagon. There, as plain as day, stood Seth and his two mates talking to a Yankee Major. I moved closer trying to hear a part of their conversation. They appeared friendly enough which really seemed odd to me.

I eased in behind some bales as they were saying: "It was nice doing business with you Major. It hurt Ted, Joe, and me to turn in our compatriots, but they were doing bad things, which put a bad light on the South. I hope you won't have that problem anymore now that you've rid the world of that bunch." Seth was counting some money as he spoke.

151

"I'm hoping you are correct. Your tip was perfect, and we were able to annihilate them night before last. Too bad you three weren't with us to see the last of that crew. If you get anymore information about such renegade groups, our reward is still the same." With that, the Major moved away towards the bridge.

Seth yelled after him, "If you have time, we'll be glad to buy you a drink in the tavern tonight."

"I may see you there."

Pausing until he was sure the Major was out of earshot, Seth turned to his two henchmen and said, "Well, with the money from the two raids and this reward, we are set for some time. We'll split these Yankee dollars over in the tavern, then tomorrow we'll head out towards Lynchburg. That's where most of the supplies for Lee's army were stored. They never did get them to us when we were at Appomattox. Things could be ripe for someone like us to relieve them of a few and sell them to the right people. There should be some easy money to be made around there."

"How are we going to get across the bridge, ain't it closed for a while?" Ted was the shorter of the two sidekicks, and he sounded skeptical as he looked up and down the river.

"Yes, but I think a few dollars will open it long enough for us to scamper across, if you know what I mean. That way we can get the jump on any others who might have the same idea."

"Well, I could use a few steins before we leave this place. We've been without for a long time now." Joe was rubbing his hands like he was ready to have more than one.

"Don't get too much in you, we still have work to do." Seth said, as they moved off towards the tavern, smiling and slapping themselves on the back as they went.

The urge to rush out and strangle Seth was almost too much to control. They would have to be stopped someway, at least Seth. The other two would wither away and wouldn't be much of a threat with him out of the way. My rage subsided a bit as I moved back up the river towards the west end of the village. But my heart continued to ache as I thought of David, John, and Ben plus all the others whose blood was on Seth's hands.

Even during the war I hadn't had the deep press to destroy, although I had been the instrument of death more than once because

152

there was no other way to survive. Maybe it seemed more impersonal when the bullets were flying in every direction. But now it was different.

I had a strong urge to kill one individual, and revenge was the motive. Certainly I couldn't get near him while he was in Bent Creek, there were too many around to see the deed. I would be caught and hanged for murder, even though he was the real murderer.

I had no doubt they would be able to bribe their way across the bridge. Lesser things had been gotten with money offered in the correct places. It would be difficult to find their trail after they crossed the James, but I would do my best not to let them get away as they moved north towards Lynchburg.

Lord, forgive me for my thoughts. If there is another way to right this vicious wrong, please show me. The war was bad enough, now my heart is writhing in anguish, as I'm ready to even the score against the enemy of my friends.

Seth and his kind will cause more problems than we have witnessed in the past. They will destroy the little good that exists today, and they certainly won't contribute anything to a solid future for our country. I'm well aware that one of your commandments is: "Thou shall not kill." But, when bad people kill the good, isn't it time to stop them before they continue their evil ways?

I thank you for any guidance you can reveal; I'm sure you will show me the way.

The sky was clear for the first time in many nights. The stars formed a sparkling dome, which glistened off the rapidly flowing water of the river. There weren't many lights showing in Bent Creek, only the tavern down near the bridge blazed streaks of light into the dark. I had no real reason to go back into the village, but here I was heading towards the tavern. I should have been on my way up the river trying to find a good place to cross. However, those rays were like magnets drawing me closer.

There wasn't any money in my pockets to buy a beverage, nor did I care for one. The wine on Communion Sundays had been a rare taste of alcohol during my early life. I had had only a sip of whiskey, and possibly two beers since joining the army, so the desire to drink wasn't the pull towards the tavern. I wanted to observe Seth and his two friends. I wanted to be in the area just in case an opportunity arose to get one or all of them alone. What I would do if I did was still unclear, but I was willing to try almost anything.

I had barely placed my foot on the first step leading to the tavern's main door when a BOOMING blast just about startled me out of my wits. It caused me to jump away from the porch leading to the door. Almost instantly, two bodies came tumbling pell-mell into the street. The light streaming through the sudden opening framed the cluster. The two untangled and faced off as the following crowd formed a cordon around them. One was a Yankee captain; the other was Joe, Seth's buddy.

Joe was on one knee with his left side to the captain. He paused momentarily before he lunged forward while at the same time pulling a knife from his belt. Sidestepping quickly, the captain fired two rapid shots from his revolver hitting Joe near the heart. He was dead before he struck the ground.

"He tried to cheat me at cards. Did any of you see him?"

"I saw him, Captain," cried out a voice in the crowd. "He was dealing from the bottom of the deck, and had been before you called him on it."

"Where are his two buddies? They might have been in on it with him. Last I saw, they were at the bar while we were playing cards."

No one noticed Seth and Ted moving away from the scene. They had started off the minute the captain had fired his pistol. The darkness covered their retreat, and they were well out of sight before anyone thought of them. I had been blocked by the crowd, and never had a chance to get near them. They just seemed to vanish into the dark night.

The major I had seen in the afternoon came down the steps and parted the crowd. "What's happened here, Captain?"

"This here fellow tried to cheat me." He pointed to Joe face down on the ground. "I caught him dealing from the bottom and called his hand. He tried to run, but I caught him at the door. We tumbled out here, where he lunged at me with a knife. I had to shoot him in self-defense. There's plenty here who'd tell you that's what happened."

Several members of the group offered their comments about the fight being self-defense. Two civilians said they would testify if the major needed them. He nodded at them to acknowledge their remarks.

The major toed Joe's body over so he could see his face. "Why, this is one of those Rebs who gave us the tip on those renegades we shot the other night. Where are his two friends?" He leaned down and went through Joe's pockets. "He has a parole and a few dollars. Not near the amount of the reward money I gave them, not even part of it. Let's fan out and find those other two. I would like to talk to them, they need to answer some questions for us."

The crowd from the tavern was predominantly Yankee soldiers who formed up in two's and three's to carry out the major's order. They were looking around for all the help they could get. Not too many wanted to go off into the dark searching for people who could be armed. They spied a Reb leaning against the corner of the steps.

"Ho there, Reb. You know where those two fellows who were with this guy," they kicked Joe, causing him to be face down again, "went off to?"

"No sir, I don't know, and I don't care. I ain't with them and never was. I's just waiting for them to open that there bridge so as I can be on my way home."

A tall soldier next to me said, "They didn't come this way. They must have beat it off to the east when the shots were fired."

Since I was one of only four Rebs at the scene, and one of those was Joe, I didn't want to be caught up in any manhunt. I ducked down trying to stay out of the light. My efforts must have worked because the larger part of the group was off towards the east.

I melted away into the darkness towards the west end of the village.

Maybe this was the revelation I had been looking for. The Lord dealt in strange and mysterious ways, and this could be his way of having Seth answer for his sins. If the major asked enough questions, Seth's sins were sure to come out.

Now I wouldn't have to worry about catching up with him north of the James. He would meet his just rights here in Bent Creek.

As I approached the general store headed west, the old lady was standing on the porch looking toward the tavern. I didn't think she would spot me, but she spoke out as I was passing, "What happened down there, Sonny?"

"Someone got shot. They said he was cheating at cards and a Yankee captain shot him. Seems he had it coming, tried to pull a knife on the captain."

"I thought you would be across the river by this time."

"It wasn't dark enough earlier, I didn't want those patrol boats to see me. Should be better around midnight. They are probably less likely to come very far up the river when it's late."

"Well, good luck to you. Be sure to look in the next time you get to Bent Creek."

"I sure will ma'am. And thanks again for the meal. You saved my life. I will never forget it."

The food package, along with my bedroll, was still under the fallen tree where it had been hidden. I was tempted to eat it before I crossed the river but knew I'd better save it for a later time.

Maybe I should stay on this side of the river tonight. However, if I did, it would be another day before I could cross. For sure the bridge would still be closed. Best to continue on tonight while conditions were favorable. Then, too, in case Seth and Ted did get away from the major, I'd better be on the other side as soon as possible if I ever expected to catch up with them.

Two faint shots echoed from the far side of the village. Could they have found Seth and Ted? Maybe, but the major had said he wanted to ask them some questions. If they were dead it was going to be difficult. Those shots were probably somebody signaling to someone else, but it wouldn't break my heart if they had been for Seth and Ted.

The river's edge was overgrown with bushes, which made travel slower than expected. After about a half mile of slogging through thorny brambles, the bank rose sharply. The cliff formation caused me to move inland. It got me out of the briers, but it added a three-mile trek before I could get access to the river again.

It must have been close to one in the morning when I found an acceptable place to enter the water. I could see the two islands in the river I planned on using as a place to rest on the swim across. Some clouds had moved in to cover the stars, which was in my favor. It would make it more difficult for any patrols to spot anyone attempting to cross the river.

The water was flowing swiftly, and it looked cold.

Chapter Ten

Suddenly the bottom disappeared and my head went under. My feet zipped out from beneath me before I was committed to becoming a swimmer. Not only was it a surprise, but also my newfound shoes left my feet and were off with the current. I came up coughing and spitting water.

I had expected to be able to wade at least a short ways into the river, but I hadn't gotten any farther than five feet from the bank. To add to my problem, the current was much stronger than expected. I was in over my head literally, as well as on my way across the mighty James, whether I wanted to be or not.

Luckily I had tied my bedroll to my back so it didn't interfere with my movement in the water. However, with all the rain from the past few weeks, the river was near flood stage, and the water was awash with lots of debris. I hadn't encountered any large pieces of rubbish so my efforts to reach the first island had not been impaired. However, my arms started to tell me I didn't have the stamina I thought I had when I first entered the river. My stroke was regular, but it was interspersed with short periods of just trying to stay afloat. This method carried me farther towards the east end of the first island than had been planned.

Due to the high water, there wasn't any perceptible shoreline along what should have been the water's edge. Low-lying limbs from the trees on the island extended into the water and made getting ashore almost impossible. Unfortunately, the bedroll on my back got hung up on one unseen limb just under the surface of the water.

159

Before I could get it untangled, my head was pulled under water and I was fighting to get air. Desperately I fought to get clear of my predicament without any appreciable success. I was going deeper, rather than towards the surface and my air supply was all but running out. Finally, it was the bedroll or me. I frantically felt for the hunting knife on my belt as the last bit of oxygen exited my lungs and severed the cord holding the bedroll. I bobbed to the surface coughing and gasping, barely able to crawl ashore.

My heart was beating like a drum, my temples throbbed, and my breathing was a labor of pain. Finally, all three slowed to a near normal pace after thirty minutes or so. I continued to lie on solid ground for the remaining part of an hour, spitting up water and attempting to get my strength back. Maybe trying to swim across this river hadn't been such a good idea after all. However, deep in the back of my mind was the thought of Seth and his friend buying their way across the bridge and getting so much distance between me and them, I would never have a chance to catch up.

Slowly I got to my feet and searched along the trees on the east end of the island in hopes of finding my bedroll. No such luck. At least my parole was still in my pants pocket, somewhat damp but intact. Not wanting to waste too much time, I moved through the low brush towards the west end of the island.

My plan was to launch into the water as far west as possible and use the current to my advantage. I wanted to give myself every feasible chance of hitting the second island. I could see it off in the mist even though it was much smaller than the one I was on. It didn't seem to have any trees on it, which would make it easier to come ashore without getting tangled in submerged growth. Also, I didn't want to be swept past it and become overly tired. For sure, I would need rest for it would be a tough swim all the way to the north shore. If I did miss it and was able to stay afloat, I would have an additional problem besides fatigue. I could end up so close to the bridge, the guards patrolling it might spot me, and that wouldn't be good.

I could see one or two lights twinkling in the distance beyond the second island, hopefully the illumination was coming from Gladstone. They appeared close, but distance at night was misleading, especially on the water. I didn't want to get overconfident and become exhausted thinking it was a shorter distance than it was. Best to wait a few more minutes before I entered the water. There was still a lot of time before sunrise, plus the overcast was keeping visibility down, which aided my probability of success. It meant there was a much less chance of being spotted by suspicious eyes.

All I needed was to have one of the Yankee patrols spot me and take me back to Bent Creek. That would give Seth all the time he needed to get away to the north towards Amherst, then on to Lynchburg. Plus, there was no telling what the Yankees would do to me for trying to cross the James against their orders.

"Hey, Pete, how much longer do you think we should stay here before we head down stream?" The voice couldn't have been more than a few yards away. I ducked lower in some bushes near the river's edge.

"We might as well stay here a little longer, Jim, then we won't have to make another trip before our relief comes on. I'm getting tired of rowing up and down this river at night. How about you?"

"Me too. This river sure does have some strong current in it right now. The only good thing is that it's easier going back down than it was coming up. Going down, all we have to do is steer and make sure we don't run into anything."

"I really don't think there is anybody foolish enough to try and get across the river up this far. Most of the people on both sides seem to be waiting for the bridge to open for traffic. I hope they catch whoever shot Mr. Lincoln soon, that way we can be on our way home instead of having to do this special patrol duty."

"Too bad there isn't any moon tonight. With this high water washing every loose log down the river, more light could be a benefit to keep us from ramming something and sinking this boat."

Of all the bad luck. These two Yankees would have to be resting just when I'm trying to swim across the river. If they stay around much longer, it will be light before I can get over to Gladstone. Otherwise, I will have to spend all day on this island waiting for nightfall again.

Also, it's freezing here in the night air. Luckily, staying huddled in this deep grass provides some warmth. However, if I don't get all the way across the river soon, I may freeze before sunrise. It sure seems warmer in the water.

"Pete, let's shove off. By the time we get back to the bridge, our relief will be ready to take over."

"Watch out. That log almost hit us. We don't want to collide with something that large. See what I mean about having more light?"

"Yeah, I see it, but it's going away from the main stream. The mid part of the river looks clear. Most of that garbage goes near the shore anyway. Let's get on the way." The splash of paddles added the finality to ensure their departure from the west end of the island.

Getting back in the water was actually warmer, although with being totally wet again, I wasn't looking forward to the cold air when I hit the second island. The current was definitely swifter between the two islands, and I was being swept along at a rapid rate. There was hardly any debris in what must be the main channel. Most of the rubbish must be routed closer to each shore, just like the two Yankees had said. I guessed the swift current didn't allow any backwash to collect in the fast water.

This time my calculations were better and I was standing in the water near the shore of the second island in less than five minutes. However, it was now really cold when I climbed onto the bank. I looked around for some vegetation to huddle under for warmth, but there wasn't any in sight. In fact, the island wasn't much more than an overgrown sandbar in the midstream of a raging river.

Guessing the north shore was no more than two hundred yards away I launched back into the water without pausing for additional rest. It seemed more important for me to get across and find a place where I could get warm. If I stayed on this island for very long, what little strength I had remaining would be sapped by the cold.

I was stroking for my life with only a few yards left to travel when something crashed into me. I had the sensation of my arms flailing the water in an attempt to stay afloat. My subconscious must have taken over, for the next thing I clearly remember was someone tugging on me. I was just out of the water's edge lying on my stomach. This person was pushing on my back in an effort to get the water out of my lungs. I coughed loudly and looked up to see an old, gray-haired gentleman. His pants legs were wet up to his knees and his body was heaving from the effort he had expended.

Hacking from deep down in my throat, I squeaked out, "What happened?"

"Well, sonny, you got hit in the head by a good size log being washed down the river. I was on the bank fishing and saw you just in time to grab you out of the water. You might have made it on your own, but I didn't want to take the chance, so I waded out to get you."

"You were fishing before dawn? Is that a good time to fish?" They were stupid questions, but it was the only thing that came to my mind at the time.

"I'll answer your questions later. Let's get you over to my shack before you come down with pneumonia. It's just a little ways from here. You got yourself a substantial bump on your noggin. We better tend to it before you start seeing double."

"It doesn't feel too bad," I flinched when I touched it, "but you are probably right. It would be better to get a closer look at it before I head out from here."

"You ain't going no place for a while. I got plenty of room and you need to get your strength back before you head out for anywhere."

I let him help me to my feet and we moved off towards his shack. As he said, it wasn't very far. We crossed what appeared to be a road, or had been at one time. We stumbled up and down the embankments, which were steeper than normal, probably to keep any flood waters from causing trouble. There were several small huts around in the area with faint wisps of smoke coming from their chimneys. This must be Gladstone; it wasn't a very large village. Morning was almost upon us as the eastern sky began to show streaks of light. We headed for the last shack in the group.

A small fire was glowing in the stove and the place felt secure and warm. There were two rooms in the cabin, one functioned as the kitchen, living, and dining area, the other his bedroom. It wasn't grand, but it seemed to fit his needs.

"I sure do thank you for pulling me out of the river. My name's Valerius, but most people call me Vee or Mac. My last name's McGrady. I'm on my way home, which is up near Amherst, a little crossroads called Clifford. Don't know what I can do to repay you, but I'm mighty grateful."

"I'm called Foster, Foster Graham. Never been up your way, but I know where Amherst is located. I've lived around these parts for quite a spell now. But, if something isn't done soon, I might be moving on myself."

Foster had a pot of soup on the stove and he ladled me up a generous portion. It tasted good and warm, the warmth going all the way to my toes. "My, this soup tastes good. I had a good feed yesterday, but there's been days when it was a long time between meals. Lost my bedroll in the river, it had a small piece of bacon and some pone stashed in it. That was to have been my breakfast for today."

"Well, sonny, I should say Vee, I think I can do better for you than wet pone and bacon. Here, try this tea. It should do wonders for you along with the soup. But first let's get those clothes dried out." He pulled a quilt from a cupboard just behind him and said, "Wrap this blanket around you while I hang those wet things of yours by the stove." Foster busied himself stringing a line to hang the clothes on while I finished off the soup.

The blanket was warm and added to the glow my body felt from the combination of soup and hot tea.

"Where you coming from, Vee? Looks like you must have been in the fighting for a while."

"Yes sir, I just left Appomattox after the surrender. I'm on my way home. Been on the way for about four days now. The bridge was shut down so I tried swimming the river. Didn't want to wait around until the Yankees opened it up again."

"Well, I'm glad to have the company. Will you be all right while I slip out for a minute? You can continue to warm up; maybe your clothes will be dried out by the time I return. If you need more soup, it's on the stove. I'll be back in less than five minutes." He was out the door as I was helping myself to more soup.

Foster was true to his word, he hadn't been gone longer than the five minutes he estimated earlier. He had some additional provisions that must have come from a local store. He was humming as he went about putting things away.

I needed to make conversation so I wouldn't fall asleep. I said, "You mentioned earlier about the possibility of you moving on if something wasn't done soon. What did you mean by that?"

164

He hesitated and then said, "Well, it's a long story which has just come to a head these last few days. I don't want to burden you with my troubles."

"I'm not going anywhere right away, particularly since you've taken my clothes." I detected a slight smile from that comment; apparently he wasn't without a sense of humor. "So, I might as well hear you out."

My eyes closed for just a second as the warmth of the room came over me. It was the first peaceful feeling I had experienced since I could remember.

Elizabeth's face was staring at me. She looked just like the last night we were together before I had gone off to fight. There were times during the fighting when I had been hard pressed to conjure up a clear image of her. Sometimes that worried me, making me think I was losing my memory. But now, with the war over, she was in my thoughts continually and I couldn't get her out of my mind. Her face constantly appeared to me in my dreams, clear and beautiful.

I should have written more letters to her. I hope she hasn't forgotten me. My plan will still be to stop by New Glasgow on my way home. If she isn't there, I will look for her until I find her. My god, I hope she hasn't married while I've been gone. Please don't let me have any such nightmares until I can see her again and tell her how much she has been a part of my dreams.

Was I really hearing her voice? It sounded so close I felt all I needed to do was open my eyes and she would be right there in front of me, although, her voice was a bit low and scratchy.

No, it wasn't Elizabeth talking to me; it was Foster saying something I couldn't understand.

"Sorry, my thoughts sort of wandered there for a second. Please go on with your story."

"Your eyes did close for a moment. Well, as I was saying, before the war there was a plan to build a railroad along the north side of the James, which would run through Lynchburg and on to Richmond. Some of the preliminary planning had been completed, but it never got much further than some survey work and some right-of-way preparation along this part of the river. There wasn't enough money or manpower to get the project totally underway. Also, the war put an end to any further thought of such a project, at least until the conflict ended.

I had been hired as a surveyor and was privy to some of the initial planning. I was sent down along the river to do some soil testing. That's how I got to Gladstone. This was to be one of two main waypoints between Lynchburg and Richmond. The other was to have been Bremo Bluff.

When Virginia seceded from the Union, I was left high and dry here with my family. My wife and son died of pneumonia in '60, so I was left all by myself. I opened a small general store and made a good living at least until goods became scarce. I was able to buy up some of the river front property and planned to use it to open a boat building business after the war. The bridge down at Bent Creek was a boon for me because any traffic headed northwest along the north shore of the river went through Gladstone. The rest stayed on the turnpike towards Charlottesville. For some reason there was never anything built on the north side of the river to accommodate travelers."

"How come you didn't have to go off to war? You were for the South, weren't you?"

"Of course I was for the South, but when the fighting first started, I was too old for them. When things got real bad, I figured there wasn't anything I could do to help. So, I just stayed here to wait out the inevitable."

"So, what problem do you have now?"

"A fellow came to town just about ten days ago. Claims he has the rights to a lot of the property in this small village. Says his grandfather rightfully owned most of the land along a five-mile stretch of the river. Alleges he was at Appomattox when the South surrendered. He said General Lee personally awarded him a medal for his outstanding service to the Confederacy. A so called friend of his arrived from Washington only days after he did, claiming to have the deeds for every decent piece of land along the north shore of the James River. And that includes everything from Bent Creek to Stapleton. Says the paperwork is being sent to him by a special courier who will be arriving any day now."

"That really seems far fetched to me. Didn't you get a deed for your land when you bought it?"

"Well, at the time, all that was required was to send the particulars to the county seat. They were supposed to set it all down on their records with a deed to be issued at a later date. I put off getting the deed because the war started right after the deal was struck."

"Do either one of these people have any hard facts which would prove they own the land? I don't think anyone could have been given such rights so soon after the end of fighting. Seems to me some sort of funny business is going on. There must be something in the wind that will increase land values. Why else would they want the property?"

"You could be correct, but I'm at a loss to figure out what it could be. Also, I'm not sure how to expose these crooks. They have money, lots of money, and they are telling people if they don't sign a release to them at their offer, they will be run off without a dime. They also have guns, which is something none of us have, so we can't protect ourselves or our property."

"What kind of deadline have they given before everyone has to have signed a release?"

"It's one week from today. One family already signed for hardly a nickel on the dollar and headed west. But, I think they were planning on leaving this part of the country anyway. There are only ten others like myself who have anything these two want. It's a small town and nobody seems to want to fight these people." Despair showed on Foster face for the first time since he started his story.

"Has anyone tried to get over to the county seat to ask them if this thing is legal? Seems to me they are trying to take advantage of a situation before anyone can check on whether they have a legal right or not."

"I've got a young friend, Tom Gill, who is coming over here in a while. He has a piece of land nearby and has become a very good neighbor. He was planning a trip to the county seat next week. It's a goodly ways from here, and transportation is hard to come by. Even if he gets there, I'm told some of the property papers were destroyed in a fire when the fighting went through early on in the war. Things been happening so fast, we really haven't had the chance to do anything. I'm about ready to throw up my hands and head west myself." Foster slumped down in a chair and dropped his head into his hands. His desperation set a new tone in the room.

167

A knock at the door brought him back to his usual self. At least the desperation on his face changed to indicate a more pleasant expression. "That must be Tom."

Foster opened the door to a six-foot hulk with sandy hair. His shoulders almost blocked out the light. He had a spring in his step as he entered the room. I jumped up to greet him as he extended his hand.

"I'm Tom Gill, it's a pleasure to meet you. I understand you had a bit of trouble getting across the James?"

"I would have had more trouble if Foster hadn't been out fishing early this morning. Otherwise, I may have been a bit farther down stream."

"Well, he's always been an early riser."

"Glad to meet you, too, Tom. My friends call me Vee, please do the same. Foster was just telling me about the two swindlers who have been trying to bilk some of the people around these parts."

"Yes, seems these two have a plan to gather up some property for peanuts that could be valuable a bit later on. It is my thought that the railroad may be coming this way again. That would make the land worth a pretty price, not what they want to pay. I think if we take a stand they will get our message that we won't be bought or chased off so easy. However, Foster and I are the only ones willing to take a firm position."

"I agree about the railroad being a possibility. It sure must be something that will increase the land's worth. Where are these fellows now? It might be a good idea to have a small conversation with them before you do anything stupid." As I was speaking, Tom took a seat in a chair by the stove. He stretched out his legs to the fire and suddenly I noticed that one of his legs was a peg. I almost blurted out, 'How did that happen?'. Instead, I diverted my eyes towards Foster.

Foster spoke up, "As a matter of fact, they've called a meeting of all concerned over in the square for this afternoon. It's the first time they've gotten all of us together at the same time. They said they were going to give us one last chance to sign."

Tom jumped to his feet, and said, "It's time we brought this thing to a head." Except for the one missing leg, he looked and portrayed the perfect specimen of youthful exuberance.

"I would like to join you two. I'm interested to listen to what they have to say. Something just isn't right about all of this."

"You're welcome to come along. The more people we have to ask questions, the better off we will be in getting to the truth." Foster chuckled, "If it is even possible to get the truth out of either of them."

The clouds had cleared and the sun was beating down on the village square. It felt good to have the warmth surging through my bones after being so cold coming out of the river.

All the people who should be there were there. The group was gathered around a large stump looking up at two well-dressed men. The two, so called owners, weren't at all what I had expected. I had been looking for rough and tumble individuals, instead they appeared well kept and overfed. The tallest, five foot eight at the best, had thinning black hair with mustache and goatee. The other was even shorter and had blond hair with a clean-shaven face, unusual for this part of the country.

The darker of the two spoke out, "It's about time you people got here. This is the last chance you're going to get. If you don't sign these releases immediately, your land will be taken over by the law when they get here. That's going to be in less than a week from now."

"You just got to pay us more than you are offering for what we have." A voice from the crowd spoke out clearly. "We've put a lot of work into these places and it's worth more than what you're willing to pay." The undertone from the crowd attested to their agreement.

"You're lucky to be getting anything. There ain't no homestead law in this state. You perched on land what ain't yours. You can take it or leave it." The dark headed man's voice rose as he said 'Take it or leave it'. According to Foster, he was the one who claimed to have been at Appomattox when Lee surrendered.

"What kind of medal did General Lee award you, sir?" A hush fell over the crowd at this unusual statement, and the dark haired one looked hard to see where the voice had come from. I stepped out from the group so he could see me clearly.

"The highest one that could be awarded. Who are you to be asking? You ain't one of these locals. Who invited you to this meeting? Why, you don't even have shoes."

Ignoring his comment about my feet, I countered with, "I don't believe there were any medals awarded at Appomattox. All we did was turn over our weapons to the Yankees, get our paroles, and then head out for home. You do have your parole, don't you?" I moved forward so I was standing right next to the stump. I could reach out and touch both men's legs. They had to bend at the waist and peer down to look into my face.

"What's it to you, mister? As I said, you ain't one of these squatters. This situation doesn't concern you. Why don't you move away or I might have to move you."

Foster had positioned himself on the other side of the stump while Tom spaced himself halfway between the two of us. Another sturdy man joined him giving us good coverage all the way around the stump.

"My friend has told me about what you two are claiming, I'm thinking you might just be a deserter rather than a hero. I was at Appomattox when General Lee surrendered, and I got my parole three days later, like everyone else who was there. There's no way you could have gotten your parole and been here for a week. They weren't even printed in Lynchburg until five days ago. Here's mine, show me yours." My parole looked limp as I unfolded it and held it between my fingers, but the signatures and proper markings showed it as official.

Suddenly hands reached out and grabbed their legs, pulling them from the stump. They both tried to pull revolvers, but couldn't with their arms pinned behind them. Tom grasped the taller one and single handedly relieved him of his weapon. Foster and the other man seized the blond one. The total number of weapons from the two included four pistols and a sabre, which had been hanging from the belt of the so-called hero.

Foster searched both men then said, "Doesn't appear you have a parole, just like my friend said. But lookey here, there's a card saying you've been living in Baltimore for the past year. Also, your blond friend seems to be from New York according to his identification. He's a long way from home, and it doesn't appear either of you have been in Appomattox recently. Got anything to say for yourselves?"

"I must of lost it. You can't prove anything on us. You people are going to be in some grave trouble if you don't let us up."

"I think you might be the ones with the serious problem. For openers, seems as if you are in fact a deserter that is if you ever did fight for the South. You and your friend appear to be opportunists, trying to take advantage of us before any type of law comes back into effect. Right now we seem to have two choices. Hang you immediately or hang you later." Foster turned his head and winked at me when he said 'hang'.

"What say men, shall we hang them now or later?"

"Now, Now, Now; came the cry from the group." And they meant it.

The next thing I was expecting to see was a rope being tossed over the nearest limb. That would have put this small group of people from Gladstone in a critical position. Foster knew it, but before he could get a word out I said, "Don't you think it would serve a better purpose to tar and feather these two so their opportunists friends will learn they better steer clear of Gladstone?"

More than one nodded in the affirmative.

Foster was quick to pick up on my suggestion. He directed two of the men to round up some tar and two others to get all the feathers they could find. It was like a holiday with a festive mood settling over the small village. Before long a blazing fire had the caldron of tar to a soupy consistency, not too hot, but hot enough to stick to skin and hold feathers.

In less than an hour, two howling individuals were on a rail being bodily carried out of town. It would be a goodly spell before either was able to sit down without some pain, and even longer before they would try their scheming ways on other Southerners.

Foster was chuckling as he rustled around in his small shack, putting some bacon and beans together for supper. Tom was by the stove working on his pipe. He had been invited to stay for some eats. It was dark outside but the river could still be heard rushing along in its pell-mell surge towards Richmond.

The gloom I had seen earlier had been lifted off Foster's back, its place taken by the reality of finally being free from those two crafty individuals. Unfortunately, they probably weren't the last to be headed into this part of the world.

"Foster, I've got to be getting on my way. You saved my life and I will be ever thankful, but I have a bit of a problem to take care of myself."

"What's that, Vee? I've been so wrapped up in things here; I never gave you a chance to put in your two cents worth. Is it anything Tom or I can help you with? We all certainly owe you. You figured out those crooks, while we were still worrying about losing our homes and land."

"No, this is something personal. In fact, I will be lucky to get it taken care of because I may never run into the individuals I'm looking for."

"Well, at least tell us what you are up against. We could have some ideas that could possibly help you, like you did for us. I do know the land north of here for a ways, and Tom has an uncle up on the Buffalo River. You are headed in that direction, aren't you?"

"Yes, and any tips you can give me on the best way north would be appreciated. As to my problem, like you said to me, it's a long story."

"And, as you said, we're not going anywhere."

"Well, some friends who I served with for the last few months of the war made a very bad decision when the conflict ended." I didn't go over how we had fought and almost died together. I left out the special missions we went on for General Gordon. I skipped most of the details of how we had gotten from Petersburg to Appomattox, or how the promised food supplies hadn't materialized at Amelia Court House or Farmville.

Instead, I centered on the waiting around in the wet and cold countryside of the Appomattox Court House area. Not knowing if we were to be put in prison or be marched off to Richmond to be placed on trial. I did express the devastating impact the lack of food and supplies had on the entire outfit. How after being without for so long might have influenced their thoughts of obtaining something to take home rather than showing up empty handed. Then I concluded on what happened as pertained to Seth and his partners. "Suffice it to say, John, David, and Ben deserved some punishment for their decision to rob, but not death by being led into an ambush by a conniving, unsavory, and disreputable person."

"Have you seen either Seth or his friends since the ambush?"

"Yes, I saw them in Bent Creek. I didn't come face to face but it had been my plan to confront them somehow. My confrontation was interrupted by a barroom brawl." The telling of the episode of the fight and subsequent killing left me hoarse.

"They could still be in Bent Creek. I don't believe the Yankees have opened the bridge as yet." Foster had the pleased look of having solved some of my problems.

"I know, but I heard Seth say he was going to buy his way across and I'm sure he did. Especially after one of his cohorts was shot when caught cheating at cards. I also heard the Yankee major say he wanted him rounded up so he could talk to him. I'm sure Seth and his friend made sure they wouldn't be around to answer any questions.

This is my problem so don't you worry about it. You have been more than enough help. You saved me from the river and you've fed me to get my strength back. I couldn't ask for any more. I feel it will all work out some way. If I don't run into them on my way home I may one of these days, and a McGrady doesn't forget."

"Well, we've had a full day and I know you want to be on your way early in the morning. I'll be up before daybreak and fix us some breakfast. I'll also put a few provisions together to keep you fed on your way home."

Tom rose up from beside the stove and said, "You know, Vee, I was planning a trip up to see my Uncle Jed. He runs a small ferry across the Buffalo. I was holding off because of the land problem, but now it's finished. I could go along with you as far as my uncle's place. That is, if you want the company?"

"I could always use the company, Tom, but I'm planning to do some meandering as I move north to see if I can come across Seth's trail. I want to get on home as fast as I can, but I think the extra time could be well spent."

"You won't have to worry about Tom if you think he might slow you down because of his leg." Foster was quick to make his point. "He can cover more ground than any man around these parts with two good legs."

"I've had two and a half years to get used to this piece of stump," Tom tapped on his peg leg. "It took awhile, but now I can stay up with anything short of a horse." He chuckled at his own little joke.

"Well, Tom, I'll be glad to have your company. I didn't mean to say you couldn't keep pace. I just thought...." the correct word didn't come to mind so the pause was longer than intended, "shucks, I'm not sure what I meant. To tell the truth, I was thinking I should be on my way tonight. Every minute I delay could mean the minute I was too late in finding Seth and his friend."

Foster spoke out sharply, "No, no, Vee. That bump on your head needs at least one good night's rest. I just pulled you out of the river early this morning. I wouldn't want you to go off and pass out in the woods someplace north of here. Anyway, I'm not sure you know exactly what you will do when and if you find Seth."

"To tell the truth, I'm not sure. But if I catch up with them, I'll think of something. They are murderers who should pay for their crime. I may not be the one to administer a just punishment, but maybe I can find someone who can."

"Vee, you are determined and I can't blame you. If I were a younger man I would go along with you, but I'm afraid I would be more of a hindrance than a help. However, Tom just might be the right person if you do run across them. You saw what he could do this afternoon."

"I can't deny Tom would certainly come in handy if it ever came to a hand to hand fight. But I certainly don't want to drag him into any of my troubles."

"You let me worry about what you drag me into," Tom's voice had a stern quality, which exuded confidence. "Now you wait for me in the morning, I will be here bright and early." He gripped me firmly by the shoulders until I nodded my head in the affirmative. Releasing me, he turned to Foster and said, "Goodnight my friend, thanks for the meal." He went out the door quietly, leaving an obvious void in the room.

Foster had cleaned up the dishes and from his movements, was ready for bed. "Tom will be a good traveling mate. I'm sure he will tell you about his leg in good time. It's a story you must hear from him." He gathered up the lantern and started for the bedroom. "Well, my new friend, we've had a long and fruitful day. Better get some sleep if you expect to get very far along the way towards the Buffalo River. I'll see you at first light." He closed his door and sent the small shack into darkness. Only the embers from the fire splintered tiny streaks of light into the night near my pallet.

I spoke loudly so I could be heard through his closed door. "Thanks again my friend. I will always remember you and Gladstone. I'll be counting the days until I can get down this way again. Sleep tight."

I sat there watching those tiny streaks of light and thought about what had transpired over a very full day.

From almost drowning, to running a couple of crooks out of town on a rail had been an adventure I wouldn't want to repeat every day. Now I was on the north side of the James and getting closer to home. It wasn't any more than a two and a half day journey to Clifford. But, it could be longer if I happened to cross Seth and his friend's path. In all probability, it would be a remote chance of seeing them again. They could be anywhere between here and points north. But the time spent in looking would be more than worth the effort if I did find them.

I'm sure my mother, my sisters, and Elizabeth would understand me taking a little extra time to look for some people who deserved to be punished for their crime. They wouldn't want a son, and she wouldn't want a man who didn't stand up for his friends.

My, I can almost reach out and touch her face; it's so clear before me. I can see her farmhouse sitting in the small valley with the nearby creek sparkling on a clear day. Please Lord; let her be home and waiting for me. Let her hopes and thoughts be the same as mine. Please give us your blessing so that our future years together will prosper.

I best get some sleep or I won't be able to travel more than a mile tomorrow before I will want to rest. It could be another long day.

I hope Tom won't mind doing a little tracking rather than striking out straight for the Buffalo River. He sure seemed to want to help and he has the strength, regardless of the one missing leg, it might take to overcome Seth and his friend.

The sound of rushing water could be heard as the river continued its flow eastward. The hoot of a distant owl echoed far away. Finally the last ember blinked out, leaving total darkness in the small room. At last my troubled mind gathered in the sleep it so badly needed.

Chapter Eleven

Tom and I had just arrived on the bluff above Gladstone. The route up from the village wound its way along a small pathway nestled in a cut of land. It was almost a natural trail worn smooth by years of use. The grade was gentle, which didn't put any strain on the climb even though we gained several hundred feet by the time we reached the top of the bluff.

The vista was breathtaking as we moved over to the edge to get a better view of the bridge below which crossed the James from Bent Creek. It was one of the first days in a long time that visibility was unlimited. It is amazing what an unobstructed panorama of grandeur can do for a person who has been blinded with the pall of battle for the last couple of years.

I had just turned to Tom and was saying, "Doesn't the peak on Pruett's Mountain stand out like a beacon. I used it as a check point when I was working my way towards Bent Creek."

Tom nodded as he stepped over next to me. His right foot had barely touched the ground when the world beneath us gave way. To say it was unexpected would be an understatement.

It wasn't tumbling head over heels that was so bad. It was being intermingled with the rocks and debris bouncing off the sides of the slide, which endangered life and limb. The ground, probably because of the recent rains, must have been ready to give way. It certainly had become unstable, and our combined weight had been just enough to make this part of the bluff collapse.

Luckily, we didn't tumble all the way to the small spit of land some two hundred feet or more below the top of the bluff. Instead, we came to rest on a ledge about halfway between top and bottom. However, we didn't exactly end up in the same place along the face of the cliff. We were separated from each other by a gap caused by the main part of the dirt and rockslide. Also, Tom ended up a few feet above my position.

"Whee, that was a quick trip which could have ended in disaster." Tom's words came in between gasps of breath. "Are you all right over there?"

"Yep," I spoke cautiously. "I don't seem any worse for the experience. Can't feel any broken bones or bent limbs. How about you?"

"Don't think I have anything which doesn't work like it did before we started down hill. We are lucky some of those rocks didn't crack our skulls, or it wouldn't have made much difference how far we fell."

"I totally agree. Now let's see if we can get back up on top where we started," I coughed out, as I attempted to scramble up the steep slope on my side of the gap. I didn't make very good progress due to the unstable ground above my position. I kept slipping back to my starting point each time I tried to advance.

"Looks like you're fighting a losing cause, Vee. Can you get over to this side? There seems to be more places to get a foot hold on this part of the incline. Let me reach down and see if you can grab my hand." Tom had advanced a few feet towards the top without much difficulty. It was amazing how well he was able to move with that peg leg of his. "I'll come back down nearer your level to help you across."

"Hang on a minute while I get myself in a firmer position. Then if you will give me a hand, I think I can get over to your side." After making sure I wasn't going to continue any farther down the slope, I stretched out towards Tom's extended hand. I was just inches short, I could barely touch his fingertips. Finally, by extending my stretch, I was able to get a positive grip. He then slid his hand up my arm a bit and took firm hold on my wrist.

"Are you ready?" I nodded as he continued to talk. "If so, on my count of three you jump this way."

His count to three was quick which didn't give me much time to worry about falling. He swung me over to a three-foot wide space like I was a rag doll. I was astonished by the strength Tom had in his arms and upper body. Maybe some of it came from the leg he had lost.

I landed with a thud and quickly grabbed hold of a small root protruding from the bank to steady myself. With both of us in such a small space, I wasn't sure the ground wouldn't fall away from us again.

"Thanks, that was almost as exciting as the fall, but I don't think I would like to make a practice of it."

"Me either," Tom said, as he moved up the incline slightly while I got ready to follow along in his footholds. "Let's get moving up this slope before we head in the wrong direction. I'm not sure this small ledge will hold both of us for very long."

"I'm hoping it will, at least long enough for us to climb to safety."

By inching past each other in turn, we gained ground towards the top. We took extra care to ensure we wouldn't go crashing down to the bottom, while expending as little effort as possible. Finally we reached the top and were on firm ground once again.

After dusting ourselves off, we took some time to inspect the immediate area we had been standing on before the ground had suddenly given way. We could see where the earth had parted as if cleaved with a knife. Our guess about being water soaked must have been correct, for dampness was evident all around where the land had surged away.

We moved back from the slide area giving ourselves a few additional feet before looking again at the vista below.

The view of the river winding eastward was overwhelming. The water appeared as a dark serpent, which sparkled in the sunlight from time to time as it coursed its way toward the sea. The mountain ridges on both sides of the river, with their individual peaks, assumed the likeness of sleeping giants sprawled out over the extended landscape. The entire scene sent chills through my bones. It had been a long time since I had taken the time to gaze out at a pleasant countryside without expecting the enemy to show up and spoil everything.

Traffic in and out of Bent Creek could be seen crossing the bridge. Tom said, "They must have found the person or persons who shot Lincoln because the wagons are moving again across the bridge."

"Yep, I see them. Wonder who was responsible for that dastardly deed? I sure hope he gets what's coming to him. It would have meant a lot to the South, had Lincoln lived."

"Well, best we be on our way if we expect to get part way to the Buffalo River crossing. I want to get to my Uncle Jed's place sometime tomorrow, if possible."

"Suits me, Tom. However, I need to scout a bit back and forth across the turnpike in an attempt to pick up Seth's trail. He may or may not have made it this far, but I've got the time to see if he did. If you have to be to your uncle's crossing by tomorrow, then best you head straight on for it."

"Oh, I don't really have any set time period I have to be at Uncle Jed's place. I know he'll be surprised to see me whenever I arrive. He wasn't expecting me until sometime next month. So, I'll be happy to give you a hand looking for any sign that would indicate Seth and his buddy have made it this far. In fact, I wouldn't mind running into the likes of those murdering scoundrels. People like that don't deserve to be running around free."

To have a newfound friend willing to help wasn't something new to me. John, David, and many others who had been a major part of my life for the past two years had provided assistance on some very difficult occasions.

However, it always gave me a very warm feeling inside when my fellow man would give assistance, sometimes to mere strangers, when help was needed most. Let's just hope that such aid will always be available now that we are again a united nation.

There's going to be a lot of need for assistance if we expect to get our lands and properties back into conditions we knew in the past. People are going to have to work together more than ever.

I'm sure Elizabeth will want to be a part of the work that has to be done in Clifford and the surrounding area. She will really make each and every day of the future a pleasant journey for me.

Shucks, I'd better find out if she is still interested in me after the past two years. I will try to keep her in the back of my mind until I determine, one way or the other, how Seth and his cohort may play in my immediate future.

If I haven't run into them before I reach Clifford, I'm not sure what I will do. I don't intend to dedicate my life to their demise, but I would sure feel better to know they get what's coming to them. People like that don't deserve to continue on in a decent, law-abiding society.

The ground was fairly level as we started for the turnpike. There were a few trees, mostly scattered pine and a few maples; so making our way wasn't difficult.

We had spent more time than I had thought getting out of that perilous situation at the bluff. It was almost noon and we hadn't made much progress towards the Buffalo. Also, all the activity had brought on a hunger which hadn't been diminished by the few regular meals I had experienced the last day or two. The thought of food, especially those last weeks of the war, would always be in my mind. It was very pleasant to have something to eat after all the wanting of the past.

We stopped in a small glade surrounded by pines. A gentle stream meandered nearby, so water wasn't a problem. With as much rain as had fallen in Virginia in the past month, water shouldn't be a problem for a long period of time.

We heated the food over an open fire, and the beans and bacon hit the spot. Just taking the time to eat and enjoy the peaceful quiet was a luxury I hadn't experienced in a long, long time. It was nice to rest after the strenuous activity earlier on when we were overlooking the James.

Tom was stretched out by a fallen pine trunk, sucking on his pipe and almost asleep when I said, "The turnpike is just over the next little ridge, why don't we head that way and check on any traffic moving north or south. If we run across anyone, we can query them about having seen the likes of Seth and his partner."

"Sounds good to me. If there isn't any news, we can split up and explore each side of the road to see if we can find any sign of them. We can join back up at an intersection just a mile or so farther on. The east branch at the intersection heads towards Norwood, you shouldn't have any problem finding it. There might even be a sign there, so wait for me if you get there first."

"I'm sure I will be able to find it, and I'll wait for you if I get there first. How deep do you think we should look when we are paralleling the turnpike?"

"Unless we come across a trail which could have been an easy path for Seth, I think a couple hundred yards will be deep enough. If we are going to find any signs of them, we should find it there. If it were I, I'd be sticking pretty close alongside the turnpike. Probably just deep enough in the woods so as not to be seen by any traffic passing by."

"I think you are correct. I'll only go deeper if I come across a trail which would appear to be an easier path for them."

"At the intersection to Norwood, the turnpike turns to the northwest heading towards Amherst. If we haven't found anything by then, we can follow the turnpike to the Buffalo River Ferry turnoff. If that is OK with you? There are several miles between the two turnoffs, so we can get a good check of both sides before we have to leave the main road. Also, we will probably have to make camp before we reach there, so we will have time to alter our plans if the need arises."

"Of course, if they've moved on along past the Buffalo Ferry intersection, we may never run across them. But I have the feeling they are still short of the Buffalo River road. Let's get on over to the turnpike before they do outdistance us and see what's going on."

There wasn't any traffic in sight when we reached the turnpike, although the roadway was well rutted from heavy wagon traffic which had been making its way north. We couldn't see any reason to wait for possible traffic, so we started northward. We could see where the road turned only a few yards up ahead. As planned, we would go inland at that point and individually search each side, rendezvousing at the Norwood cutoff.

Our plans changed drastically as we rounded the turn. The grisly spectacle brought back vivid memories of scenes, which would probably never be erased from our minds. It was like we were back in the war once again.

A Yankee wagon was overturned. Two Bluecoats were lying near the wagon tongue and behind some broken pieces of the wagon frame. One held a musket, but apparently hadn't been able to put it into

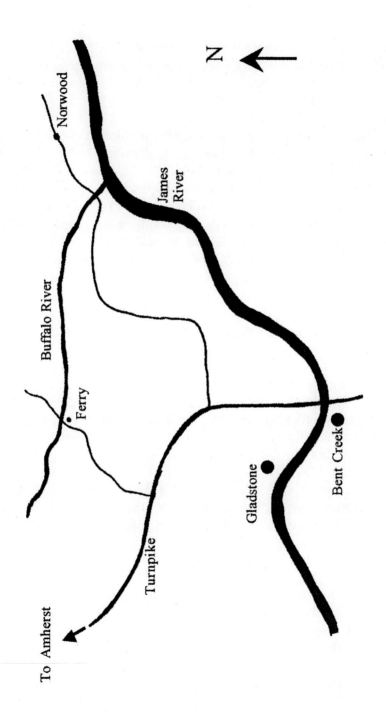

action. The other was crumpled behind the man with the musket. He had a pistol in his hand, but his body was turned away from the turnpike. The pistol could have been fired. A third man was sprawled out halfway up the bank. He must have been trying to get into the woods for cover.

Boxes from the cargo were spilled all along the shallow ditch on the east side of the turnpike. Several boxes had broken open exposing parts of uniforms and bedding.

It was then we noticed the man on the bank move. It was ever so slight, but a definite attempt had been made to slowly inch his way further towards the woods. We rushed to him to see if we could be of assistance. He moaned as we reached his side.

"Who did this to you?" We turned his face out of the dirt and held him so he could get more air. We could count several wounds to his back, none of which looked good.

The man's breath was coming in short gasps, and he coughed as he said, "Two men, one was big with a large barrel chest and shocking red hair. The other was smaller with black hair." His cough sounded like the death rattles I had heard so many times in the last two years, but his words continued. He seemed to want to get his story out. "They rushed out at us from the woods on the far side while we were stopped to adjust the harness on our team. Their shots bolted our team, causing the wagon to turn over in the ditch. The team broke loose and stampeded down the road. At least those renegades didn't get the horses. We didn't have much of a chance to fire at them before they were upon us with pistols. My two partners were hit first after the wagon turned over. I was thrown over on this bank and was trying to make the woods when two shots hit me. Bill down there did get off a shot and I think he wounded one of them. I heard one of them scream out, and it wasn't a Rebel yell. I'm not sure which one he hit, but one for sure. One of them shot Bill at point blank range to make sure he wouldn't be firing again; I think it was the big one. After that, they must have thought we were all dead, cause they didn't follow me up the bank. They sounded awful mad when they saw we weren't carrying anything but bedding and old uniforms."

"Take it easy friend, let's see if we can do anything for those wounds." Tom's voice was as gentle as if he were speaking to a baby.

184

"Ain't you two Rebs? Wouldn't think you would care much one way or the other what happens to me, but thank you anyway." Blood seeped out of his mouth as his coughing increased. It was difficult to understand his words, which turned out to be his last. Moments later he slumped in Tom's arms as he touched the faded gray of my jacket, his eyes searching to understand what was happening. Tom laid him down and closed his eyes just as a wagon and two riders approached from the north.

As the wagon and two riders pulled to stop beside us, I said to Tom, "Sure sounds like Seth and his friend from the description he gave. I'll bet it wasn't Seth who got hit. He probably had his little friend out in front screening him. Wonder how bad the wound was?"

"Don't know, but maybe these Yankees caught sight of them when they were coming down the pike. Looks like they are headed back to Bent Creek with an empty wagon."

"What happened here? You see who did this?" The only officer of the group, a captain, yelled out as he brought his horse to a stop.

"No sir. We just happened upon this debacle a few minutes ago. We didn't even hear the firing so it must've occurred a bit earlier. We were trying to help this poor fellow on the bank, but he just died. He did have time to tell us two renegades hit them while they were stopped to see about their team's harness. Said his buddy down there by the wagon tongue might have hit one of them before he was killed. Did you see anyone like a big barrel chested man with red hair when you came down the road?"

"No, didn't see anyone like that. How do we know it wasn't you two who killed these men?" The captain had his revolver out while he was asking us questions.

"Well, for one thing you don't see any guns on us, do you? Also, here's my parole." I slowly pulled the paper from my pocket. It was the second time I had had a chance to look at it since I put it there for safekeeping. "I'm heading home from Appomattox, and it ain't been easy going."

"Your buddy there got one of those paroles?"

Tom spoke up with, "I got my discharge papers after the second Bull Run, thanks to some of your likes. I also got this there." He rapped on his wooden leg with his knuckles to make his point.

"OK, I guess you've made it clear it wasn't you two. But do you have any idea who it was?"

"Yeah, from the description the fellow on the bank gave us before he died, it sounds like a big, red-haired renegade who was leading a gang south of the James. He got some of my friends killed when he lied to them about his plans. I'd been hoping to run into him; I've got a score or two to settle when we meet up. He's also giving a bad name to the majority of us who fought honorably."

"Well, he must be long gone from around these parts by now. I've got to get this wagon back to Bent Creek or I would scout around for him and his buddy. We will take those bodies with us, and I'll let the people know what happened up here."

"There was a major who wanted to talk to a big, red-haired man about some irregularities when I was passing through Bent Creek. I'm sure he will be interested in hearing about this."

We helped the Yankees move the bodies to the back of the wagon. We used some of the blankets from the broken boxes to cover them. It was going to be a bumpy ride in the back of that wagon to Bent Creek, but I was sure the passengers weren't going to mind.

"We'll also try to carry some of those broken boxes with us." He motioned for his sergeant and the private to move some of the boxes to the wagon. Looking at my feet, he said, "Don't see any shoes in the bunch of clothing, otherwise I'd offer you a pair."

"Thanks anyway. I've been making it pretty well barefooted this far. Might as well continue on the same way."

Tom stepped forward and said, "You could leave one or two of those muskets, just in case we run across the two who did this deed."

"Sorry, but we'd both be in trouble if I did that. You Rebs ain't supposed to have any weapons, not for a while anyways. So, I'll take the guns along with their bodies. That way neither of us will get in trouble. Thanks for trying to help out here, too bad you came onto this after all the action had occurred."

"Well, we'll still be looking on both sides of the turnpike as we move on north. If one of them is hurt, they might not be able to move along so fast. It might give us a chance to run into them. Don't exactly know what we'll do if we find them since they have pistols, and we don't. But, we'll think of something when the time comes." Tom hunched down by the broken wagon as he spoke.

The other two Yankees had gotten back up on the wagon after storing what boxes they could. They were ready to depart and signaled to the captain.

The captain saluted and spurred his horse as he said, "Well, you two have a safe trip, wherever you're headed. I hope you run across those two, they could cause a lot more trouble if they're not caught soon."

A truer statement couldn't have been more exact. I had seen first hand the growing carnage being left by the likes of Seth.

The sun was well into the west as they rounded the bend. They were out of sight before the dust settled.

Tom and I had moved off the turnpike several hundred yards. We had gone down a slight grade to a small creek whose water was clear and cool. We figured we were just a bit short of the Norwood turnoff but since night was beginning to fall, we might as well make camp for the night. Our short attempt to search the surrounding area for any signs of Seth and his partner came up empty. We would wait until morning when we could be more thorough.

"Do you reckon Seth and his buddy are anywhere close by? If one of them is hurt, no telling how far they might have traveled after they hit the wagon." Tom scratched his head as if he were in deep thought about what he just said.

"Hard to tell. Reckon we won't know until we run into them." I threw down my new bedroll, courtesy of Foster, and started moving some rocks to make us a fireplace. "I'll go fetch some firewood and we can get us a fire going so we can have some hot food. When it gets darker, I'll see if I can find a place to look around. Might spot a fire or some smoke which could give away their location."

"Well, if we do run into them, we won't be without assistance." Tom pulled out a pistol from under his shirt.

"Where did you get that?" I was really amazed to see him with a gun.

"The dead Yankee on the bank had it tucked in his belt. Since the Captain didn't see it, I thought I might as well keep it for future use. You got any problem with that?" He was tucking it into his bedroll as he spoke.

"It's fine with me. I was just surprised but glad to see it."

Our meal was finished and I had gone off to look for a spot, which would give me a view of the surrounding area. I found what I was looking for just across the small creek near our camp. I looked in all directions, but nothing was visible that would cause us to think anyone else was nearby. That meant we would spend our time searching both sides of the turnpike tomorrow on our way to the Norwood turnoff. If nothing turned up, we'd do the same until we reached the Buffalo River Ferry intersection.

Tom was stretched out with his pipe when I returned. He had added some wood to the fire and it was down to some nice glowing coals. The screech of an owl, somewhere off in the woods, was the only sound to be heard. It was pleasantly quiet and peaceful after the turmoil of the day.

"Guess Seth and his friend had time to put some distance between the wagon and themselves before night set in." Tom's comment was more of a statement than an inquiry.

"Yep, but hopefully not too much. Maybe we can spend less time in the early part of our search tomorrow if we don't see any positive signs."

"Do you want me to put another piece of wood on the fire, or are you ready for it to burn down?" Tom said, puffing on his pipe.

"I'll add one more, it may be a while before I go to sleep. I'm going to lie here and see if I can put some sense to the happenings of the last few days. For one thing, it was sure a stroke of luck for me to run into Foster and you. I don't know how much further I could have made it without you all's help."

"As determined as you are, Vee, you'll make it all the way home, regardless of how much help you get."

"Well, that's kind of you to say so, Tom. But it was nice running into the likes of you in Gladstone." Tom didn't appear to make a retort, so I continued with, "If it isn't the wrong thing to ask, how did you lose your leg in the early part of the war?"

Tom settled himself with his back against a pine tree. He nodded his head slightly, pointing his pipe in my direction and saying, "It's a long story, but if you aren't too sleepy, here's what happened as well as I can remember. It's been almost four years ago. The date was July '61 and I was a sergeant in General Stonewall Jackson's brigade. We were positioned along the southern bank of Bull Run, a mile or so downstream from Stone Bridge. That was the bridge on the

Warrenton Pike that crossed the run about two and a half miles south of Centreville. The entire Confederate line stretched from slightly west of Stone Bridge, to as far down the run as Union Mills Ford. Centreville was where the major portions of the Yankee force was supposedly located. We were aligned to protect and defend Manassas Junction, it being the key juncture for the railroads coming out of Alexandria heading southward as well as over into the Shenandoah Valley.

General Beauregard, the commander in the field, had drawn up his plans to attack the enemy before they could get out of Centreville. I'm not positive about exactly what happened, but the Yankees didn't wait for our attack. They assaulted our left flank west of Stone Bridge before we could move on them. This put things in a pickle, because our western flank wasn't heavily defended. If the Yankees turned it, Manassas Junction could have been overrun before we could have done much to stop them.

General Jackson had us on the move to a position just to the east of Stone Bridge when he learned of the attack on the left. "Old Stonewall," he got the nickname of "Stonewall" during this battle, changed our direction of march and we went headlong towards the sound of firing. As we approached the area, Rebs were falling back in the face of heavy enemy fire. We, along with at least two other units, had converged without knowledge of the other. We met the enemy head-on and were able to slow the Bluecoats who were advancing up the slope on the south side of Bull Run.

The fighting was fierce, neither side giving any quarter as the encounter continued. We pushed them back a bit, but they returned with a vengeance. A key point was when the general called for us to "Give them the bayonet." It was a rallying call, which brought many of the disorganized units around us back into the battle. Momentarily, we pushed them back again but only for a short period. Those Yanks came back in full strength determined to take the hill. When one went down, another would take his place until we started to give back ground we had already won.

Around about this time, I'm not positive of the exact timing of events, two batteries of Federal artillery charged forward and unleashed their guns against our artillery. But they made one mistake. They outdistanced their infantry support and were left without any covering fire. There were some Rebs to our left who took advantage of this.

They, along with a small cavalry unit and other infantry, were able to bring musket fire to bear on the Yankee cannoneers. Part of our boys joined in as best we could even though some of us weren't in position to fire on the artillery site. But that didn't stop us from pouring as many bullets in as we could make count. The entire effort was able to silence both batteries within minutes. This action broke the main thrust of the Yankee advance at that particular spot in the battle."

"I know what it means to not have infantry supporting artillery. That's what happened to us at Petersburg. We got run off our position because we didn't have any infantry support. We were almost wiped out, just managing to escape because our major had a good withdrawal plan. Unfortunately, he was killed as we made our get away.

It sure sounds like things were pretty tight for you men nearby the Stone Bridge. I always thought the battle at Manassas Junction was all in favor of us Confederates. From what you say, it was a battle that could have gone either way." I moved to put some more wood on the fire. Tom shifted and continued.

"Well, it was surely in a tender balance as far as I could see. It was the first big battle I had been in, but it looked to me as if we could have lost the field had it not been for those Yankee batteries making the wrong move they did. That allowed our artillery to zero in on those Bluecoats, which sent them running back to the north of Bull Run. Of course, there was still a lot of heavy fighting left to do.

We moved some men down towards the bridge to make sure we could protect that approach from any Yankee advance. I had just gotten into position when my military usefulness came to an end. Don't know for sure exactly where the shot came from that hit my leg, but the bullet shattered the bone below my knee. The pain nearly caused me to lose consciousness, but I managed to keep my wits about me. I laid there on the battlefield for a long time with the fighting raging around me. It wasn't until late in the afternoon before our boys were able to make a final meaningful rush that broke the Yankee line.

Must have been about forty-five minutes or so before that final charge that two men dragged me to a safer spot. They replaced the

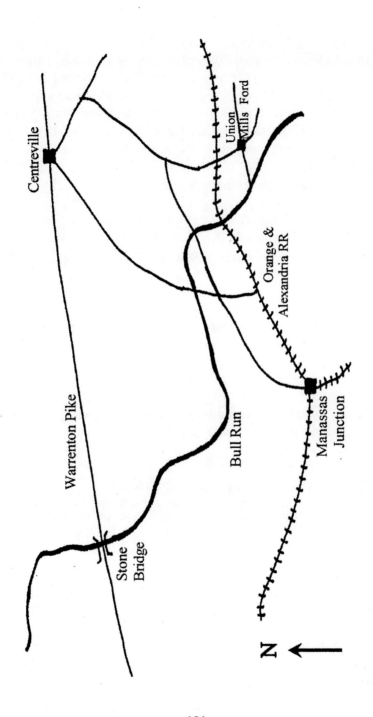

makeshift bandage I had put around my leg to stop the bleeding. I almost fainted when I looked down at my leg. It was in bad shape and I knew I would be lucky to keep it. Later, I was moved to a hospital in Manassas where they took my leg off. The doctor said there was no way it could be saved. I was too weak to argue with him. I guess I was one of the lucky ones though. There were a lot of boys in that hospital who didn't come out alive. I'll never forget the stench from all the wounded and dying.

It was about three months before I got the wooden leg, and it took me another two months to learn how to use it. Now, it seems like I've had it all my life. Like I said earlier, that time at the Stone Bridge might have been a blessing in disguise. Don't rightly know if I would have made it through the entire war and still been alive at the end. I figure losing the leg gave me a new lease on life. Don't get me wrong, I'm glad I fought when I did, and I would have gone on fighting until the end. But I ain't sorry about the way things turned out either."

"I guess none of us know what would have happened if things had been different. I say thank the Lord we are both here well and fit tonight. Wonder if Seth and his buddy are the same?" As I rolled out my bedroll, I noticed Tom was doing the same, taking care not to disturb the pistol.

"Goodnight, Vee. Thanks for asking me about the leg. I had wanted to tell what happened to me for sometime now. Hadn't had anyone who I thought would understand how it really was during the fighting, until you came along. See you in the morning; we have a ways to go and some searching to do. Good night."

"Good night to you, Tom. I hope I can get to sleep without thinking about your battle at Manassas Junction. I'll try to concentrate on how we will run into Seth and his buddy tomorrow. If we don't, I'm afraid my mind will be totally confused. One thing for sure, we know they made it this far, so they must be headed in the same direction we are. We've got to find them. We must find them. Sleep well."

My mind was too full to get to sleep. I should have asked Tom about his leg during the morning hours, then I would be able to sleep without nightmares.

How many times had I thought about being wounded and losing an arm or leg? Would I have been able to get home? Would Elizabeth want a man without all his parts?

I didn't have to worry about any such thing now that the war was over, but visions always seem to come back when things get quiet.

Ah, those crickets are beginning to chirp; maybe their chattering will lull me to sleep.

The gunshot echoed for what seemed like a minute. Both Tom and I sprang up at the same instant, looking in all directions to determine a source.

"It must have come from over in that direction," Tom said, pointing to the north of our location.

"It sounded like a pistol shot to me. A musket would have been even louder. It seems like an odd time for someone to be hunting, it isn't even light yet."

"I don't think that was just any hunter, Vee. If I had to guess, I would say our quarry might be involved. Maybe Seth and his friend have run out of rations. Could be they shot some type of game. If so, they may try to cook it and that would bring out some smoke to follow."

"Let's clean up this place and get on back to the turnpike to see what we can pick up. That shot sounded like it was at least a mile or so away. It could be further knowing how sounds carry in these woods." I began to roll up my bedding.

"Let's not hurry too fast. If they don't get a reaction right away, they may think no one heard their shot. After all that happened yesterday, I wouldn't think they would want to bring a lot of attention to themselves. Then again, the shot might not have been for game, maybe it was for a more sinister reason?"

Chapter Twelve

There was a bit of morning fog as we made our way back to the turnpike, but we expected it to burn off before long. Breakfast had been some leftover beans and bacon; nothing was wasted since we both had experienced hunger at one time or the other. For me, it had been most recent and I didn't plan on ever going hungry again, if at all possible.

We were all but certain Seth and his buddy hadn't dallied long in this region. If anywhere, our guess is they would be further on towards the Buffalo River Ferry turnoff. However, the gunshot early this morning hadn't been very far away. For that reason, we planned to search every stretch of countryside until we reached the Norwood intersection, and if no signs were found by then, we would continue our hunt onward to the Buffalo River.

Making way rapidly wouldn't be easy, for the land was thickly wooded along this tract. Although, according to Tom, there were some open fields when we approached the Norwood cutoff. However, he continued on to say our relief would be short lived, because the part of forest after the cutoff would be much more difficult due to heavier undergrowth than we would see in this stretch of forest.

"I'll take the east side, Tom, and you can have a look to the west, if that suits you. Let's go until the sun gets directly overhead or until we reach the open area near the Norwood cutoff. We can return to the turnpike there to make sure we're still on track. If we hear any traffic, other than Yankee wagons, we'll attempt to check it out before it gets out of sight."

"Maybe it would be better if we weaved back and forth as we move along. Then neither of us would be very far away from the turnpike at any one particular time. That way, if we hear traffic, one of us will get a look at it before it passes us by."

"Sounds good to me, Tom, although, I don't know if seeing any more Yankee wagons is going to help us, one way or the other. Every one of them we've met up with wants to check our papers. I don't want to wear out my parole showing it to every Yankee we come across." I grinned as I said the part about wearing out the parole.

Tom smiled and started to move off the road to our left. He parted with, "Yeah, we just want to make sure Seth and his friend aren't in any of them. I'll meet you down the road in a mile or so, and we'll check any findings. If you come across anything interesting before then, sing out and I'll join you. See you later."

"OK, see you in a while."

Moving back and forth through dense foliage was hard going on bare feet. In places the undergrowth was heavy and passage was difficult. It would have been much easier to take the path of least resistance or a convenient animal trail and still be able to cover almost the same amount of ground. Of course, most of the animal trails I saw would have led me away from the turnpike, rather than allowing me to parallel it as we had planned.

It was near time to get back to the turnpike and meet Tom, so I took up a course to avoid the thickest of the undergrowth. I was making good time when suddenly I tripped and fell forward into a thicket of briers. As I extracted myself, trying not to get scratched by the briers, I turned to determine the cause of my fall. That's when I saw it. A foot was poking out of a pile of recently cut pine branches.

It took me only seconds to view the remainder of what was attached to the foot. The body had been covered hurriedly so pulling the branches away from the corpse didn't take long. The body was face down so after I cleared the foliage away; I rolled the body over to discover a large wound directly in the face. It was a nasty injury and left little to recognize other than it was a man, shorter than six foot tall, and with coal black hair. However, there was something about

196

the dead man that looked familiar to me, but I couldn't seem to remember just where or when I had seen him before.

Those features and coloring belong to someone I've seen recently. Where had it been? There couldn't have been too many places, because I can count my encounters with people on one hand since I departed Appomattox.

Think, think, I know I've seen him before.

That's it, he is, or was, the shorter of the two men with Seth. I saw him last during the fight outside the tavern in Bent Creek. The light hadn't been good that night, but I'm sure he was Seth's other companion on that fateful evening.

He must be the one shot by the Yankee troops back by the broken wagon. Yes sir, there's a wound on his lower stomach area and it looks like he lost a lot of blood before he got this far. He must have been almost dead when he got shot in the face. Only person who could have done such a deed is Seth. Why would he want to finish off his friend at this point?

I'm beginning to believe Seth doesn't know the meaning of friendship. I reckon both sides had bad men fighting for them. Seth was certainly a prime example of one on our side. Just goes to prove war can change men from better to worse than they were before they started fighting. In the case of this war, a person needed to be real good at the start if he planned to come out even close to the same way.

I hope I haven't let my thoughts or future conduct become so tainted by what I've been through. To me, I haven't noticed any change, but here I am trying to hunt down a killer of men. Am I any better?

I cupped my hands and yelled as loud as I could, "Tom, Tom, I've got something here." I waited momentarily for a response, but didn't hear a reply. Without shouting again, I moved through the trees to the turnpike, while making sure I marked my path so I wouldn't have any trouble finding the location again.

As I emerged onto the turnpike, I spotted Tom several yards farther along to the north where he had exited from the trees on the west side. I waved my arms and yelled again to gain his attention. He saw me beckon and didn't waste any time in hastening to my position.

He certainly didn't let his peg leg slow his progress; he was there in a matter of seconds.

"What have you found, Vee?" He wasn't even panting from the brisk sprint to my position.

"It's a body of a man who's been shot in the face. However, he looks familiar to me. I think he's Seth's last remaining companion. He was with Seth in Bent Creek when their other associate was shot outside the tavern. Remember I told you about that incident?"

"Yeah, I recall your story. That's when you think the Yankees first wanted to talk to Seth about the massacre where your friends were killed?"

"Correct. This body also has what I'm sure is an earlier stomach wound. He must have been the one shot by the Yankees when they were attacked at the broken wagon yesterday. It has to be Seth who shot him in the face early this morning, although I'm not sure why. It did make identification a bit more difficult, but I was finally able to place him. He hasn't been dead very long. Come on, I'll show you where I left the body."

"Lead the way. If he was the recipient of the shot we heard earlier this morning, then Seth couldn't have traveled much further north. He would stay in the woods to keep out of sight, and you know how hard it is to make good time through the forest."

"You are certainly right about not making any speed through the undergrowth and briers," I acknowledged, as I started back up the bank towards the trees. I saw my mark near a tall pine and said, "Here is where I came out of the woods. The body location isn't too far away." My marked trail was easy to follow, and we found the body exactly as I had left it.

Tom spent some time looking at the body and the surrounding area before he uttered a word. "The shot to the face was the final thing that killed this man, although the stomach wound would have ended him before very long."

"Yep, being gut shot would have killed weaker men long before this one died. The Yankee who died in your arms said his buddy got off a shot before they were killed, and it seems he sure made it count."

"This one," Tom moved the body farther away from the branches as he spoke, "lost a lot of blood between here and that wagon. He must have been almost dead by the time they got this far. I'm sure he was a burden for Seth. Must have finally been too much for him to lug along, so he finished him off, then hid him under these branches. Seth could have ended his life in several ways, but he chose to shoot him in the face." Tom shook his head slowly and continued, "The only possible reason I can think of for such a drastic ending, would be to make him unrecognizable. Sure would hate to have to count on any friends like that to get me through to safety."

"Well, best we bury him. Don't know who we would turn him over to if we could. For sure, I'm not taking him back to Bent Creek and I doubt that captain we saw yesterday will be back this way." I started scraping a shallow grave with a broken branch. Luckily, the ground was soft from all the rain, which made the task easier.

Tom gathered some stones, which we placed at the head of the mound to finish the job. We didn't have anything to mark the grave other than the stones and a large piece of bark. We both stood for a moment in silence. Tom took off his hat and put it over his heart, "May this soul have better luck with his future friends than he did here on earth. Amen."

We reached the Norwood cutoff in a matter of minutes after returning to the turnpike. We hadn't detected any new signs of traffic we hadn't seen the day before. The area in the immediate vicinity of the intersection was mostly open fields with the exception of a small stand of pines on the north side of the road. Just as we were turning to follow the turnpike, two Bluecoats with bayonets on their muskets leaped out of the trees.

One of the Yankees with three stripes on his sleeve yelled out, "Where you two headed?"

"We're bound for the Buffalo River turnoff, about three miles up the road." I reached in my pocket for my parole as I spoke.

"Careful there, Reb, don't pull anything out of that pocket you'll be sorry for later." The Bluecoat's muskets went up to an alert position.

"Just reaching in to get my parole to show you. We don't have any hankering to do any more fighting. We done had all we need and now we are on our way home."

"We heard a shot earlier this morning. Best we could figure, it wasn't more than a mile or so away. Did y'all hear anything?"

"Yeah, we were south of here about two miles when we heard the shot. Don't know who was doing the shooting, but we ran across a body back down there in the woods, shot in the face and dead as could be." I pointed back down the road as I explained what we had seen and heard.

"Who was he?" asked the sergeant, as both men relaxed their weapons.

"Not sure, but we think he was one of two renegades who attacked some Yanks back towards Bent Creek yesterday. Your three boys had been shot up bad, one was still alive and before he died he described the leader as a big, barrel-chested man with red hair. Seen anyone looking like that pass this way?"

"Nobody of that description has passed this way in the last few days. We've only seen our wagons moving on to the north."

"He must have bypassed you then, because we don't believe he'd hang around these parts for long."

"If he'd stayed on the turnpike, we would have seen him. What happened to our dead boys? They weren't left there on the road, were they?"

"Certainly not, one of your captains and two others in an empty wagon headed south took the bodies back into Bent Creek. The one who died while we were there said they had hit one of the raiders before they were all gunned down. The fellow we found back a ways had a bad gut shot which must have come from that hit. The shot we heard early this morning, was one full in his face to finish him off. We suspect his traveling partner did the shooting because his mate was almost gone and he couldn't carry him any longer. A bad way to end up." Tom's words seemed to hit the mark because the two sentries kept nodding as he talked.

I jumped in with, "We plan to continue on towards the Buffalo. We're gonna keep an eye out for the redhead as we move along. Any problem with that?"

"Naw, we wish you luck. We've just been posted here to make sure our wagons don't take a wrong turn on their way towards Amherst. We're hoping to get some relief before long. We's ready to go home ourselves. Is there anything we can do to help you?"

Before I could open my mouth again, Tom said, "You don't have an extra pistol you could spare? We might need something more than a stick if we meet up with the redhead."

"Wish we had Reb, but you know you ain't supposed to have any weapons. We could be shot giving you any and I don't plan to finish this war by getting killed by my own kind."

"No hard feelings, Yank, just thought I would ask." Tom winked at me as he said the last.

There was a long pause as we just looked at each other. Finally I said, "Guess we'll be moving on, Yanks. Hope you make it home before long. I know how it is to be away from the people you love."

"Yeah, and good luck to you. When you get to the Buffalo River Ferry road there's a couple of our buddies guarding that intersection.

We were all together at Appomattox Court House on those last days of the war. We were sure glad to see it end."

"So was I. My friend here got his peg leg at Manassas, so he'd been out of it for a while." Tom nodded, not wanting to add anything further to the conversation.

"Tell them hello for us. Their names are Mathew and William. Mathew is the roly-poly one."

"Sure will," I said, as we turned and headed north up the turnpike.

It is almost more than I can understand. Here we are exchanging pleasant remarks with people who had been our enemy only a few days ago. The irony of it all further enforces in my mind the stupid blunder this war has been on our country. I promise I will do everything in my power to ensure this misfortune of mankind never happens again.

It might be well to fight to preserve the virtues our forefathers established for us when they first declared our freedom. But, not to fight our brothers over things which honorable men should settle peaceably. I'm sure Elizabeth will agree; we will raise our children to honor their neighbors and their country.

My plan is to have several children. We need to repopulate our world to replace the many young men lost during this awful conflict.

I must be a bit crazy. I'm taking for granted Elizabeth will marry me; much less want a large family.

201

My conscious thoughts recently haven't had much room for Elizabeth. However, I'm sure she has dominated my subconsciousness, for when I close my eyes her beauty abounds in my dreams.

I pray she will have me when I get back to Clifford, and that she will agree with my plans to have more than one or two children.

We proceeded up the turnpike until we were out of sight of the two Bluecoats guarding the Norwood turn off. There we sat down to ponder our next move.

"Vee, I say we move on directly towards the Buffalo River cut off and check with the Yanks there to see if they've seen anything of Seth. I don't figure he would hole up any place between here and there. In fact, he's probably gone on towards Amherst rather than to the Buffalo River ferry."

"You could be right, Tom. He could have bypassed the sentries at the next intersection just like he did the ones behind us. After the disorder in Bent Creek and the massacre at the wagon, he must know the Yankees are looking for him. Then again, he just might head directly for the ferry rather than chance running into Bluecoats who are no doubt in force in Amherst."

"If we use the turnpike, it will save us the trouble of thrashing our way through the heavy forest which cover both sides of this road. I've had enough of that rough underbrush to last me for a while." Tom suddenly looked puzzled; he spoke quietly as he continued, "If he heads straight for the ferry, that could mean trouble for my Uncle Jed. But, maybe all he will want is to get across the Buffalo on the ferry and head off north without bothering anybody."

"I doubt your uncle has much to worry about if Seth comes his way. He will only want to get across the river as quickly as possible. Does your uncle have any help with that ferry?"

"Yeah, he can't do all that burdensome work by himself. Adam has been with my uncle for years now. Uncle Jed bought him before the war and made him a free man the same day. They've been the deepest of friends ever since."

"Well, if we head on towards the cut off and then on to the ferry, we could get there before Seth does, if in fact he is headed in that direction. He would be staying in the woods, which would slow his travel. Let's get on the way." I started to rise when I said, "Do you hear something?"

The rumble of wagons coming from the south reached our ears. We moved to the bank alongside the turnpike and squatted down to wait for them to pass. When they came into view, there were three of them with two outriders flanking each wagon. The wagons were weighted down with equipment and boxes. The boxes carried items they used to overpower us those last few months.

They pulled to a halt abeam our position. Either they were ready to take a breather or they wanted to check on us. It was probably both from the lather on the horses and the looks of the men. A captain in a rumpled uniform climbed down from his sweaty horse and said, "You two must be the Rebs our sentries back there at the intersection said we would overtake."

"We are," I nodded, without saying any more.

"Can you prove it? We've heard about the killings back towards Bent Creek and the trouble there, so we aren't taking any chances." The captain walked over to us as he spoke.

I pulled my parole out of my pocket and showed it to the captain. He took a closer look than most had, but nodded his agreement that we were who we said we were. "Where you headed?"

"Clifford, by way of the Buffalo River ferry. My friend here," I motioned towards Tom, "has an uncle who runs the ferry. He plans to stay on with him for a piece. I'm going on to my home."

"Where in the world is Clifford?" The captain seemed earnest in his question. I'm sure he wasn't familiar with this part of the country and was just trying to be friendly.

"It's a little crossroads not too many miles east of Amherst. There's a general store and a few houses, which make up the town. Also some farms nearby, which is where I'm headed."

"Well, as soon as we give these horses a breather, we're heading on towards Amherst, then on to Washington. Should take us a couple of days, but we'll make it if we don't get any more rain. Crossing some of these rivers hasn't been easy."

"We'll probably see high water again at the Buffalo, but the rivers should be coming down soon since the rains have stopped," said Tom. They were the first words he had spoken since the Yankees pulled up next to us. He had only been watchful and alert, like he expected the Yanks to pull their guns at any minute.

The captain mounted his horse in preparation of leaving and said, "We're gonna be on the lookout for that redhead we've heard about. You two ought to be, too. From the sound of him, he doesn't care whether he's killing Yanks or Rebs."

We watched as the dust subsided from the wagons. It was almost noon so we pulled back into the forest a ways to have some food. Didn't take us long to get a small fire going and heat some beans. Tom had packed some cornbread, which he pulled out of his knapsack to complete our lunch.

"If we move along at a good pace, we could make the Buffalo by morning, that's stopping for some rest before we get there." Tom was ensuring the fire was out as he spoke.

"Suits me, Tom. The sooner we get there, the closer I'll be to Clifford. That is if we don't run into Seth before then."

"I'm beginning to think Seth will get out of these parts as soon as he can. He must know the Yanks want him bad. I'm not sure he realizes you and I would like a crack at him, too. What are you gonna do, Vee, if you don't run across him before you reach your home?"

"Not sure, Tom. I would like to avenge my friends, but in fact, they brought their demise on themselves. I maybe can forgive them for their waywardness, but I still feel Seth betrayed them. He also soiled what we Rebs stood for during all our years of conflict. That I can't forgive." I let the silence fill in the moment before I said, "If I don't run across him before I reach my home, I won't destroy the rest of my life trying to hunt Seth down. I'm sure someone, somewhere, will give him what he has coming. A person like him won't get through this life without receiving his due."

Just as we topped the small rise only yards from the Buffalo River Ferry turn off, we were surprised to see the Yankee wagons halted at the intersection. There appeared to be some confusion since part of the mounted guard was in defensive positions.

"Halt where you are," came the command from two troopers shielded behind a log dugout.

"What's the problem? You just saw us back a ways and you know who we are and where we're headed." Tom spoke up as we came to a quick stop.

Before we could get an answer, the Captain commanding the group came around the barrier and waved us forward. He didn't look very well as he said, "The two guards who were watching this intersection have been killed. Looks like someone slipped up from behind and shot both of them from close range. The odd thing is, one of them was stripped naked, while the other one is still in uniform."

"I'll bet the roly-poly one, Mathew, as I recall his name, was left with his uniform on. The other man must have been big, but not as rotund. Am I right?"

The captain looked at me in amazement, "How did you know the fatter one wasn't left naked?"

"Well, your two sentries back at the Norwood intersection had told us to tell their two buddies hello. They said Mathew was the roly-poly one. The big, red-haired, barrel chested renegade we are all on the lookout for couldn't fit into a short fat man's uniform. Apparently he plans to continue on north as a big redheaded Yankee."

"You could be correct. He stripped him clean. He also made sure he wouldn't mess up the uniforms, because he was careful to shoot both of them in the back of the head. I don't think they ever knew what happened."

"How long do you think they've been dead?" Tom pressed him for an answer.

"I'd guess the ambush happened not much more than an hour ago. Took us a minute or two to find them after we stopped, they had been dragged off into the woods. We are supposed to make contact with the checkpoint sentries as we move north. We were surprised when we didn't see them when we first arrived."

"Come on, Vee. Let's move out of here." The captain looked surprised as Tom pulled on me to hasten my departure. "I've got the feeling a big redheaded Yankee is going to be trying to cross the Buffalo at my uncle's ferry. With his disguise, he probably won't have to keep to the woods. He'll hopefully stop for the night, so he won't be getting there until morning. If we travel all night, we've got a chance to arrive before he does something bad."

"He's our problem, Reb. Anyway, he could be headed towards Amherst and not the ferry."

"Could be possible, but I'm not taking the chance. And, to whose problem he is, it's who crosses his path first as far as Vee and I are concerned. Right, Vee?"

"Correct, Tom. Good luck to you Captain, sorry about your sentries, but there isn't any reason I can see for Tom and me to stay on here. If you catch up with Seth, and that's his name, I hope you'll see he gets what he has coming. We'll try to do the same."

The light had failed some hours ago, so moving along this rutted road had to be done with care. We didn't want to step into a rut and sprain an ankle. Such an injury would delay our planned arrival at the ferry, hopefully before Seth. We did stop to rest for five minutes out of every hour. Tom claimed it was a tactic used by General Jackson, which had enabled his army to move with the speed it did. I had to admit the five minutes every fifty-five minutes was just enough to revitalize the body. The rest provided the needed energy to continue on toward the goal we had set for ourselves.

I had hoped we might spot a campfire as we advanced towards the Buffalo and the ferry. If Seth did stop to rest, he could be thinking it was safe to have a fire. However, up to this point, there had been nothing but blackness on a partly cloudy night.

We were on one of our five minute breaks when Tom said, "As I remember, we should be getting to the ferry in another hour. That will put us there just as the first streaks of light are coming over the eastern horizon. The land begins to slope to the river in a mile or two. So, it will be all down hill from there. Usually my Uncle doesn't come down to the ferry until after he has his breakfast, but there's a bell which can bring him down earlier if there is enough traffic."

"How much traffic has to stack up before he will send the ferry across?"

"Usually, one wagon will be enough. He gets paid to keep traffic moving. If it's just one person and a horse, he will take his time before he operates the ferry."

"How does the ferry operate?"

"It is a pulley type. You've seen them before, haven't you? The ferry moves along attached to a heavy rope. It takes a strong man to shuttle it over and back. That's one of the reasons it works out so well for Uncle Jed to have Adam working with him. When the river is running swift, like it is now, it could take both of them to manage the clumsy system. Of course, the people riding the ferry are expected to help with the rope. Maybe he won't be in such a hurry if only one man wants to cross. That could mean Seth might have to wait a while, which will be to our advantage."

"Yeah, your Uncle Jed could take his time to do more than just eat his breakfast. That way there could be a delay before he would be ready to move the ferry to the south side of the river."

"You could be correct, but I'll bet Seth won't be waiting without raising a lot of cane. If he wasn't riled before he got to the ferry, waiting might set him off. From what you say, Vee, he doesn't have all the patience in the world." Tom seemed to freshen the pace even though it was still difficult to see exactly where we were walking.

We were fortunate the darkness was beginning to ease so with any luck our chances of falling were being diminished. I was still amazed how well Tom moved with his peg leg; it was all I could do to stay up with him.

The morning glow was really starting to peek through the trees as we began the snaking downhill grade leading to the river. According to Tom, we only had about a half-mile remaining before we reached the ferry. That's when we first heard the sound of the bell.

The first clang sounded normal, just like someone had given the clapper a couple of quick tugs to bring some attention to their position. Silence followed for maybe a minute, then the next sound was that of a person who wanted assistance immediately. The jangle of the bell hurt our ears as we moved closer to the river. The clatter covered any noise we made as we moved close enough to see a tall redheaded individual in a Yankee uniform, vigorously pulling on the hammer.

Tom held up his hand motioning for us to advance through the trees to a position closer to the ferry landing. He whispered, "Let's get to a location where we can get a clear shot at him."

"Let's not use the gun if we don't have to, Tom. Maybe we can take him without having to shoot him?"

"I doubt the possibility we can subdue him without shooting him first. He's a big man. I don't want us to get into a brawl, only to have him get away. He also has a pistol and we know he's willing to use it."   ·

"You may be right, but let's wait until shooting becomes our last resort. I've got this big stick I picked up back a ways, it might just be the weapon we need to even things up."

The intense noise of the bell drowned out every other sound in the area, when suddenly the clanging stopped. The abrupt silence lasted only a matter of seconds. It was quickly followed by a pistol shot, which echoed across the rapidly flowing river.

"Hold on there young fellow," came a voice from the far side.

Tom whispered, "That's my uncle's voice."

"Get that ferry over here you old coot before I put the next shot between your eyes," Seth yelled at the top of his lungs.

"Well now, sonny, you might want to look slightly to your left. See that musket aimed at your head. Adam there don't take kindly to people demanding us to move this ferry because of any threats."

Tom and I moved a bit closer so my whisper was barely audible, "Good for your uncle. He and Adam might take care of this situation without us getting involved."

All I got from Tom was a nod. He had his pistol in a ready position. Again, I touched his arm and gave him a negative headshake. He shrugged his shoulders in tacit agreement.

"Listen old man. I'm on official government business for General Grant, and I need to cross this river without delay. I'm authorized to use force if need be, but it would be better if you cooperated without giving me any trouble. That way I wouldn't have to report you to the authorities when I pass through Amherst." Seth hadn't taken his eyes off the musket Adam had aimed at his head.

"If you're headed for Amherst, you are on the wrong road. You should've stayed on the turnpike." Uncle Jed hadn't made a move to start the ferry across the river.

"Well, this is the way I'm going to get to Amherst, now move that ferry over here." Seth's voice had calmed a bit, but he hadn't put his pistol away.

"As soon as you holster your pistol, Adam and I will start across. And, if you pull it out again, it might be the last move you make." Uncle Jed sounded like a person who wasn't to be tampered with.

"OK, OK, I'll put the gun away, but you better be getting on the way when I do. I've waited longer than I had planned now." Seth hastily put the pistol in his holster and sat down to wait for the ferry.

What Uncle Jed and Adam couldn't see was Seth's left hand. As he rested his back against the trunk of a pine, he slowly extracted an additional weapon hidden in his belt. By folding his arms, the weapon was hidden from anyone looking across the river. He must have been a walking arsenal for I could see another weapon bulging under his tunic.

It wasn't an easy task pulling the ferry across the swift water of the river. Adam was doing the major portion of the work, while Uncle Jed ensured the rope ran smoothly through the pulley.

"Hurry up, it's been almost twenty minutes since I arrived here. I'll make sure the proper people hear about your tardiness, if you don't get a move on."

At that comment, Adam stopped pulling on the rope. Uncle Jed followed the pause by saying, "Sonny, you're sure making it difficult to take a liking to you. I've been running this ferry for longer than you been around, and I ain't worried much about what the proper people think about my operation."

Seth slowly got to his feet, and extended the hidden pistol towards the ferry. The shot hit the railing of the ferry, very close to Adam. Its echo seemed to ripple across the water. "You've got thirty seconds to start your ferry in this direction. If it ain't moving by then, the next shot will be for you."

"If you shoot us, ain't no way this ferry is gonna get over to your side. Then your only chance of getting to the north side is to swim for it, and that might be a bit difficult the way this river is running today." Uncle Jed remained steadfast.

Another pistol shot splattered the wooden planking between Uncle Jed's feet. "I may not care whether I get to the north side or not. Get that ferry moving or you won't care which side I'm on."

Uncle Jed nodded to Adam and he reluctantly started pulling on the rope again, edging the ferry closer to the south side landing. Seth stepped closer to the edge watching every pull on the rope as the ferry neared his location. It seemed like things were moving in slow motion. Finally the ferry banged into the landing with a loud thump causing the entire structure to shake as if pounded with a giant sledgehammer.

Without looking at Tom, I used the crunching sound as my cue to go into action. I sprang down onto the landing behind Seth swinging my heavy stick wildly, but making solid contact with his right shoulder. It caught him completely by surprise, dislodging his pistol, and sending him to his knees at the water's edge. However, my advantage was fleeting for it didn't take him but a moment to regain his senses and get to his feet. In the same motion he pulled his other pistol from its holster and swung the barrel in my direction. I thought I was about to meet my maker.

Instinctively my eyes closed, only to open again suddenly when the blast of gunfire echoed along the river's edge. I couldn't tell from which direction the shot had come, but when Seth crumpled to his knees with a large hole between his eyes, I assumed Tom had been the one who fired. He had agreed it would be a last resort before he fired, and to me that moment had arrived. Instead, Tom was rushing behind me towards the ferry; while Adam was lowering his musket with smoke still coming from its barrel.

Seth, undoubtedly, had changed his focus at my sudden entry onto the landing when he should have kept some of his attention on the ferry. Adam had been his real threat all along.

Uncle Jed bent over Seth and said, "This gentleman is no longer with us. Don't know what his problem was, but we could be in some trouble for shooting a Yankee now that the war is over."

Tom held up his arms as if to stop traffic, and said, "Uncle Jed and Adam, this here madman with me who uses a stick instead of a gun is my friend, Vee." I nodded at both Jed and Adam. "The man on the ground wasn't no Yankee. He was a bad Confederate who deserved to die. He caused the deaths of several of Vee's friends, not to mention five or more Yankees between here and Bent Creek. He probably would've killed you once you got him over to the other side. Vee and I've been trailing him for the past two days, and thank the Lord, we got here in time to help out; although, it looks as if you two might not have needed our help."

"Naw sir, mister Tom. Mister Vee jumping down all of a sudden like he done, sure give me time to draw a bead on him before he could shoot anybody. We's glad to see you both." Adam deftly primed his musket as he spoke. He was making sure it would be ready, just in case.

"Well, what do you suggest we do with this body? We can't leave him lying here on the landing." Uncle Jed rolled the body over making sure his original diagnosis was correct. "Yeah, he's sure a big one. Glad we didn't have to take him on bare-handed."

"We could dump him in the river and let the current take care of him. Or, we could bury him back in the woods and leave the grave unmarked." Tom rubbed his chin as he spoke.

"Might be a lot of questions asked, if and when his body was found later downstream." Everyone nodded in agreement. "Of course, we could turn his body over to the Yankees and tell them what happened here." That comment drew doubting shakes of the head.

Uncle Jed waited a moment for any other suggestions before he said, "I think Tom's idea about the unmarked grave would be best for me. I doubt the Yankees will spend much time looking for this monster. For sure, he won't be causing any more problems for the Yankees or us. Most of them are eager to get on back North. They've had about all the fighting they want, just like our boys. So, as long as we know what happened here, and with the knowledge the world won't be bothered again with the likes of this redhead. I say we get on with his disposal. Anyone disagree?"

We all stepped to the task at hand.

Adam's late-morning breakfast was one of the finest I had experienced in a very long time. Real eggs and bacon along with mouth-watering biscuits topped with the sweetest honey in the world. It made me even more anxious to be getting on towards Clifford.

Tom and his uncle both wanted me to stay on for a few days, but I was determined to be on my way. "I'm not much more than a full day's walking from home. I also plan to be stopping by New Glasgow to check on someone I've been thinking about for these past two years. I should be able to get to her farm by early morning."

"Well, Vee. I'm mighty glad I decided to come with you this far. I wouldn't have missed all the excitement for anything." Tom extended his hand, "You will always be welcome, both here and Gladstone."

"Give my best to Foster when you get back to Gladstone. I sure owe you fellows a great debt. Hope I'll be able to repay you one of these days."

"I think you already have. Take care, Vee."

I should have stayed the night with them for the sun was close to setting as I passed over the second ridge away from the Buffalo River. What I had thought to be a wonderful breakfast was in fact a late mid-afternoon meal. Guess in my haste to head for home I didn't realize how time was getting on to dark. The sun was dipping behind the mountains and the evening sky was a crimson band sweeping across the horizon. Complete darkness would arrive soon and I hadn't planned to travel without decent light to see the way. So, another night under the stars wouldn't hurt none, there sure had been plenty up to now.

Adam had sent me off with a packet of food, which more than likely would last me until I got to Clifford. Not only was he handy with a musket, he was one of the better cooks in this part of the state. He and Uncle Jed seemed to have a nice life together.

My bed was once again a carpet of pine boughs. A few stars peeked through some low-lying clouds. The cricket's song was eternal and the slight stirring of the pines kept me company as sleep began to drape over me. Tonight Elizabeth would dominate my dreams. Home was closer than it had been for the past two years.

Chapter Thirteen

My campsite had been just off the road about a mile and a quarter from the ferry. Maybe I should have stayed the night with Tom, Uncle Jed, and Adam. But, by traveling while there was still a slight bit of daylight, I would be able to arrive at the Kimbrough farm in the early morning hours. It also gave me some quiet time to get things in the proper perspective.

Seth had brought his demise on himself, but I had been part of the instrument that caused him to meet his final downfall. Could I have done something else to save him from dying at such an early age?

From the day I first met him after the fighting ended, he was headed for a fateful ending. My only real regret is not convincing my friends to avoid his likes. If so, they would still be alive.

I guess I'm glad to know he is dead. If Tom and I hadn't run into him I would always be concerned as to his whereabouts. Wondering if he was still causing problems for whomever he made contact with. Jumping down on that landing with just a stick in my hand wasn't one of the smartest moves in my life, but thank the Lord for Adam.

Yes, now I can put Seth out of my mind and get on with the rest of my life. Time to turn the page on a new and bright future.

Sleep had been deep and the gray streaks of dawn gave me a fresh outlook on life. There was barely enough light to eat the bacon

213

sandwich Adam had packed for me, but the sky had brightened by the time I finished eating. It wasn't long before I was moving along the road at an easy pace. This time I didn't have to forge my way through the wooded terrain bordering the road.

Halfway between the last ridgeline and the next, the land opened. I expected to see some farms, but all that greeted me were fields of scrub grass with a lone pine here and there. It was on the climb to the last ridgeline that I felt the weariness of the past few days set in, but I continued on anxious to catch sight of the Kimbrough farm.

I had been on the road from Appomattox for what seemed like months. Actually it had only been a little over a week, and I was ready to end my trek. When I topped the crest and spotted Elizabeth's house, all my fatigue seemed to vanish.

The farmhouse hadn't changed from what I remembered. It appeared faded from this distance and possibly in need of some paint. But what building didn't now that the war was over. The lead used in paint had been high priority for other items much more valuable to the war effort than having things neat and trim. However, I really couldn't recall all the features of Elizabeth's home, I had only been there once or twice before going off to fight.

Off on the far horizon a neighbor's farm could be seen. Houses comprising the main part of New Glasgow were further to the east. The Baptist church steeple stood out like a beacon. The tracks of the main railway running between Lynchburg and Charlottesville glistened in the morning light like two silver snakes moving across the land. The scene was peaceful and serene, something I had longed to see. I was almost home.

The path leading to the Kimbrough farm descended across open fields and ended close to the barn. It was eerie quiet. The only sign of life was a small wisp of smoke coming out of the chimney near the rear of Elizabeth's house.

That means someone has a fire going in the kitchen. I was hoping to see people in the field, maybe even Elizabeth out back feeding the chickens. It would be an easier meeting than having to go bang on the door. Would they remember me? Would Elizabeth answer the door?

The bellow was loud enough to wake the dead, "Everybody, come here and look. Vee McGrady has come home at last." Mr. Kimbrough grasped my hand and pulled me into the house. "My boy, are we ever glad to see you. Have you eaten? Come on and sit down while Momma fixes you some food."

Mrs. Kimbrough hugged me and seemed to be shedding a tear. "Let me get you some coffee. You look like you haven't eaten in days."

"Thank you m'am. I'm plenty full, but coffee sounds good. I had a wonderful meal yesterday over by the Buffalo River ferry. Is Elizabeth home?"

Elizabeth's younger brother and sister came in the room and both had smiles on their faces. They gave me separate hugs, which really made me feel at home. They had a thousand questions, but I interrupted with, "Is Elizabeth home?"

Mrs. Kimbrough understood my frankness and answered, "She's over in Clifford staying with your folks. Been there for a week come next Sunday. She's taken a teaching position at the academy nearby your place. She said it was about time she got on with her life and teaching has always been a good role for a young lady. But, if you want my guess, I kinda think she wanted to be nearby when you returned."

"I sure hope you're correct for I've thought of nothing else but her. Funny when you're away from something you know is right for you and you are unable to tell that person how much they mean to you. My only nightmare was wondering if she would still be here when the war ended. I hope I can get your blessing when the time arrives."

"I don't think our blessing will be any problem, Vee. We are mighty proud of what you've done and we are doubly happy to have you back safe and sound."

Eventually, I was able to convince the Kimbroughs I should be on my way if I expected to get home while there was still daylight. They really seemed happy and glad I was finally back from the war. They gave me most of the news about my folks who were all well and awaiting my return. Momma Kimbrough wanted to fix me some food to take along, but I was able to convince her I would be home in time for supper. Plus, I still had some of the food Adam had prepared for me.

I looked back and waved as I moved towards the village and the road, which intersected the main highway between Amherst and Lovingston. They were all outside watching my departure.

Crossing the railroad, which was at the edge of the village, wasn't a problem. There wasn't any traffic on the tracks and it looked like not many trains were back in business since the fighting had stopped. I guess the Yankees were using what equipment there was available to move their supplies north. In the past, I normally would have been leery crossing railways, because the Confederates hadn't controlled much of the rail traffic during the waning days of the war.

Approaching the turnpike, I met up with some wagon traffic. They were all Yankee wagons moving north and most had outriders as security. However, none of them seem interested in me and I wasn't challenged to show my parole. As the last of four wagons passed my position, I dashed across the road and onto some familiar ground.

The countryside dropped off slowly into a timber-covered valley. I knew this area like the back of my hand. I had hunted these woods since I was a little boy. I was only a mile or so from home now.

Entering a small clearing, I spied a tree with my initials carved deeply into the trunk. I could remember the time as if it were only yesterday. I had bagged a four point deer and our family had venison for weeks afterwards. Nearby was an old blind my daddy and I had built to use when the wild birds moved through our part of the countryside. It was still standing, although it would need some repair before it could be used again. I spied the trail where I used to set my traps. Always could count on two or three rabbits. Those had been good days; I sure hoped they would return.

Shock and hope was all that entered my mind. I wasn't sure but across the green pasture leading to our farm, stood what looked like a body with its hair blowing in the gentle breeze. I don't know if it was the distance or tears welling in my eyes, but to me it looked like Elizabeth waiting for me on the knoll above our farm. Then I saw two dogs bounding towards me. Duke and Sam were completing the welcoming committee. As I broke into a trot, they met me halfway and were nipping at my heels all the way into Elizabeth's arms. I'm not

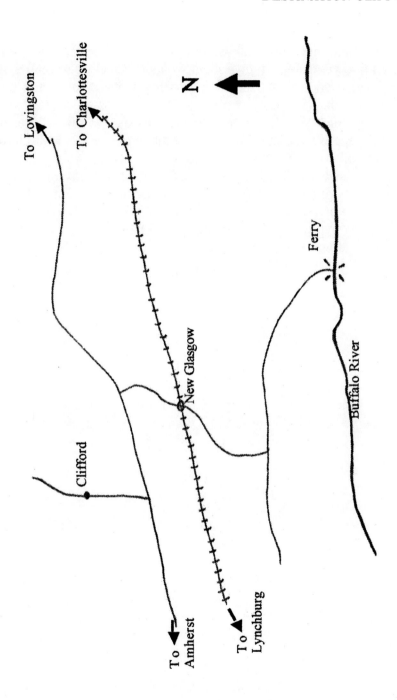

sure, but it seemed our minds had been together from before I departed two years ago. It gave me a wonderful feeling to realize my dreams had been real and not some fading fantasy concocted by a lonesome mind.

Her voice was like music to my ears as she said, "Vee, my dearest, I hope we can make all the past memories wither away into a bright future."

"My sweet Elizabeth, I have dreamed of this day more times than I can tell you. In my mind, the scars of battle will eventually fade from our countryside, and we of Virginia will hopefully heal our wounds the way the earth heals itself. It will be up to us to do our part in this reconstruction process."

As my arms tightened around her, she whispered, "I'm ready my love."

The daylight was waning, but the brightness of our lives was only increasing its shine as we walked slowly down the hill towards the farmhouse. It had been a trying four years of war. But for the most part, our family had survived as well as could be expected. Brother Ben was our casualty and we would remember his brightness and live with his loss. Hopefully, Elizabeth and I would make our many dreams come true in the future years. Only time would tell.

Epilogue

My Great Grandfather and Great Grandmother, Valerius and Elizabeth McGinnis, were married on November 13, 1867. They settled on a small farm near Clifford. They had nine children; all were born on the farm in Clifford. Thomas - 1868, Mary Lena - 1870, William Hill - 1873, Nannie - 1875, Frank - 1877, Charles - 1879, Fredrick Wills - 1882, Bessie - 1887, and Mabel -1893. Nannie died shortly after birth, and Bessie died at age five. The others went on to long and productive lives.

Valerius became Magistrate for Amherst County and served in that position for forty years. He attended and stayed active in the various Confederate Veterans gatherings, but was forever loyal to the Stars and Stripes from April 12, 1865, until his death.

Elizabeth and Valerius moved from their farm in Clifford to Lynchburg in 1930. They lived in the home of their daughter, Mary Lena and granddaughter, Alpha until their deaths.

Elizabeth died on June 6, 1932, and Valerius died on March 1, 1935.

About the Author

Lieutenant General Walter D. (Dan) Druen, Jr. USAF (Ret) was born and raised in Lynchburg, Virginia. He attended VPI after service in WW II. November 1950, he entered the USAF's Aviation Cadet program. He amassed over 5000 hours of jet fighter time during his career, which included combat tours in Korea and Vietnam. He retired in August 1982.

He entered the General Aviation business with the Hughes Corporation and later Triton Energy Corporation. He concluded his second career in January 1991.

His third career, writing, began after leaving the corporate world. He has published two books on Fighter Pilot humor. *Sometimes We Flew*, and *Sometimes We Flew Too*.

He resides in Las Vegas, Nevada with his wife of forty-nine years.

Printed in the United States
19244LVS00002BA/305